BUTTERFLY DREAMS

a novel

BUTTERFLY DREAMS

a novel

ANNE MCCLARD

Aristata Press

Library of Congress Control Number: 2023939137

Book Design: Anne McClard
Book Cover Design: Anne McClard
Editor: Erin Cusick

Photos and maps: Anne McClard, except where otherwise noted [aerial photo of S.
Jorge, Daniel Viera; aerial photo of Ilheu de Topo, António Faria].

Epigraph: printed with permission of the author, Vasco Pereira da Costa, from his
poem "São Jorge," which appeared in translation in *The Sea Within: a selection of
Azorean Poems,* translated by George Monteiro and Onésimo T. Almeida.

ISBN 979-8-9878524-6-0 (paper)
ISBN 979-8-9878524-5-3 (hardcover)
ISBN 979-8-9878524-7-7 (ebook)

This book is a work of fiction. The places described, however, are real. The temporal
aspects of the story are deliberately vague and are not intended to accurately
represent historical events. All characters are wholly fabricated, and any resemblance
to real people is purely coincidental.

Aristata Press, Portland, Oregon

To my ancestors and descendants

I leave behind that broken biscuit the hills of Terceira.
São Jorge is a dragon stretched out in the channel.
My eyes troll slowly along the peaks that top it.
Sharp cutting, they callous the feet that walk them.
The clutches of the monster are low-lands which float
unstable
Over shoals licked by tides.
From its eyes scintillate rays. Sparks come from its
Forked tongue
Humiliating the Topo lighthouse.

— EXCERPT FROM POEM "SÃO JORGE"
BY VASCO PEREIRA DA COSTA

ARCHIPELAGO OF THE AZORES

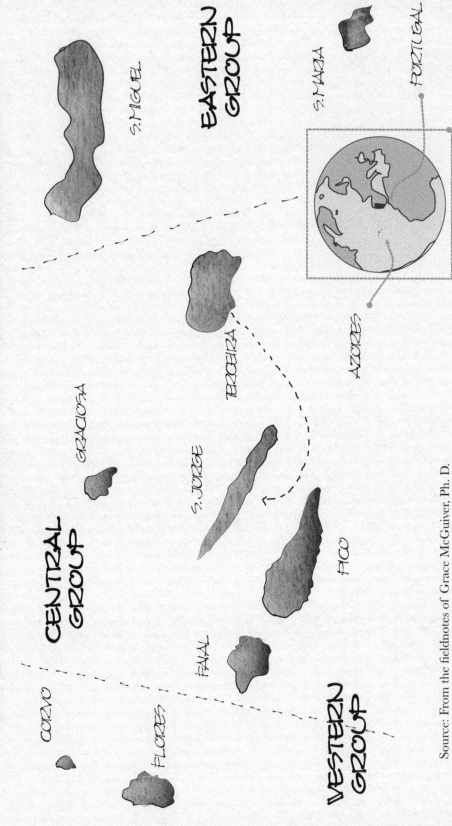

S.MIGUEL

EASTERN GROUP

S.MARIA

PORTUGAL

AZORES

TERCEIRA

GRACIOSA

S.JORGE

CENTRAL GROUP

FAIAL

PICO

CORVO

FLORES

WESTERN GROUP

Source: From the fieldnotes of Grace McGuiver, Ph. D.

ISLAND OF SÃO JORGE

TOPO

MAGNUS?

ZOETAS

TIA CARMINAS

MANUSS

GRACIOSA TROUGH

WIDEST POINT - 6 M

NORTE GRANDE

PICO DE ESPERANCA
3,400 FT.

NORTE PEQUENO

POST OFFICE

MY PLACE

FAJÃ DOS VIMES

CALHETA

MAGNUSS APARTMENT

STEEPLE

URZELINA

VELAS

PICO CHANNEL

ROSAIS

NOTE-END-TO-END S. JORGE IS ONLY 35 MILES AS THE OWL FLIES

Source: From the fieldnotes of Grace McGuiver, Ph. D.

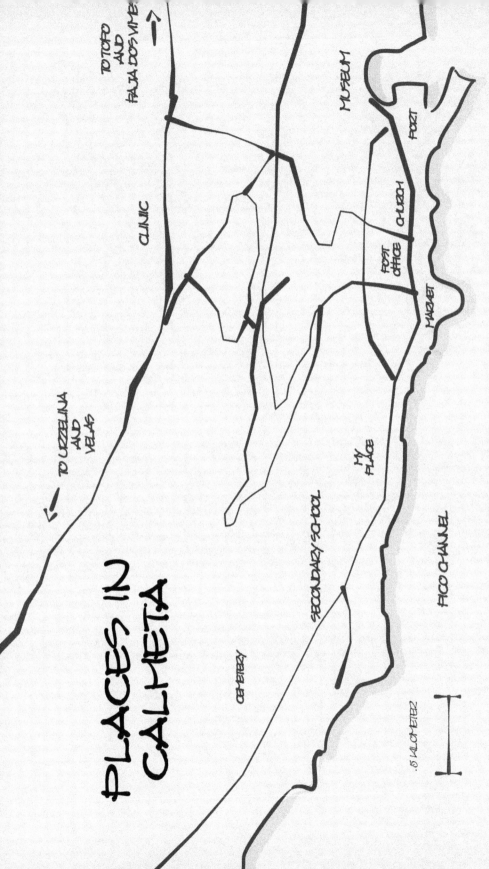

PLACES IN CALMETA

TO TOPO AND FAJA DOS VIMES →

TO UZZELINA AND VELAS ←

CLINIC

MUSEUM

PORT

CHURCH

POST OFFICE

MARKET

MY PLACE

SECONDARY SCHOOL

CEMETERY

PICO CHANNEL

.5 KILOMETER

Source: From the fieldnotes of Grace McGuiver, Ph. D.

PROLOGUE

THE PHRASE *You will miss him when he is gone* plays again and again in Grace's mind. She *does* miss him, more than she could ever have imagined. How could she have guessed that her trip to her anthropological field site in the Azores on the *Holy Ghost*, an ancient cargo boat, would unleash such a deadly series of events?

ORDINARY TIME

1

THE HOLY GHOST

GRACE

As THE *HOLY Ghost* rounds the bend of the far eastern tip of São Jorge, Grace sees her home for the year laid out before her, a massive water beast wading in cold deep waters. She sees the full length of the island, reptilian, dragon-like. It's as if she has been here before, but no, probably just a trick of her exhausted mind. São Jorge bears a striking resemblance to the Iao Valley of Maui or maybe the Na Pali coast of Kauai. Verdant cliffs drop gracefully down to the sea; countless waterfalls spill from its heights to its depths. Yet Hawaii's gentleness is absent; São Jorge seems harsh in the cold North Atlantic wind, and the volcanic blackness of the earth feels sinister under the present blanket of dark clouds. *This is not a tropical paradise.*

The captain approaches and wordlessly offers Grace some *lapas*. He holds several limpets out to her with a gnarled grease-stained hand, and looks her in the eye as he raises an eyebrow as if to ask, *Would you like one?*

Her mother once told her about Portuguese fishermen in California and how they ate live limpets off the rocks near Catalina, but Grace has never seen one up close before. She picks the smallest one and inspects it. It resembles a tiny Chinese rice hat.

The captain smiles and gestures to his mouth. *Try it, eat it,* he insinuates. Her stomach rises into her throat at the sight of the poor creature's undulating salmon-colored belly. Its antennae reach helplessly through the air as she tries to eat it. She suppresses a gag. She must have grimaced, because the captain laughs as he snatches it back, and puts it into his own mouth. He chews with obvious delight. *Perhaps cultural anthropology is not a good choice for a person with such a squeamish disposition.*

Three other passengers are on board: a woman and her two children. The woman has stared suspiciously at Grace for the entire trip. Her kids are cute: a boy who must be five or so and a girl who looks to be about seven. The children enjoy the *lapas* the captain gives them. They giggle as they pop them out of the shells and into their mouths.

Looking at Grace with a sweet smile, the little girl asks, "The senhora doesn't like *lapas?*"

"I don't know. I've never eaten them before. I think I don't like eating live animals."

The girl giggles.

"Rosa and Afonsinho, get over here," their mother hisses. She looks worried. "Don't bother the nice lady." The children scramble back to their protective huddle.

The sea is rough, but Grace keeps her eyes on the horizon to stave off nausea.

SEVEN WEEKS HAVE PASSED since Grace's arrival in São Jorge. She gazes through the window as the bus descends the steep winding road into the village of Urzelina. She has made this trip from Calheta to Velas six times—almost every Thursday. The ocean glistens below. Across the channel, she sees the island of Pico languishing in the sea like a great bathing woman; a hip, waist, an enormous breast reach upward. A wispy cloud rises into the sky. The great earth mother feeds milk to the heavens. Grace closes her eyes for a moment.

Halfway there.

Today the bus is unusually crowded. Rui Veloso, "the father of Portuguese rock and roll," blares from the radio. The acrid smell of sweat, the bouncy pop refrain, the motion of the bus, and reflections from the sea are taking their toll. She opens her eyes.

A colonnade of tall palms graces both sides of the road. Behind the palms, white walls obscure houses of nobility, obscure the former glory of the great colonizers. These grand houses fascinate Grace. When she asked her friend Ângela Maria about them, she said, *Most of those are houses of sorrow. Full of woe, unhappiness, death, and even murder.* Graces wishes to find her way into one. She has always loved a good mystery.

Even more than these houses, Grace marvels at the church steeple that stands in the center of town, submerged in hardened lava, a remaining testament to the power of the earth and the mercy of o Divino Espírito Santo. The people say the Holy Ghost spared the town of Urzelina from absolute destruction during the last eruption of Pico da Esperança. Mountain of Hope, indeed.

Catching the eye of a woman who stands in the aisle, Grace smiles and offers the empty seat next to her. "A senhora, *por favor,* feel free to sit here."

"No, thank you," the woman responds flatly. She gestures to a seat up ahead. Three children crowd together across two seats.

Grace hasn't noticed the kids until now. The woman moves toward them as if shielding them from Grace's view.

Grace turns her thoughts to her research and sifting through old newspapers for historical gems pertaining to the island's festivals. She feels safe, protected at the archives, a place where she knows what she is doing. People always think she must be outgoing since her job involves talking to people, but to the contrary, she's a bit shy, an introvert. She was surprised when she learned that she shares this trait with many anthropologists. She is a perpetual outsider looking to belong.

Today, perhaps if she is lucky, she will come upon something interesting about the Festa do Espírito Santo. So far, she has learned darned little about it after being here for almost two months. Finding people to interview has proven more challenging than her methods class led her to believe it would be. She feels awkward explaining to people what she is doing here and asking strangers personal questions about their lives.

The ride seems endless today. Normally, somebody strikes a polite conversation with her out of curiosity. *You must be that American living in Calheta,* they say, beginning a conversation that usually lasts for the entire ride. Today feels different; something intangibly heavy hangs in the air, seeps deep into her skin.

She arrives in the town of Velas at nine fifteen, but the archives don't open until ten o'clock. As has become her custom, if six times makes a custom, Grace stops in at the Café da Ilha for a *galão* to fill the vacant time. She always looks forward to the half hour spent sipping warm sweet milk and coffee while eavesdropping as she pretends to read or take notes in her notebook.

"Bom dia!" the owner says as he approaches the table. "Will you have the usual today, *Lourinha?*"

"Yes, please." How nice that he has given her a nickname. If a man in New York had ever called her Blondie she would have told him to fuck off, but in this context she feels validated instead; she's achieved considerable acceptance after such a short time, or so she thinks. Something to be proud of. She digs through her bag to find a pen.

He returns with her *galão*. As he sets it down, he says, "I hear there's a storm up in Topo."

"Really? Funny, I didn't see a single cloud on my way here this morning." The image of the enormous breast, its wispy cloud rising from its nipple, comes to mind. "Just the cloud above Pico." Still, she supposes it *is* possible since she didn't look toward Topo; Velas sits at the far western end of the island, and Calheta, where she lives, halfway between the two.

"Well, perhaps it will pass." He pushes his hands into his pockets. "Hope you don't get caught in it."

"I'll be careful." Grace enjoys his concern for her, but honestly, she is twenty-seven years old and can take care of herself in foul weather. How bad could the storm be anyway? She strains to hear the conversations at the two other tables.

"The poor little child . . ." The woman lowers her voice, as if in response to Grace's presence at the neighboring table. Grace manages to hear "The mother is claiming . . ." Grace hears the word *murder*. Seems unlikely. She strains to understand the conversation at the other table—something about a mysterious illness in Topo. Jorgenses, as the people of São Jorge are known, spend inordinate amounts of time talking about weather and health, and today is no different. She supposes there is little else to talk about in a place like this. She finishes her drink and bends over to tuck her notebook into her bag. Sensing someone looking at her, she looks up, but nobody's there.

A wet wind whooshes past her when she opens the door and begins to step over the threshold into the street. She turns toward the proprietor and says, "Perhaps there is a bad storm brewing after all."

He smiles warmly. "Yes, I told you . . . Be careful, okay?"

"I will. Thank you. Until the next time." She proceeds, holding her hand over her eyes to protect them from the pelting rain.

2

SAINT CATHERINE'S FEAST

GRACE

FOUR HOURS PASS SLOWLY in the windowless archive as the storm that rolled in earlier rages outside. The power goes out, leaving the room pitch black. It isn't the first time this has happened. She uses her phone to illuminate her work. When the door opens behind her, the dim daylight of the reception area brightens the room briefly. Probably the archivist checking in on her. No, it's someone else who uses a phone to navigate through the dark reading room. Grace can now tell that it is a man by his silhouette. He's tall and slim. A chair screeches as the stranger pulls it out to sit at a reading table on the other end of the room.

Grace continues to read *O Jorgense*, a newspaper from the turn of the twentieth century. She would leave if there were somewhere else to go, but the return bus isn't until three. She finds an article on Santa Catarina, patron saint of students and workers. Just-in-time knowledge since her feast day is just two days away.

The room smells of musty old newspapers. Her hands are so cold that she can barely hold her pen to take notes. She wishes she could take photos of the papers, but a sign by the door reads "No photos allowed." The archivist explained that they don't want people using flash photography with such delicate documents, so she's left to the old ways, transcribing by hand. She feels watched again. This time, though, she knows who the watcher is—the tall slim man. Only the glow of his face is visible across the room and she can't tell anything about him. She would say hello, but another sign reads "Talking not allowed."

She nods a greeting to the glowing face, and he nods back. She thinks he smiled just a bit. It comforts Grace to know that she has the company of a living person, even if she doesn't know him. Although she feels safe here, the archives are depressing and lonely. Fieldwork is not what she had hoped. She has no idea what she is doing. Nobody ever told her that her first *real* fieldwork experience would be so terrifying.

The silent man gets up and glides past her, brushing against her back ever so lightly as he walks by. He doesn't say anything. Her heart races as she tries to ignore the intrusion on her personal space. He leaves. He should have said *excuse me* at least.

As Grace signs out around two in the afternoon, the archivist is quite chatty. He might have one of the loneliest jobs on the planet, working in isolation on an isolated island.

"Quite some weather today—eight-meter waves on the north side," he exclaims, "but nice thing in here is that these thick stone walls keep it all out."

"Indeed," Grace replies, "if I hadn't seen the storm blow in, I wouldn't have even known it was happening, at least until the lights went out." She laughs.

"Oh, sorry about that. These old buildings . . ."

"No worries! At least today I had some company in the dark." Grace grabs her coat from the rack.

"Oh yeah, that fellow from Switzerland," he says, "or maybe Sweden? One of those countries . . . they're all the same to me."

Grace supposes from his perspective all foreigners are kind of the same—outsiders, like her.

"Huh, that's interesting, I wonder what he's doing here?" She doesn't expect an answer.

"Not too sure. Geology or some such thing, I hear. Lives here part of the time and up in Topo the rest of time, or at least that's what people say . . ."

What people say. What do people say about her?

"Hoo hoo," Grace coos through Ângela Maria's back door. She's worked hard at imitating the high-pitched voices of the women of São Jorge; it requires talking at a pitch several notes higher than her natural voice. This time her voice cracks.

"Oh hello, Graça Americana! I am just finishing the dishes." Ângela Maria waves a dish towel through the air. She looks happy to see Grace. "I was getting worried about you in this storm." She touches Grace's shoulder and kisses her on each cheek.

Ângela Maria treats Grace as if she were a child, even though Ângela Maria, at forty-three years, is of an age to be Grace's older sister, if Grace were fortunate enough to have one.

"You worry too much." Grace plunks herself down at the kitchen table. True. Ângela Maria worries about everything for everybody. Her face dons the wrinkles of someone ten years older. What lies in Ângela Maria's past? Did she lose someone close to her? Was she victimized in some unspeakable way? Perhaps one day Grace will find out what lies buried beneath Ângela Maria's usually cheerful demeanor.

"How about a little *vinho* and *castanhas*?" Ângela Maria asks. Steam plumes up from an aluminum pot on the stove behind her.

"No, thank you." She no doubt will ask again until Grace accepts. "I'm not too hungry. My stomach's a little upset from the bus ride."

"Oh come, you'll feel better with a little wine!" Ângela Maria takes two glasses out of the cupboard.

"Well, okay then. If you insist." Grace stands and walks over to look into the boiling pot. Shiny brown chestnuts bobble up and down. "Let's not eat as many as we did on Saint Martin's feast day —it made me sick!"

"Oh yes, I agree. We overdid it." Ângela Maria hands Grace a juice glass filled to the brim. "To your health!"

"And to yours!" Grace responds. She takes a sip of the home-made wine—still young, simultaneously sweet and sour, low in tannins, and sulfite-free; almost grape juice. Ângela Maria's kitchen is cozy, and Grace feels at home here. It reminds her of being in her grandmother's kitchen when she was a girl on the reservation in Montana: foreign and familiar at the same time.

"How did your research go in Velas today?" Ângela Maria asks. Her interest is genuine.

"Fine, I guess. The storm knocked the electricity out, and it made it hard to see, but other than that it was fine."

"Oh yes, our lights went out today as well, but only for an hour or so." Ângela Maria strains the chestnuts and sets them on the table. "I always hate it when the power goes out."

A sad look sweeps across Ângela Maria's face, a dark look Grace has seen one other time—the day she moved into the apart-ment on the ground floor. *God willing, you'll be happy here,* she said as she showed Grace the space for the first time. Grace thought then that perhaps Ângela Maria hadn't wanted to rent the place, but that wasn't the case.

Grace sits down. "What did you do today?"

"Oh, the usual. Babysit." Ângela Maria says *babysit* in English. "The little ones were here in the morning. Their mother picked them up at lunchtime, and after that I went into town to buy a few little things that I need to finish the skirt I am wearing to the dance on Friday night."

Grace struggles to get the shell off a chestnut. "Well, sounds like your day was better than mine."

"Oh really? What happened that was so bad?" Ângela Maria reaches over, gently takes the chestnut from Grace.

"I don't know. More of a feeling. People didn't seem as friendly as usual." Grace takes the perfectly peeled chestnut from Ângela Maria. "I can't tell you exactly what it was, but I kept feeling like people were talking about me and giving me strange looks."

Ângela Maria rises to get the wine jug from the counter and refills their glasses. "I wouldn't worry about it. People talk. People look. You're something new. It'll pass. *A maldade está nos olhos de cada um.*"

Grace hates it when Ângela Maria speaks in proverbs. She lacks the cultural and linguistic knowledge to interpret most of them. "I suppose you're right," she says as if she understands. Evil is in the eyes of the beholder. Does this adage allude to the evil eye? Or is it saying that everyone sees evil? She has read about the evil eye and is unsure whether one can talk about it openly. The thought of asking about it at once excites Grace and fills her with dread. She would hate to bring up a taboo topic, but maybe she could ask Senhor Estêvão when they meet the next morning for his so-called English lesson.

"Perhaps the sudden change in the weather has made things seem worse than they are," Ângela Maria suggests.

"Yes, I think you're right. I'm sure I'll feel better tomorrow."

Grace and Ângela Maria sit talking for some time longer, covering topics that have become habit—family in America and sick relatives.

Abruptly, as if remembering some forgotten thing of importance, Ângela Maria says, "I saw my cousin Zoeta today—she's the one you met who lives near Topo." She fidgets with her empty glass. "She says there's some mysterious sickness up that way and that one little boy has been taken to the hospital in Velas—they're afraid he might die." She pours herself a little more wine. "Poor little thing."

"Do you know him?" Grace asks. Ângela Maria is clearly deeply troubled by the boy's illness. This must have been what the women in the coffee shop in Velas were talking about. Amazing how quickly news travels on an island. *What people say.*

"No, no, I just feel for the poor little guy," Ângela Maria says.

"Did Zoeta say whether they know what caused it?" Grace gets up and takes her plate and glass to the sink, starts to rinse them.

"Oh, leave it. Miguel is yet to come home for dinner, and I'll have to wash dishes again anyway." Ângela Maria stands, holding her apron; she twists it tightly around her hands. "They aren't sure, but at least they don't think it's contagious."

"That's good, because I'm headed up there this weekend to do an interview with Padre João, and I wouldn't want to catch anything." Grace moves toward the door. "I'm exhausted. I'm going home to bed." She stoops to hug Ângela Maria. "Thank you for the chestnuts and wine. Good night."

Ângela Maria responds, "Have dreams of gold. Until tomorrow *se Deus quiser.*"

Grace smiles. Ângela Maria always adds *if God wills it* to her good-byes. The intensity of her voice signals sincerity, the sincerity of someone who believes deeply in the will of God, which Grace does not. Feeling the slightest bit drunk, she steps outside onto the landing, then stumbles down the steps to her apartment in the *loja* below.

GRACE AWAKENS ABRUPTLY when the fish vendor's motorcycle passes by, as it does every morning at approximately the same ungodly hour. No need for an alarm clock. Next, the milk vendor stops beside her bed, the head of which abuts large wooden doors that open to the street. He honks his horn to let Ângela Maria know he's there. Grace hears Ângela Maria's footsteps overhead as she scurries out to meet him. She tucks her head under the covers, hoping to find sleep again since the sun hasn't risen yet—she dreads getting out of bed in cold darkness.

The *loja*, the ground floor of the house, is intended for storage, not living. Too damp; too little light. Before departing New York for São Jorge, Grace received a letter from Ângela Maria offering to rent her the space. *We hope you will find the loja acceptable. Although it isn't up to American standards, I am sure you will find it comfortable and affordable.* Grace hastily accepted the offer, glad to have one trouble-some detail of fieldwork taken care of in advance. Nonetheless, she didn't know what to expect of her accommodations since American homes lack an equivalent space; the *loja* is neither garage nor basement, but has attributes of both. Like a garage it's above ground with large doors opening to the street; like a basement it is below the main floor of the house, damp and dark.

Ângela Maria and Miguel converted the space into a guest apartment five years earlier to accommodate Miguel's cousin from America who came to spend the summer. The apartment includes a little bathroom complete with toilet, sink, and a shower without a curtain. The so-called kitchen contains a single cabinet for storing dishes and dry goods, a small built-in counter with a hot plate on top, and a tiny refrigerator. Brown ceramic tiles cover the floor; rough plaster walls rise to the ceiling. *Bichos da Calheta*, to which Grace has grown accustomed, coil on the wall as if part of the decor. Other than these friendly millipedes, the only adornments are a crucifix that hangs across from the bed, and a picture of the Virgin Mary over it. The bright pink, yellow, green, and white handwoven wool bedspread gives the place an air of home. Grace likes it.

She flings her feet over the side of the bed and makes a dash across the cold floor to the light switch. The bare incandescent bulb's yellow light instantly makes her feel warmer. She reaches into the bathroom to turn on the shower.

RAIN. *Chuva*. Rain.

Grace spends the morning drinking coffee and entering notes into her laptop. Suddenly she remembers she promised to meet Senhor Estêvão at his shop for his English lesson at ten o'clock. It is already nine forty-five. She throws on the Black Diamond rubber raincoat and boots that Jake gave her as a parting gift.

Ângela Maria introduced Grace to Senhor Estêvão after Mass on Grace's first Sunday in Calheta. A couple of weeks later, he approached her to see if she would give him English lessons. Grace agreed to it, thinking that Senhor Estêvão might make a good key informant for her research, and also she knew there wouldn't be many social opportunities for her with men, gender segregation being the norm.

As she steps through the door to his shop, a bell tinkles, signaling her arrival.

"Good morning, Senhora Doutora!" Senhor Estêvão's wife chimes.

Grace dislikes being called Doctor, but Senhor Estêvão and his wife insist. They are overly concerned with propriety. "Good morning, N—" Grace fumbles for her name.

"Norinha."

"Yes, I'm sorry, Norinha. I have come to meet with Senhor Estêvão for his English lesson. Is he here?" She scans the shop but doesn't see him.

"He told me you would be coming."

Norinha is fake. She smiles too broadly. She's cold.

"He is on his way here now. He had some business to attend to for the *baile* tonight." Norinha organizes items under the glass counter in make-busy fashion.

"Oh, of course, the dance." Ângela Maria mentioned it as well.

"You *are* going, aren't you?"

"I'm not really sure. Where is it?" Grace asks.

"Up at the secondary school. Students in their final year always sponsor a dance during the week of Santa Catarina. Why don't you join us? We'll have a table, and we can make room."

"Oh no, I wouldn't feel right about barging in on your party, and besides, I don't really know how to dance." Grace adds, "I am quite shy." Grace prefers quiet observation over active participation. Ironic for someone in her budding profession.

"Nonsense. I won't hear it. You'll have to learn. Maybe you would like to buy a new dress?" Norinha comes out from behind the counter.

Grace hasn't worn a dress in years, nor did she consider dressing up for dances when packing, and she can't afford to buy new European clothes; she barely has enough money to pay her rent and buy food for the whole year.

The door chime rings. Saved by Senhor Estêvão. "Good morning, senhor! Are you ready for your English lesson?

"Yes, yes, as ready as I can be." He wipes his feet carefully on the mat. "I apologize for my tardiness. I was doing some business up at the *sociedade*."

"Yes, your wife told me . . ."

"I think you are going to be pleased with me. I've been reading a story about New York City in *National Geographic*." He pulls a tattered *National Geographic* out from behind the counter to show Grace.

"Great. That's my town!" *National Geographic* is a magazine of the exotic for her. As a girl she ferreted through piles of them to find photos of naked natives. The idea that the natives of São Jorge might be looking at *her* culture as something exotic strikes her as funny.

"Yes, *your* town—my thoughts precisely." Senhor Estêvão gestures toward his back office. "Well then, please, let's begin."

Grace steps past Senhor Estêvão. The top of his head comes to her chin. He is a small man, although not fragile or weak; he is sinewy and strong, like her in that way. Norinha busies herself straightening up the jewelry in the glass case. She doesn't mention the dance again.

Senhor Estêvão leads the English lesson, as he leads in all that he does. He fancies himself something of a director. He's mentioned several times that he directs the *Grupo Folclórico*, a singing group called *O Trio*, and a theater group. He enjoys being in control.

He patronizes her, refers to her research as the *little book you're writing*. She lets this pass, ascribes it to his archaic attitude toward women.

During their first meeting, he said, *I can't understand what your father must be thinking to let you go off playing in the world alone.*

Grace said, *My father doesn't think I am playing.*

Well, you certainly pulled the wool over his eyes, then! Senhor Estêvão exclaimed. He later said, *At your age a woman should be concerned with getting married and having children.* To which Grace responded, *I am engaged to be married,* a half-truth. In fact, Jake and she *are* planning to marry after they both finish their degrees. Senhor Estêvão's desire for propriety and order in his world was apparently satisfied.

Today's lesson consists of Senhor Estêvão reading aloud from his magazine and asking Grace questions about pronunciation and meaning. After forty minutes of this, Grace suppresses a yawn. Had she been given control, she would have done things differently. She hoped their lessons would be conversational—give and take. Senhor Estêvão, however, wants to have his turn, and then for Grace to have her turn. His turn is long, her turn short. Grace waits patiently for her cue. No point in rushing him.

"Well, I think you have heard enough of my voice for the morning." Senhor Estêvão closes his magazine, carefully placing his laminated bookmark in the seam. "Do you have any questions for me today before we wrap up?" He stands, removes his jacket, and drapes it over the back of his chair.

"Well, yes, I do have one." Grace flips through her notebook, where she has written down all of the adages that she has heard since arriving in São Jorge. Most come from Ângela Maria. "Here, I am wondering what this adage refers to. *A maldade está nos olhos de cada um.*"

"Obviously"—Senhor Estêvão dons an erudite expression—"this adage refers to mortal sins, such as greed and covetousness. The eyes are the sensory organ with which we are most likely to commit these mortal sins. No?"

"Of course. I should have figured that out." Grace *had* figured that out. "I've read that in many parts of the Mediterranean world people believe in something called *o olho mau*. I wonder . . ." Grace squirms, avoiding Senhor Estêvão's eyes.

"No." He looks amused, then puzzled. "*O olho mau . . .* you must mean *mau olhado* or *olhado*, as the people call it." Senhor

Estêvão walks to the window that frames a view of the *vila* of Calheta against its backdrop of the sea and Pico. As he often does, he puts his hands together behind his back. He gazes, focusing on some distant point.

In Grace's experience, men who put their hands behind their backs can't be trusted; they usually have something to hide. What could a man like Senhor Estêvão have to hide? She studies his perfectly combed curly black hair, starched white shirt, and carefully pressed pants.

Turning, he says, "*Olhado* is superstitious rubbish. These days few people believe in it. Very few people. Only ignorant peasants believe in such nonsense."

"Oh really?" Grace probes, "Tell me, since I have only read about it, and I don't know if what I've read is accurate. What exactly is the evil eye?"

"People believed one person could look at another person in a certain way, bringing bad fortune, but as I said nobody believes this anymore." Senhor Estêvão sits back down across from Grace. "Still, you *will* find people here on this island who believe. But then, some people here believe in witches and other such silliness too."

Only ignorant peasants.

"What kind of bad fortune?" Grace feels compelled to press on, although her time is up.

"Mostly illnesses in children and animals, but nowadays we know about viruses and bacteria." Senhor Estêvão's tone indicates to Grace that he is finished with the conversation. "And now, my little *doutora*, I have some important business to attend to, so I hope you will forgive me for cutting our conversation short." He moves toward the door.

Grace follows. "Of course, our time is up! As always, I've enjoyed talking with you, senhor." Grace extends her hand to shake. Senhor Estêvão's hands remain behind his back. "Thank you so much."

He bows his head toward Grace. "Well, yes. Oh, and I was wondering if we might regularly meet on Tuesdays at the same time? Will that work for you?"

"I think so. I'll let you know if for some reason it doesn't. Until then." She walks through the shop. Senhora Norinha has stepped out. What a relief; the dance issue has been left undecided.

For the first time, she feels a modicum of success. She managed to engage Senhor Estêvão in conversation about something that matters. She knows that she has hit him in a sensitive spot by the circles of perspiration that bled through his white shirt.

3

NOSSA SENHORA DO ROSÁRIO

GRACE

ON THE WAY home from Senhor Estêvão's, Grace stops at the post office. Senhor Silva, the postmaster, greets her with a friendly smile. "You have a letter today," he says as he turns and reaches into the sorter. "Letter from home?"

Not that it is any of the postmaster's business, but it is a letter from Jake. "Yes, from my fiancé." Grace stretches the truth again. "He's coming at Christmas." *Thank God.* She misses him so much. She tucks the letter away to read later and heads toward home.

Before going to her space in the *loja*, Grace pops her head through Ângela Maria's back door. "Hi there!"

The neighbor girl sits in a high chair, and Ângela Maria tries to coax her into eating some puréed mush that she calls *papas*. "Oh hello, yourself, what's up?"

"Not much, I just stopped in because I was hoping to catch Miguel before he heads out in his boat for the afternoon."

Ângela Maria clicks her tongue to say *What a shame.* "You just missed him! What did you want with him anyway?"

"I wondered if I could borrow his car tomorrow morning to go up to Topo." When she moved in, Miguel said she was welcome to use his car from time to time if she paid for gas.

"I'm sure it'll be fine," Ângela Maria says. "He's taking his boat over to Fajã dos Vimes to fish early tomorrow and won't need it."

"What a relief," Grace says. "I dread the idea of taking the bus up to Topo."

Ângela Maria nods in agreement. "Yes, this way you can go up and back on the same day without having to hitch a ride back. I don't want you to experience that again."

"Exactly, I'm still traumatized by it." Grace once missed the bus out of Velas and got picked up by a drunk couple. She was then held hostage in their house in Urzelina for hours after they insisted on stopping for a drink. She didn't arrive home until midnight. "I definitely feared for my life."

"As you should have, not just because they're drunks, but because people say he murdered his first wife and threw her in the ocean to be devoured by sharks!"

People say . . .

Grace shivers at the thought. "Yeah, not sure I believe that, but I'm sure glad we didn't drive off a cliff in the night."

Before leaving, Grace hesitates a moment. She really wants to ask Ângela Maria about the evil eye, but she can't bring that up now, not when Ângela Maria is babysitting.

"Well, thanks, I'll see you in the morning?"

"Until tomorrow, God willing." Ângela Maria wipes the baby's face off and sets to cleaning up the mess.

LATER IN THE AFTERNOON, Grace hears the neighbor arrive to pick up the baby. She overhears Ângela Maria say, "Oh, she was a perfect princess! She ate all of her food and took a long nap. She should be ready for the dance tonight!"

A few minutes later Ângela Maria knocks on her door.

"Hey, I was wondering if I could talk you into coming to the dance with me and the kids? We have a table, and Miguel will be out fishing."

"Oh, I'm not sure . . . I don't have the right clothes . . . I don't know how to dance . . ."

"Nonsense, those are all just excuses. I insist," Ângela Maria says with finality. "And besides, Santa Catarina is a big deal for Calheta; she *is* our patron saint, for whom our church is named. The dance begins at eleven. Be ready at ten thirty."

THEY ARRIVE at the dance just as it gets started. Grace feels totally out of place. Everybody is much more dressed up than she is. She wears black jeans, a pair of equestrian-style boots, a gray cashmere sweater, and a short leather jacket; it's the dressiest outfit she has.

Ângela Maria and the kids go off to make rounds with their respective friends. Grace sits at the table alone, trying her best to blend in, to disappear.

"Oh, I see you decided to come after all!" Norinha appears out of nowhere.

"Yeah, Ângela Maria didn't give me a choice." She laughs uncomfortably, hoping Norinha doesn't feel slighted.

"I bet you wish you would have bought that dress . . ." Norinha gives Grace the once-over.

Blood rushes to her face. "Yes, that would have been good, but I couldn't . . ."

"Oh, it's fine. You know where to go for the next dance, every *festa* has a dance."

Senhor Estêvão suddenly appears next to Norinha. He puts his arm possessively around his wife's waist. "Good evening, Senhora

Doutora," he says. "Would you do me the honor dancing with me?" He holds his elbow toward Grace.

"I really don't know how . . ." Grace falters.

"Nonsense," he says, turning to Norinha, "I am a very good teacher, aren't I, Norinha?"

"Absolutely the best," gushes Norinha. "You must let him teach you!" Norinha looks at her husband affectionately.

Miserable best describes how Grace feels out on the dance floor, towering above the crowd. She sticks out like a sore thumb. She is certain that the whole village is laughing at her. Senhor Estêvão guides her expertly around the room, controlling her like a giant *márionetta*. Humiliating.

Ângela Maria is at the table when she gets back. "Bravo!" she says. "You did great! See? Aren't you happy you came?"

Grace lies, "Yes, thank you for inviting me." She can't wait to get home. When she leaves at two o'clock in the morning, a major feat, even the youngest children are still up enjoying the fun. A teenage boy at the door teases her for being the first to leave. "I hope your *carro* doesn't turn into a pumpkin."

The reference to Cinderella doesn't register immediately, but when it does, Grace laughs awkwardly late—if only her prince would show up the next day.

THE FOLLOWING MORNING, Grace drags through her routine. Upon stepping out her door into the yard, Ângela Maria's chickens greet Grace with their usual flutters and clucks. She's finally accustomed to their incessant noises. Poking her head into the doorway upstairs, she calls out, but no one answers. A note, weighted down with car keys, sits on the table.

Dear Grace,

I had to run up to my parents' house. Here are the keys to the car. Miguel said he filled it with gas. Hope that your meeting with Padre João goes well and that you have a good day in Topo. Don't worry if people are not friendly. People there are so fechadas. Until later, God willing.

Your friend,
Ângela Maria

Ângela Maria's comment about Topo amuses Grace. She has said before that they are *closed*. When Grace asked what she meant, Ângela Maria responded, *Well, they're not open, like the people of Calheta; they're unfriendly to outsiders.* It makes sense to Grace. *Topenses* live in greater isolation at the remote eastern end of the island, which is nearly always socked in with fog. Naturally, they would be more closed.

Grace chalks these disparaging comments up to village rivalry. People from Calheta bad-mouth other places on the island. People from other parts of the island bad-mouth Calheta. Tit for tat.

Levi Strauss 101: Open and Closed, Dry and Wet, Sunny and Cloudy, Light and Dark, Right and Wrong, White and Black, Happy and Sad, High and Low, Hot and Cold, Motion and Stillness, Raw and Cooked, Good and Evil

THE SUN SHINES as Grace ascends the steep narrow road out of Calheta, passing Revelinha and Ribeira Seca. When she reaches the top of the island, she drives eastward into the bank of fog that hovers over hedge-lined pastures. In the distance cows graze, their outlines barely visible. *Bovine ghosts.* A fine mist covers her windshield, making it difficult to see. She passes the turnoff to Fajã dos Vimes when suddenly, as if from nowhere, a tall thin man looms at the side of the road—the foreigner she saw in Velas at the archives.

Ordinarily, Grace doesn't pick up hitchhikers, but it seems improbable that he'd be a rapist or mass murderer. Besides, on an island this size, if he were a criminal, he would surely be caught; there is no place to run. No way to leave. She stops the car, leans across the passenger seat, and pushes the door open. "Do you need a ride?"

"Yes, I would appreciate it."

He speaks Portuguese with a thick Swedish accent. Portuguese with a lilt; it sounds funny, but charming.

"I'm headed to Topo," he says.

"Climb in, then. I'm headed that way too." Grace likes his face; it is kind. His disheveled sun-bleached hair and the handmade wool sweater he wears give him the appearance of a Nordic fisherman, Grace's type in her pre-Jake days. "I'm Grace McGuiver." She reaches out to shake. The firmness of his grip surprises her. He slides into the passenger seat and closes the door. She guesses he's well over six feet tall, maybe six three or four.

"I know who you are." He smiles broadly, revealing a mouthful of imperfect teeth. "I'm Magnus Sorenson." He adjusts his knapsack on the floor between his feet. "It's a pleasure to meet you." His knees are jammed up against the dashboard. He tries to adjust the seat, but it's broken.

"Yeah, sorry about that," she says, and she is. He looks uncomfortable. "How do you know who I am?" She's at a disadvantage. She knows nothing about him.

"Uh, well, it's a small island, and news travels fast. You are news, especially in Topo, where there isn't much *movimento.*"

People also describe Calheta as a place without movement; nothing ever happens there. "Hmm . . . I hadn't thought of myself that way."

"So, you are an American?" he asks.

"You should know." Surely, if he already knows her name, he knows she's an American too.

"A *real* American?"

"Of course. What's that supposed to mean?"

"I mean, you speak Portuguese so well. I thought maybe you were a Portuguese American. I've met a lot of those," he says.

"Oh, no. Definitely an American-American, as American as it gets." Many people here speculate that she is Portuguese. Some refuse to believe that she doesn't have a Portuguese ancestor lurking somewhere in her lineage. Her proficiency in their language is all the proof they need. Indeed, it hadn't taken her long to learn the language, just a summer in a language-immersion program and a month practicing in the Azores. It doesn't hurt that she studied French for ten years and Spanish for three. Magnus's Portuguese isn't bad. He has adequate command over syntax, grammar, and vocabulary, but he lacks fluency and an ear for some of the sounds.

"Good. Then English is your first language," Magnus says in flawless British English with the slightest hint of accent. "For some reason, I have had great difficulty learning Portuguese. It is the damnedest thing. I speak German, Dutch, English, Danish, and Swedish fluently."

"Perhaps you're no good when it comes to Romance." Grace sees by his expression that he doesn't get her joke. "You know, Romantic languages . . . ?"

"Of course. I get it now." His blush turns to seriousness. "Yes, that appears to be the case." An awkward silence.

He better exhibit a sense of humor soon. If there is one thing she doesn't like, it's a man who takes himself too seriously. Jake seldom takes himself seriously, and he doesn't take other people seriously either; always joking around, always the funny guy. Nobody makes her laugh the way he does. She misses him, and in this moment she realizes how much she looks forward to his Christmas visit.

"So, what brings you to this godforsaken place?" Magnus asks.

"I don't think it's so godforsaken!" She surprises herself with her vehemence; her allegiance to São Jorge has developed in such a short time.

"Okay, so what brings you here?"

She keeps her eyes on the road. "I'm working on my dissertation research for a doctorate in anthropology." She hopes that'll satisfy his curiosity because she doesn't feel like explaining her topic; she doesn't even think she can.

"Anthropology, huh? So what kind of bones are you digging up here on the island?"

Grace often has to answer these kinds of questions. "I'm not an archeologist. I'm a cultural anthropologist. I study living peoples, not dead ones."

Magnus looks amused, like a cat toying with a mouse. So typical of Continental Europeans to be so smug. "Oh really? So what have you learned so far about the fine people of São Jorge?"

Trying to suppress her annoyance, Grace answers, "Well, not a whole lot at this point. I've been here for less than two months." She clears her throat. "I'm doing research on the annual festival cycle." She omits the rest of her spiel.

"That's nice. I guess you could say I'm not that big on the soft sciences. I like hard, verifiable facts—rock-hard facts." He laughs as if he has said something funny.

Grace never thinks of what she does as science, soft or otherwise. She's more into the art of it, along the lines of literary criticism. She doesn't bother telling him that; he likes rock-hard facts, real science.

"Well . . . what do you do?" she asks.

"I'm a geophysicist."

"That must be interesting." Grace doesn't have a clue what a geophysicist actually does.

"I'm surprised you think so. What do you know about geophysics?"

He's testing her . . . so arrogant. She can't wait for this ride to be over. "Well, not too much, honestly. It has something to do with the physics of the earth I suppose." Grace tries to sound confident.

"Very good!" he says. "I'm studying volcanic activity here in the Azores."

"Well, you're in the right place."

"Yes, I am in the right place, and so are we. My place is around the next bend." Magnus reaches between his feet and pulls his knapsack into his lap. "Well, Grace McGuiver, it was a pleasure to meet you, and I look forward to seeing you again."

"It was a pleasure meeting you too. We're bound to run into

each other somewhere." Grace brings the car to a stop. She hopes she doesn't run into him too often. What a pompous ass. Magnus gets out of the car, extends his hand toward her. She shakes it. "Until the next time."

"Yes, until the next time," he says, and then disappears into the fog. Grace can't see a house, or even a yard. He just disappears. She pulls out into the road feeling deflated. Maybe she *is* wasting her time. After all, her research isn't likely to reveal earth-shaking findings like his.

Rock-hard. Verifiable facts.

The fog makes everything surreal. As Grace crawls along the road, buildings appear and disappear. A knot forms in her stomach. Padre João told her not to be late, saying, *I'm a busy man.*

Nothing about his manner makes her feel at ease. Ângela Maria introduced them after Mass on her first Sunday in São Jorge, the same day she met Senhor Estêvão. His conversation with her had been curt.

Are you Catholic?

Grace hemmed and hawed. *No, I was raised Episcopalian.* Her face flushed as she stretched the truth. She didn't think he would understand if she said she was raised a heathen, so she latched on to her father's religious upbringing.

Well, I guess that is okay. Closer than it could be. End of conversation, no smile, no nothing. He turned to greet the next parishioner.

Grace dreads her interview with him today. She's already had enough of men who know everything, and whose work and play are of such great importance that she should feel ever so grateful that they deign to spend an hour talking to her.

Nossa Senhora do Rosário appears out of the fog. The church looms large over the small *vila*. Grace glances at her watch—five minutes late. Padre João's secretary told Grace that he had only about an hour free. He is in Topo *taking care of the needs of some parishioners.* If only she hadn't given Magnus a ride, she would have been on time.

Grace parks the car and steps into the heavy, cold, and silent air of Topo. As she climbs the steps of the church, she knows she will find the doors locked; it feels deserted. The secretary *did* say that he would meet her at this church, didn't she? She walks around the building and tries the side doors; they too are locked. Mud cakes onto her feet. If only she had worn her rubber boots instead of her *good* shoes. She tries to scrape the mud off on the concrete landing of the only remaining untried door. She jiggles the handle—no luck. Is it better to sit in the car or to be visible? Visible to what? She hasn't seen a soul, save for a dog that passed by. Perhaps the padre has been and gone, because she *was* late.

Grace decides to sit in the car so she can work on her interview questions. She flips through her notebook to the predated page. Senhor Estêvão and Ângela Maria insisted that she talk to Padre João about Espírito Santo. Grace scheduled the interview to carry out their wishes. She knows the story he'll tell won't be the one she wants to hear. Nonetheless, she probably needs to get the church's official line on it, so that's what she plans to do. While she is at it, she will take his temperature with a question about the evil eye.

A distant tapping sound disturbs her focus. Someone is knocking softly on her window. A boy of eight or nine years stands there, bundled in several layers, eyes peeking out between a hat and scarf. Grace rolls down the window. *"A senhora Americana?"* he asks.

She looks into his dark eyes. "Yes?"

The boy nervously looks down. "O Padre will not be able to meet with you today. He sends his apologies."

Shit. "Oh, well, thank you for letting me know." The boy turns and disappears before Grace has a chance to say anything else. She tosses her notebook over to the passenger seat as she closes the window. She starts the car and waits for the fog to clear off the windows. Closing her eyes, she rests her head on her forearms, which are folded across the top of the steering wheel. What a frustrating waste of a day this has been.

MAGNUS

Magnus felt oddly happy as he left Grace's car. To be sure, things didn't go as well as they might have, but at least he met her. He had seen her at the archives and thought she was pretty in that wholesome American way. She was so intent on her work, scarcely ever looking up, even with the lights out, that he could see she didn't want to be bothered.

Now he sits in his dark *lab* staring blankly at the lava-flow screen saver on his computer. Perhaps she is just shy, he thinks. The glowing lava flow creeps slowly down the face of the screen until the entire screen oozes and vibrates red, dissipates, and starts over again.

He hates to admit it, but after more than a year in São Jorge, he feels lonely. Now he's gone and made an ass of himself. What compelled him to tell her that he doesn't care much for the soft sciences? He has a knack for insulting people unintentionally. Adriana broke up with him shortly after he told her father that he thought organized religion was to blame for nearly every ill in the world. He listed them all off. It wouldn't have been so bad, but her father was a Lutheran minister who prided himself and his church for its involvement in liberal social causes. In truth, Magnus doesn't believe what he said, but he's polemic; he loves to argue and to poke at people.

He's made only one friend the whole time he's been in São Jorge—a fisherman in Fajã dos Vimes, and he isn't a *true* friend. Magnus rents a shack from him where he stores his motor boat when he's not using it. They scarcely talk about anything except for the weather and fishing. He doesn't even know if Zé is married or if he has children.

Magnus fidgets with the paper in his printer, checks the ink, and types a couple of notes. He decides to go into Topo for a coffee and a shot of *aguardente* to warm up. Maybe he'll run into Grace.

He doesn't want her to think he's looking for her, so he stays solidly on the path to the café, but there's no sign of her. Glancing down the street one last time, he steps out of the cold into the stale warmth of the Café da Vila.

"Bom dia," he says to the owner. When in Topo, he comes here every day, sometimes twice a day. He doesn't need to order. The owner begins the process of making his coffee.

Although Magnus has been here countless times, the man rarely attempts to converse with him. Once, they exchanged a few friendly words about the Swedish national soccer team, and another time they spoke of the weather. Like the rest of the people in Topo, the proprietor of the café seems indifferent to him, disinterested. What could they possibly have in common?

The owner sets the coffee and *aguardente* down firmly. "You're back earlier than usual today," he observes.

"Yeah, it's too rough to go out." In good weather, Magnus takes his boat around to the north side of the island and into the channel between São Jorge and Graciosa to monitor the Graciosa Trough for suboceanic volcanic activity. During his year in São Jorge, he hasn't witnessed a single vapor column, although he travels the trough religiously every week, weather permitting. Only once has he ventured out in bad weather, a decision that he regretted. Magnus continues, "I was lucky to get a ride back to Topo with the American woman who is staying in Calheta."

The owner leans closer. "Really?" He walks over to the television and turns it down. The midday telenovela is on. He turns back to Magnus. "And what business does she have in Topo?"

"Well, I don't really know." Magnus puzzles over the café owner's interest. "I didn't think to ask." He kicks himself for not asking. If he had asked, he would know where to look for her. He downs his *aguardente* in one swallow. It burns, sending its characteristic warmth across his chest and into his face. "She's an anthropologist, though, so it probably has something to do with that. You know, she's probably up here to learn something about your culture."

The owner scratches his stubble-covered chin. "Perhaps." He turns away mumbling what Magnus registers as, "Or maybe she came up here to stir up more trouble."

Perhaps she has a relationship in Topo, a love interest? *To stir up more trouble* . . . perhaps an argument? How would the café owner know about that? "Did you say 'to stir up more trouble'?" Magnus asks.

The owner moves behind the bar and begins wiping the counter. "Doesn't concern me. Shouldn't concern you. *Falai do mau, pagai no mau.*"

How irritating. Magnus hadn't started the conversation in the first place. He drinks the last of his coffee. "I'm not sure what you mean."

"If you talk about evil, you'll find evil, or it'll find you."

Now Magnus is completely confused. *Has Grace done something horrible?* He stands up, pulls some money from his pocket, and lays it on the table. "I suppose you are right. Should I steer clear of the American?" he asks, fishing for a clue.

The man laughs maliciously. "*Conforme*, depends . . . depends what you want with her."

A chill runs down Magnus's spine. He decides to let the subject go. Perhaps if he talks to Grace again he can find out what's going on, what she might have done. Maybe he can even help her.

GRACE

TEARS well up as Grace drives out of Topo. Life would have been so much better if Jake had come to the field with her. When she asked him to come along, he gave the idea serious thought—it would be fun. They went back and forth on the subject. Grace's advisor insisted that they needed to be married, or at least pretend to be married, but when she brought marriage up with Jake, she could see that it scared him. They talked about getting married and having kids all the time, but always in some abstract future. Grace didn't want to pretend.

Although Jake's predisposition to fun enticed him to go with her, his practical side did not. Frugality runs deep in his personality; he's an economist, after all. In the end, this is what kept him from coming to the field with her. He said it would be better for both of them to pursue their own paths for the year. That way, they could finish their respective degrees at the same time, saving both time and money. Then they could consider marriage.

"Damn you, Jake," she says aloud. She made sacrifices for him. She chose Columbia over Stanford because he was there and then delayed her fieldwork by a year so he could join her. Her advisor warned her that it would be tough as a single woman doing fieldwork in the Azores. Perhaps she should have stayed in the United States and studied one of the many immigrant communities there, but she felt pressured to go abroad. *Real* anthropological fieldwork requires leaving the safety of the familiar, at least that is how she rationalized her decision to come to the Azores by herself.

She rounds a sharp corner. To her dismay, Magnus stands on the side of the road, hands in pockets, as if waiting for her. He signals her to stop. She stops and opens the passenger-side window. Will he notice that she's been crying?

Magnus puts both hands on top of the car as he leans down to look in. "Is everything okay?" he asks.

Grace forces a smile. "Yeah, couldn't be better." She sniffs dramatically. "My mold allergies are acting up."

"Oh, I see." Water drips off his nose. "I wondered if you feel like coming in for a cup of Swedish-style coffee?"

That is the last thing she wants to do. She looks at her watch. "I would love to, but I really can't do it today. I need to get this car back to Calheta," she lies. "Thanks so much for the invitation. Maybe another time?"

"Okay then, another time." Magnus reaches through the

window. "Until then." He looks her directly in the eye, and they shake hands. He disappears again.

A narrow escape. Grace can't wait to get back to Calheta to her *loja*, make some tea, crawl under her covers, and read a good novel.

4

EVIL EYE

Evil is in the eyes of the beholder.

ÂNGELA MARIA

Ângela Maria does not believe in the evil eye. She also believes in it. Her ambivalence stems from the knowledge that most Azoreans don't believe in such things nowadays. She heard many stories growing up, like all Azorean children do, but has had no firsthand experiences. Sometimes she wonders if her mother conjured those tales—about the evil eye, the witches who had pacts with the devil, and werewolves who devoured children at night— just to keep her eight surviving children under control, to try to increase their chance of survival in a dangerous world. She might have done the same if she were responsible for so many children. Perhaps if her father hadn't spent so much time away. Sometimes it seemed like he came home just long enough to impregnate her mother. Well, one can't be too sure in these matters. Her mother was not the *only* one who told these stories.

To be on the safe side, Ângela Maria made sure that her children, and even her chickens were protected. Tia Carmina, the renowned *benzadeira* of Fajã dos Vimes, saw to it with blessings and incantations, and Ângela Maria augmented Tia Carmina's magic with amulets, gifts to her children. If ever someone complimented her children, she was quick to follow up with the phrase *Guarda de Deus*, "Protection of God." No, she has never personally seen a case of *olhado* or been a victim, but she has always been careful. Her mother, on the other hand, claims to have lost her oldest sons to it. Ângela Maria wonders whether she should tell Grace what she knows. But Grace wouldn't believe her anyway.

A maldade está nos olhos de cada um.

Knowing that Grace would be stopping up for the car and wanting to avoid her, Ângela Maria made her Saturday egg delivery to her parents a bit earlier than usual; she isn't ready to talk to Grace. Now, at nine o'clock in the morning, she walks home carrying a bag of warm fresh-baked sweet potatoes in a plastic bag. She hopes that she hasn't made the round trip too quickly.

Her parents are getting older, but they are still self-sufficient. When she arrived at their house this morning, her father was working in his gardening shed. Her mother was baking in the wood oven in the outside kitchen. She must have started the fire in the wee hours because the oven blazed and the gigantic sweet potatoes oozed caramel—just the way Ângela Maria likes them.

Back home, Ângela Maria climbs up the steps and opens the kitchen door. Good, Grace has already left. Ana and Mário are still asleep. She puts the bag of sweet potatoes down on the table and goes to the cupboard to retrieve a plate. How happy Ana and Mário will be to see these when they finally get up.

She loves Saturdays: no babysitting, no rushing to get the kids out the door to school. The day stretches out before her like a luxurious bed all to herself. She plans to go to the *minimercado* and then to Senhor Estêvão's store to pick up a few items. She wants to start working on Ana's dress for the New Year's dance. First, she needs to clean up the dishes she uncharacteristically left unwashed in the sink. She plugs the drain and turns on the hot water.

Grace's presence has been a blessing that has eased Ângela Maria's solitude. Before her arrival, loneliness permeated every pore of Ângela Maria's body in spite of the companionship of her remaining children. Although her friendship with Grace is new, they have an inexplicable bond; she feels she can tell Grace almost anything. Almost. As she dries the last dish and sticks it in the cupboard, the sound of someone clamoring up the back stairs startles her. The door flies open. It's Miguel.

"What's the rush?" Ângela Maria asks.

Miguel, breathing hard, says, "We were down at the port getting the boat ready and a policeman stopped by." He pauses to catch his breath. "They're looking for the American girl." He wipes sweat off his brow with a handkerchief.

"Why on earth are they looking for her? What do they think she has done? What could she have possibly done?"

Miguel gets a drink of water. "I have no idea. I asked, but they said it was official police business—that they were not at liberty to talk about it. I don't like it."

Feeling faint, Ângela Maria pulls a chair out from the table and sits down. "I'm sure it's nothing." She runs her fingers through her short black hair. "I know you don't completely trust her, Miguel, but she's a good girl. I know she is." A silly thing to say, after all, she doesn't really *know* Grace; she just met her. What *is* her family like? What kind of people would let their daughter go someplace so far from home, where she has no relatives to vouch for her, to protect and help her?

"How the hell do you know she's good? For your sake I hope so . . . We don't need any more trouble." Miguel slams his glass down. "Just tell her when you see her that she is supposed to report to the police station first thing Monday morning. Well, I gotta go. Zé's waiting." He leaves as quickly as he arrived.

Ângela Maria shudders with anger. Miguel opposed renting the *loja* to Grace, to anyone but family. He argued that *American*-Americans don't have morals, not the same morals as Azoreans. As further proof, he said, *And she doesn't even believe in Our Lady*. Grace hadn't exactly said she didn't believe in Mary, but when Miguel asked her, she said, *I believe in Mary, but I don't think I believe in her the same way as you.* Ângela Maria watched Miguel carefully and could see that the answer Grace gave failed to win his approval.

Miguel distrusts outsiders generally, like many others here. Ângela Maria convinced him to take Grace in by appealing to his sense of familial obligation. His cousin, the one for whom they allegedly finished the *loja*, was Grace's teacher at the university. He asked them for help on Grace's behalf. She left the decision to Miguel; he *is* the man. In the end he decided it would be all right, and besides, they could use the extra money.

After he leaves and she recovers from her anger, she hurriedly dresses for running errands. The joy of her expansive day has vanished. She plans to stop at the post office to call her cousin Zoeta in Topo; she needs more information before talking to Grace. Ângela Maria will help her, no matter what the trouble.

ESTÊVÃO

Senhor Estêvão leans over his desk, in theory working on the accounts. Saturday mornings are peaceful in the store. He enjoys the solitude. He flips through his desktop calendar, reviewing his appointments for the coming week. He has penciled in his "lessons" with Grace for the entire year. He likes her, especially the way she treats him—with such great respect.

During their lessons, she listens to him attentively, never taking her striking blue-eyed gaze off him. Her eyes, although blue, appear almost Asian. Dangerous. He loves their look—exotic. Trouble. When she speaks to him, she always casts her eyes down, and he loses sight of them, compelling him to talk again. People say bad things about her. A shopkeeper can hardly avoid hearing such things, especially with a wife that gossips. Yes, Norinha gossips with the clientele. She has made it clear that she is not fond of Grace. She refers to her as *desgraça*.

Senhor Estêvão, however, doesn't subscribe to the bantering of women. The frivolity of such talk once landed him unjustly in prison for several years in Angola during the Salazar era. The banter of women stole a piece of his youth. Yes, that is how he ended up here . . . now . . . in this position.

He'd been at the university in Luanda studying finance. Back then, people knew him as Raposinho, the sly little fox. His friends predicted that one day he would be a powerful politician. He had connections and came from the right family. He too thought this would be a likely course for his life. His life took a different turn, however.

Being a man driven more by desires than ideals led to his involvement with a *mestiça* woman, the half sister of one of his classmates, who was white. Oh, the clarity of her chestnut-colored skin. Her scent fills his memory even now, arousing him.

The complication arose because the same classmate's white sister and he were engaged. When his fiancée learned of the relationship between him and her *mestiça* half sister, she vowed to destroy him. Although he could never prove it, he is certain she spread the rumors about him, rumors of his fraternization with anti-government Blacks, the rumors that ruined everything.

Norinha knows nothing of Raposinho nor much about his life in Angola. He told her that Blacks killed his family on their farm during an uprising and that talking about Angola only brings him pain. Consequently, they don't talk about it often. In truth, Blacks set him free from prison during an uprising, presuming him a sympathizer. His family had long before disassociated with him, fearful that they would be implicated in his alleged involvement in anti-government activities. Until recent years, he's had no contact with his former self.

After being freed from prison, he changed his identity and fled Angola on a fishing boat to the Azores, where his father's family originated. The captain of the boat lived on the island of São Miguel, which is where he met Norinha, who was visiting her cousin, the captain's wife, in Ponta Delgada. As it so happened, she came from São Jorge, the same island as his father. Their relationship began out of desperation; she needed a husband and he needed a living and a life. Love eludes him. The only woman he has ever loved is his mother.

The tinkling of the entry chime brings Senhor Estêvão to the surface. He glances through the crack of the half-open door. Dona Ângela Maria. "I'll be right with you," he calls out to her.

"No hurry," she says.

She's a good girl, can be trusted to browse without worry. Lucky for him that her family adheres to the old island ways. Senhor Estêvão straightens the papers on his desk and checks himself in the mirror before stepping out of his office.

GRACE

GRACE, happy to see the sun again, descends into Calheta in the early afternoon. She stops at the *minimercado* and buys a few things, including a frozen chicken, a rare treat since they only stock them sporadically. Maybe she can make a pot of soup.

After parking the car carefully in its spot at home, she climbs the stairs to return the keys. The door is open, Ângela Maria visible inside.

Ângela Maria looks surprised to see her. "You're back so soon?"

"Yeah, the padre didn't show." Grace hands her the keys. "Tell Miguel thank you for letting me use his car. It ran great." Hungry and tired, she doesn't feel like talking. "I topped up the gas."

"Think nothing of it." Ângela Maria puts the keys on a hook by the door. "Poor thing. Driving all that way and getting stood up. What could have kept the padre from seeing you?"

"Don't know." Grace told her about the boy who delivered the padre's message. "That's how it goes."

"Are you hungry?" Ângela Maria motions toward a plate on the table.

"I am but, forgive me for saying so, those don't look too appetizing; they look like rocks." Grace takes a closer look, reaching out to touch the crusty mound.

"They're sweet potatoes cooked in the wood oven—you'll love them."

Grace welcomes Ângela Maria's nurturing. "I'm starved." She picks one up to inspect it. "What is this white stuff on the outside?"

"Cornmeal." Ângela Maria cuts a potato in half, revealing its beautiful red-orange flesh. Caramelized sugar has collected between the flesh and the skin to form a gooey layer. Putting half a potato on a plate for Grace, she asks, "Would you like a little tea? I already started water." She gestures to a pan on the stove.

"Sounds great." She takes the plate from Ângela Maria and sits down at the table. "How do I eat this? Do I eat it with a fork?"

"You can use your fingers." Ângela Maria dumps some leaves into the water on the stove—fresh leaves. "I talked to my cousin Zoeta today on the phone, and she told me that the first boy who got sick is still in the hospital, but the other children are better. Strange, isn't it?"

Grace takes her first bite of potato. She has never tasted anything like it. Exquisite, like pie in a skin. "Do they know what it is yet?" she asks.

"The doctors are puzzled." Ângela Maria sets two cups of tea on the table. "Zoeta said the family is certain that it is . . ." Ângela Maria pauses. "Something very bad."

Clearly, Ângela Maria didn't say what she started to. What could be so hard for her to say?

"Grace, I'm very worried about you."

Grace takes a sip of the watery tea. "Why?" Then she says emphatically, "I'm fine. I really am."

Ângela Maria's forehead contorts with worry. "The police stopped Miguel this morning." She puts both hands around her teacup. "They were looking for you."

"What?" Maybe she has misunderstood. Perhaps her

Portuguese isn't as good as she imagines. "Why would the police be looking for me?"

"We have no idea," Ângela Maria says. "He told them you went to Topo for the day. You're supposed to report to the police station first thing on Monday morning." Ângela Maria focuses on Grace, as if assessing her response. "Grace, have you done anything? Anything wrong?"

"Absolutely not." Grace is shocked that Ângela Maria even asked such a thing. "What *could* I have done?"

"I'm sure it's nothing serious. After all, if they wanted to arrest you or some such thing, they wouldn't wait until after the *festa*." Ângela Maria stands up. "Police are like that. They get you all worried about nothing. I guess when police come looking, we always jump to the worst conclusions, *não é?*"

"Yeah, you're right," Grace says. "I'm sure it's just some little thing, like maybe they want to make sure I have a driver's license, or maybe they need me to sign something."

Something definitely is going on, though, and she needs to find out what it is. First, the strange trip to Velas, then the equally discomfiting trip to Topo, and now the police are looking for her. Paranoia? Perhaps, or maybe someone wishes her ill.

ON SUNDAY, the feast day for Santa Catarina, Grace heads upstairs to join in the celebration. The soup alone is enough for Grace, but the food keeps coming.

Ângela Maria's sixteen-year-old son, Mário, laughs at the way Grace looks at the fish. "What? You probably never saw a fish cooked with its head on!" Mário spent a year in America with his aunt and thinks he knows everything about American culture. *Americans get all their food out of cans.*

"Not true!" Grace says defensively. "You'll be surprised to learn that I myself have cooked fish with their heads on. I also know how to gut a fish." Grace can say this honestly. She fished often growing up in Montana. Her mother taught her how to catch and clean fish. "But I have never seen a fish that big served at the table—and whole." The enormous silvery fish completely fills the long platter.

"We saved this one for today," Ângela Maria says. "We always have the best on a feast day." Ângela Maria serves everyone potatoes. "Miguel caught this one in August, didn't you, Miguel?"

Miguel's mouth is full. He nods. He hasn't said a word since Grace's arrival. She doesn't know why he hasn't warmed to her. She's tried to start conversations with him many times, but to no avail. Ângela Maria tells her not to worry about it; *He's the quiet type.*

Ângela Maria, seemingly embarrassed about Miguel's nonresponse, makes an effort to smooth the gap. "I remember when I was a girl, my father brought home a nine-kilo lobster."

Grace does the conversion in her head, *almost twenty pounds.* "That's incredible! We don't grow them that big in the US," she says. She wonders if they are tough and rubbery at that size.

When they finish the second course, Ana, Grace, and Ângela Maria clear the plates from the table. Miguel and Mário watch television. Ana begins washing dishes.

"A Graça, I think you have a visitor!" Ana stands on tiptoe looking out the window.

Grace leans over to see. Sure enough, Magnus-the-arrogant-Swede paces below. He must have knocked on the *loja* door. Grace thinks about ignoring him but decides against it since by now everyone in the house, even Mário and Miguel, looks curious, or so she thinks. "Just my luck," she says, smiling out of embarrassment.

Ângela Maria is already out the back door inviting him up. "Are you looking for Grace? She's up here!"

Grace, strangely ashamed, blushes. She hasn't told Ângela Maria about picking him up on the way to Topo.

Magnus moves timidly toward the stairs, speaking awkwardly, "Yes, but I don't want to bother her if she is busy. I don't want to intrude." He sticks his hands in his pockets.

"Nonsense. Come up. We are about to have dessert."

"Well, okay, thank you."

"Magnus, what a surprise!" Grace tries to look happy to see

him when he enters. Mário and Miguel stand up for a moment while Grace introduces Magnus to everyone, then they resume their television watching. "Magnus and I met yesterday on my trip to Topo." It seems better to fess up right away; she doesn't want to arouse suspicion. "He was hitching a ride, and the weather was so miserable up on the *serra* that I didn't feel like I could pass him by."

Magnus smiles and nods in agreement.

"Of course," says Ângela Maria. "One must help out when one can." She takes Magnus's jacket to hang up. "Please have a seat, Magnus." She motions toward the room where the men sit. "We'll have dessert soon."

"That sounds lovely." Magnus joins Mário and Miguel in front of the television. The announcer screams, "Gooooooooooal!" Magnus, obviously comfortable with the male element, cheers with the others.

Grace helps Ângela Maria with the plates, trying to ignore Magnus's every move in the other room with Miguel and Mário. "What kind of cake did you make?"

Ângela Maria carries the round single-layer cake to the table. "*Bolo Alemão*," she says.

It doesn't look anything like the gooey German cakes one finds in the United States. "What's in it?" Grace asks, more to make conversation than out of genuine interest.

"Sugar, butter, orange rind, eggs, flour—it's a simple, quick cake to make—good when you have fresh oranges around." Ângela Maria cuts the cake into thick wedges. Looking over to the men, she says, "Cake's ready."

Ângela Maria seats Magnus diagonally across the table from Grace. Grace observes Magnus as he digs into the cake. He looks extremely content.

"This cake is delicious," he says. "Very much like a cake my mother makes. The best cake I've had since arriving here!"

Ângela Maria blushes. "Well, I'm thrilled that you like it so much."

Things go smoothly enough. Magnus doesn't say anything to offend anyone, and Ângela Maria asks all the questions, which is good; it means Grace doesn't have to say as much. She learns a lot:

Magnus rents a room in Velas, where he spends about half his time; in good weather he travels by motor boat, not by car; and his house in Topo is close to Zoeta's house.

When the meal is over, Grace helps clear the table. As she sets the last of the dishes in the sink, Ângela Maria whispers, "I don't think he came for dinner."

"Yeah, I know, but I don't have anything to say to him . . . we didn't exactly hit it off the other day." Grace glances over at Magnus, who talks to Miguel about some *futebol* star in Sweden.

"I gather that. Maybe he knows that too. Why don't you go for a short walk with him?" Ângela Maria dries her hands off.

"Okay, I guess I should give him a chance," Grace says.

Ângela Maria looks pleased with herself.

Grace waits for a place to interrupt the animated conversation. "Magnus . . . interested in a little exercise? I was thinking about taking a walk."

Magnus jumps to his feet, a bit too eagerly. They thank Ângela Maria and Miguel and leave, heading toward Fajã Grande at a relaxed pace.

"So, I don't suppose you were really just in the neighborhood like you said." Grace kicks a stone.

"Well, not exactly." Magnus looks down as he walks. His toes turn out like a duck. "I wanted to"—he looks up at Grace—"apologize for being such a jerk yesterday." He looks back at his feet.

"I hadn't noticed. Were you being a jerk?" she asks facetiously.

"I don't know what gets into me. Sometimes I can't help myself. I want you to know I really don't think anthropology is stupid. I don't know anything about it."

"I guess you already figured out that I don't know squat about geophysics. So there. We're even."

"You probably know more about it than I know about anthropology," he says. "I guess you could say I'm not really a people person. Anyway, that's what I came to say."

Grace averts her eyes from his earnestness. "I accept your apology. I was just a little irritated." They walk in silence for a few minutes. "Well, I have to go get ready for work. Today is the *festa* for the patron saint of Calheta, and I need to get my recording equipment in order, so we better go back." They turn back.

Magnus starts to ask Grace something and then stops.

"What?" Grace asks.

"Oh, nothing. I . . ."

"Come on! Ask. I'll answer anything. Promise."

"I wondered what sort of work you were doing in Topo yesterday. I'd like to learn more about what you are doing."

"That. I went there to talk to Padre João about the Festa do Espírito Santo. He stood me up." Grace tells him about waiting for the padre. "When I saw you as I was leaving, I was crying. Just at the end of my rope, as they say."

"I noticed that."

"I'm pretty depressed. I'm not getting anywhere with my research. I'm floundering, honestly. I don't know . . ." For now, she won't mention the police thing—not until she knows what it's about. She doesn't know him well enough.

"Do you go to Topo frequently?" he asks.

Is this Magnus's way of flirting? "No, actually, that was my first time there on my own. I went through once on a driving tour of the island. Why do you ask?"

"I was thinking you should stop in for tea the next time you are up that way."

"I might just do that," Grace says. She is warming to him. His awkwardness gives him appeal. Perhaps she had judged him too harshly before. They may actually become friends.

In front of Ângela Maria's house they exchange good-byes and also phone numbers. "Thanks for accepting my apology," he says as he turns to leave.

MAGNUS

As MAGNUS MAKES the steep hike up to the main road, he is satisfied. He's accomplished what he wanted. Now he knows Grace won't avoid him. Perhaps they will even become friends. Although Magnus is relieved that Grace is not involved with anyone in Topo, he remains puzzled. She has never been there, except to pass through. She cried from frustration with her work, not over something that happened. He fusses over the facts as he walks to the road leading out of Calheta. Maybe he should have told her about what the café owner said. No, that would have upset her. He plans to find out what is going on.

5

BLOODY MONDAY

GRACE

MONDAY MORNING FINALLY ROLLS AROUND. Grace hasn't been able to sleep the whole night. She alternates between obsessing over her visit to the police station and thinking about Jake. The snippets of sleep she managed to catch were marred by a repetitive dream in which Magnus spoke in the smug voice, not the kind one, and asked, *But can you prove anything? What can you prove? What is your hypothesis?* Grace tried hard to think of the answers to these questions. Each time she verged on a solution, she awakened, only to fall back into the same unsolvable riddle moments later. She's grateful when the sky begins to lighten.

She gets up, anxious to put this day behind her, makes her coffee and waits. She hears Ângela Maria outside, feeding her chickens as usual. The chickens chatter and cluck, and Ângela Maria responds in kind. Grace hears a knock on the door. It's Ângela Maria.

"Good morning!" Ângela Maria says.

She gives Grace kisses on both cheeks. Grace returns the kisses awkwardly.

"You poor thing! You look like you hardly slept a wink last night."

"Yeah, I guess I'm a little worried about this police station thing," Grace says.

"Well, I saw that you were up, and wanted to check in on you. Are you hungry? I have some fresh buns and São Jorge cheese out upstairs." Ângela Maria puts her hand on Grace's arm as she speaks.

"No, thank you. You know me. I drink coffee and milk for breakfast." Grace takes a big gulp of coffee to demonstrate.

"It's not good for you to drink that stuff first thing in the morning." Ângela Maria chides her. "Well, I have to run upstairs—I have a pot of water boiling on the stove." She begins to leave.

"Oh, Ângela Maria . . . ," Grace says suddenly. "I don't know where the police station is!"

SHE HUMS AS SHE WALKS, perhaps because humming always soothes her, forcing her to take deep breaths, afterward expelling the air evenly. How it works matters little; she needs calming. Three cups of coffee was too much. Today she hums Joni Mitchell's the "Circle Game." As soon as she stops humming, her mind wanders to fantasies of terrible things that are going to happen at the police station. She hums some more.

Grace opens the door marked inconspicuously with "Polícia," and steps into a tiny office; it is smaller than most stand-up cafés. Somebody is whistling a tune from behind a closed door. She taps a service bell that sits on the counter and looks around as she waits. A bulletin board hangs by the door. No most-wanted posters—only a few court notices and some pictures from a party. In one of the photos, five men sit around what appears to be a dead pig; the surrounding grass is stained red with blood. They each raise a glass and don big camera smiles.

"*A matança.*"

Grace startles at the sound of a man's voice from behind. When she turns, she sees a uniformed policeman leaning on the counter, smiling, as if he has played a joke on her intentionally.

"You probably never've seen a pig-killing party before, have you?" The officer lifts the hinged countertop and approaches her. He stands uncomfortably close. She smells his aftershave. "Let me guess, you are the American, Grace McGuiver." He says her name *Mic-ee-ver*. "Just like the television show, no?"

Grace forces a laugh as she steps back to create space. "Yes! People here always recognize my name from that show. Mine is spelled differently, but—"

"Well, we've all seen it and love it," the officer states matter-of-factly.

"I admit I never watched it before coming here," Grace says. "I don't quite get the appeal—"

"American ingenuity in practice!" He goes on as if he has given some thought to it. "You Americans are quite the problem-solvers! We admire that."

"I'm not sure about that, but I do have a problem I'd like to solve . . . Why am I here? Have I done something wrong?" Her face flushes, and she feels the all-too-frequent red blotches rising on her neck.

"Oh, no no no, nothing like that." The officer picks up a stack of papers from the countertop. "Just routine business for your visa." He straightens them by tapping them on the side, clears his throat. "It says here," he reads off the paper, "that as a condition of getting your residency visa granted, you need to have some blood tests."

"Really?" Grace can't remember reading that in the paperwork she received from the consulate. "For what?"

"Let's see . . . AIDS, hepatitis, and other infectious diseases." He looks up at her. "You have such pretty eyes . . . ," he muses aloud in a creepy sort of way.

She ignores it. "Okay. That's not a problem. Where do I have to go for the test?"

"I'll take you." The officer puts the papers in a folder.

"No, no, that's not necessary. I can go where I need to if you'll tell me . . ."

"I *must* take you. I have to see that the paperwork gets done properly. Those were my instructions from the consulate." The officer touches Grace's shoulder as he guides her out the door. "We need to go up to the clinic. The nurse is only on duty this morning," he says.

They get into what appears to be the officer's personal car. There are no official markings on it, and other than the fact that she has met this man in the police station and that he's wearing a uniform, she isn't entirely sure he *really is* a police officer. Rivulets of sweat trickle from under her arms. She reassures herself that Ângela Maria knows where she went. Thank God Ângela Maria stopped in early to see how Grace was doing and gave her directions.

Grace has been past the clinic many times, so she will know shortly whether they are really going there. The car climbs the hill out of Calheta. "So does everyone who wants residency have to get a blood test?" she asks.

"Wouldn't know. First time I've been asked to personally escort someone." The officer's answer seems genuine. "Should only take a few minutes," he says, turning into the driveway at the clinic.

When they enter, there are only a few people in the waiting room, but they all stare with curiosity. She can't blame them—the foreign girl at the clinic under police escort. The officer tells Grace to wait while he talks to a woman at the reception desk. He signals Grace to follow a nurse who appears at a side door. "I'll be here when you are done," he says.

The nurse leads Grace to an open exam room. Grace has had her blood drawn many times in rooms exactly like this. "Please, be seated," the nurse says in English. "This won't take no time."

"Your English is excellent," Grace says as she sits down.

"Oh, thank you. I don't think so."

"No, really, where did you learn it?"

The nurse busily prepares to draw the blood. "In America. I lived there from the time I was four until I was ten. Can you push your left sleeve up?"

Grace pushes her sleeve up, and the nurse ties a rubber cinch around her arm. "Where'd you live?" She's happy and relieved to be having a normal conversation.

"Lowell. My brother still lives there. Do you know it?" She says *Low-ell*, with the accent on the second syllable, the Portuguese way.

"Not too well, but I've heard of it. In Massachusetts, right?" Grace turns her head away as the nurse sticks the needle in. Squeamish.

"Yes, the most beautiful state in America." The nurse starts to fill a second vial.

"You think so? Where else have you been?" Grace is less interested in her answer than in avoiding sight of the blood she is losing.

"Oh, let's see, I have been to New York City and to the Vale San Joaquin in America *de cima*."

She'd been to Massachusetts, New York City, and the San Joaquin Valley in California—America *de baixo*, and America *de cima*—lower and upper America. "Well, it *is* a big country . . . and there are a lot of states in between!"

"Where are you from?" The nurse finishes the second vial, pulls it free, and begins a third.

"One of the states in between—Montana . . . the most beautiful state in America . . . Why do you need so much blood?"

The nurse checks her paperwork. "Oh, they want to make sure they have enough to rerun the tests if there are any problems."

What kind of problems? Not a chance she has AIDS or hepatitis, or anything else for that matter, but what if she does? Would they kick her out of the country? The nurse finally withdraws the needle. It stings. She presses a cotton ball on Grace's arm and applies a Band-Aid.

"You're done!" She labels and places the tubes carefully in a rack. "It was a pleasure to meet you. My name is Zulmira. I'm sure we will see each other again sometime." She extends her hand.

Shaking hands, Grace says, "Zulmira. That's a beautiful name. I'd say it was a pleasure, but . . ."

Relieved that it is done and indeed was nothing, she exits to the waiting room, where the officer waits. He drives her home. As she gets out of the car, she sees Ângela Maria peering out the window, anxious to hear what's happened.

6

CONFESSION

ÂNGELA MARIA

ÂNGELA MARIA SLEPT HEAVILY the night before Grace's visit to the police station. She enjoyed the *festa* and was exhausted, but she awakens feeling as though she has not slept at all. The minute she's fully awake, nonspecific anxiety floods into her consciousness, a feeling that plagues her frequently. Oh yes, now she remembers one of the many things she has to worry about—Grace and the matter with the police. To avoid bothering Miguel, she gets up quietly, grabs her clothes, and dresses in the bathroom.

She sets a pot of water on the stove and puts some fresh *papo-secos* on the table, along with *queijo de São Jorge* and *marmelada*. Then she grabs the garbage pail and goes to feed the chickens. Outside, the cold moist air clings to her skin; she can see her breath. The hens cluck with anticipation. Ângela Maria loves this part of the day.

As she scatters food from the garbage pail, she says in falsetto,

"Oh yes, you will have a feast today." She always talks to the chickens, attributing their fatness and prolific egg laying to her tender treatment. Her chickens lay two eggs per day when many people are lucky to get just one. She notices that Grace is up and knocks softly on the door.

Ângela Maria offers Grace breakfast, knowing that Grace will decline. She doesn't understand how Americans grow to be so tall and strong with such unhealthy eating habits. It is good she stopped in though, as Grace didn't know where the Police station was, and it is not obvious. The poor girl. What happens with the police matters little. Grace is in serious trouble, the kind of trouble that can't be fixed without divine and supernatural intervention, the kind of trouble that one falls into innocently. Ângela Maria puts two teaspoons of Breakfast Blend *cevada*, a roasted barley beverage that resembles instant coffee, into a mug and adds hot water. Clearly, Grace has done nothing wrong. At the same time, she has done everything wrong.

On the way to Mass the other day, Grace asked, *What could you possibly have to confess?* Ângela Maria laughed, saying, *Well, you would be surprised. There are two kinds of sinners: those who do it without knowing, and those who do it on purpose. I am the kind that doesn't know it, didn't do it on purpose, and that is the hardest kind of sin to fix!*

Ângela Maria sits down at the table. She hears a door open in the hallway. Miguel. She rises to make him a cup of Breakfast Blend. He's still in the bathroom. She sets him a place across from her. As he emerges, she says, summoning the most cheerful voice she has, "Good morning!"

"Huh." He moves his head in a gesture of acknowledgment.

"Did you have a good sleep?" Ângela Maria asks.

"Fine." He sits down at the place she has laid for him, takes a bun, cuts a hunk of cheese off, and begins eating it.

Ângela Maria watches him from across the table. He's a handsome man. Unlike many men his age, he's still fit; he hasn't developed the belly that most of them have. He's been a good father, an adequate provider, and perhaps not as good a husband as he could have been. He has trouble keeping his pants on, like many men. Had Ângela Maria been born twenty years later, she would have divorced him by now. Truth be known, were she of marriageable age today, she might not have ever married him, or anybody for that matter. Perhaps she would have gone on to finish her secondary education, maybe even to the university, like she plans for her children. Things were different in those days. In some ways they were simpler. Girls grew up, married, had children, and took care of the home. That was that. Once upon a time, this seemed like everything she would ever want.

During Miguel's and her courtship, she eagerly awaited their awkward chaperoned meetings, and then their walks up to Fajã Grande, holding hands, full of the yearning for one another that only young lovers feel. Where did this yearning go?

Now she watches him chewing his food and feels nothing toward him. Their courtship was long, marked by endless absences when he was out on the fishing boats. The days leading up to his proposal seemed eternal and inevitable. She supposes that she is lucky, though, since some women give in to desire before marriage, like one of her cousins, who became pregnant. Her cousin's young man went off to sea and never returned. He didn't die or anything; he just didn't come back. That was common in those days; young men left and never came back, leaving mothers, sisters, and lovers to deal with the dirt they left behind. At least Miguel came back.

Ângela Maria sighs loudly. "Well, Graça is off to the police station."

"Good. I hope they arrest her." He shoves a piece of bread into his mouth.

"Miguel! You don't really mean that," she says. "What in God's name is wrong with you that you dislike her so much? What has she done to you? Or maybe I should ask what wouldn't she do for you?" Her anger at Miguel swelled.

"No, it isn't like that, not this time, Ângela Maria." Miguel plunks his cup onto the table. "I don't trust her. All of this talk about the illness in Topo, now the police looking for her. I knew she was trouble the minute she walked in the door. We don't need it—that's all."

"What are you talking about?" Mário asks.

Ângela Maria looks up. How long has Mário been standing

there? How much did he hear? How much does he know? "Oh, nothing. Just about Graça."

"Well, if what I think matters, I like her." Mário walks to the cupboard and grabs a plate. He brings it over and sits down.

"And I think her new boyfriend is cute!" Ana's voice chimes in from the doorway.

"He isn't her boyfriend; they met a few days ago!" Ângela Maria says. "You better mind your own business."

"Mark my words." Ana sits down and picks up a bun.

Ângela Maria cleans the house thoroughly this morning. She even takes all the books out of the bookcase, moves it, and dusts behind. She finds cleaning therapeutic; it's better than confession. Confession does little to expend nervous energy.

No matter what trouble Grace is in, Ângela Maria vows to help. She won't let Miguel come between her and her friend. Things can be put straight; they always can. She tidies the figurines on her dresser. Perhaps Miguel will come to trust Grace over time. Miracles have happened before.

At last she hears a car pull up in front of the house. She moves the curtain aside to see out the dining room window. Thank God, it's Grace, and she's smiling.

Anthropological Field Methods 101: No matter how much one reads about doing fieldwork, there is no substitute for actually doing it. First experience feels like sink or swim, often more sinking. Try to focus on the research goal even when faced with physical discomfort, suspicion, and resistance.

GRACE

THE RAIN POURS DOWN, and the wind howls. It's been like this for days. At ten o'clock in the morning, Grace still lies in bed, snuggled under the heavy wool blanket and bedspread. She's unmotivated. On Tuesday she went to give Senhor Estêvão his English lesson, the day after the blood draw. He's changed—loosened up, thankfully.

On Thursday she went to the archives in Velas. Otherwise, she's done nothing, nothing worth writing in her notebook, nothing worth telling anyone about. She did little research, other than visiting Ângela Maria's parents one day. She learned how to distill *aguardente*, how to carve a cork, how to make *carne assada* and *pão de milho*. She also drank too much *aguardente*, tasted good wine, some vinegar, and ate the *carne assada* with *pão de milho*. She's restless. She needs to do more.

Since their walk after dinner on Sunday, her mind keeps wandering to thoughts of Magnus. Grace half expected to find him at the archives on her Thursday visit. Disappointed, she stayed and worked for only an hour, spending the rest of her time milling around in shops. At every turn, she hoped Magnus would appear, but he never did.

She's depressed. Fieldwork is not romantic; it is damn lonely. She wishes she could go home for Christmas. This will be her first Christmas spent outside Montana. Hard to believe that she made it to twenty-seven and has never spent a Christmas away from home. Even during her last four years at Columbia, she always managed to get home.

She talks to her mom by phone every other week. Her mother calls her on the house phone, so it is preplanned. Her dad isn't much of a phone talker. Typically he gets on the phone and says, *Hi, Runs-with-the-Moon*—he likes to use her Blackfeet name. Her mom, the Blackfeet Indian, never uses it. Then he says, *Everything all right?* After hearing that it is, he says, *Okay, I love you. Here's your mom.*

Grace drags herself out of bed. She pulls on her jeans, a T-shirt, and a sweater. On her way to the sink, she stubs her toe. A four-inch centipede, the kind with long legs, struggles to climb up the side of the basin. No matter how hard she tries, she can't get used to living with these creatures; they move too fast. She fills a glass and pours it over the centipede, watching it struggle as it slips down the drain. *Thou shalt not kill . . .* Well, there is a sin to confess. She feels a tiny bit guilty. Mostly, she is happy it is gone.

Damn—she forgot to get coffee. She dresses in her Black Diamond rain gear. Although people laugh at her for wearing it, she loves it. She admits she looks kind of funny in it—like a fisherman out of a Winslow Homer painting. Most people in São Jorge don't even use an umbrella. *It's water! A little water never hurt anyone.* Grace begs to differ. She likes being dry.

But even her rain gear is insufficient on a day like this. As she walks toward the café, the wind blows needles of rain into her face, forcing her to look at the ground as she walks. She decides to stop at the post office, which is halfway.

She's hoping for a letter from Jake. In his last letter, he promised news of his visit. He's too cheap to pay for international long distance on his mobile, and she's too poor to afford it, so they haven't spoken on the phone, just a few texts. Sure enough, a letter has arrived. She tears it open, anxious to read the details of his plan. *Shit.* He isn't coming: "waited too long to buy tickets . . . really sorry . . . ." A tear rolls down her cheek. *Damn him.*

"Everything okay at home?" the postmaster asks.

"Oh yeah, I think so. Thanks," she says. Senhor Silva is a nice man, but she doesn't think he's the one to share sorrows about her love life with. She heads back out into the rain. She needs coffee.

ADVENT

DECEMBER 1 - DECEMBER 24

7

SIGN OF THE BUTTERFLY

ESTÊVÃO

"LOOK AT THIS! Isn't it the most darling thing you've ever seen?" Norinha labors over the Barbie display with a friend. Holiday Barbie wears a billowy pink satin ball gown.

"Just darling!" her friend agrees.

Both store windows will soon display bright-pink Barbie boxes from top to bottom for Christmas.

The sound of his wife's falsetto grates on Senhor Estêvão's nerves. As usual, he sits at his desk working on accounts. The business, which belonged to Norinha's family, has been good to them. The Sousas go back a long way in Calheta. By the time he and Norinha married, they were both nearing thirty, on the older side, and her parents were getting older too. Her mother's health was failing. Shortly after their marriage, his father-in-law asked if he would mind taking over the store. Mind, why he *planned* on it. Yes, it is a marriage of convenience. He certainly would not have stayed with Norinha for any other reason.

". . . that American girl . . ." Senhor Estêvão's ears perk up. The two women always gossip about Grace. Perfect. He counts on it. He's planted seeds in fertile soil.

"Dona Ângela Maria says she has a fiancé in America—I don't believe it. Look at the way she flaunts herself!" says Norinha.

"I know! Did you see what she wore to the Mass for Santa Catarina? Unbelievable! Everywhere she walks, heads turn. She acts like she doesn't notice it, but I think she notices it all too much!"

Senhor Estêvão doesn't think Grace dresses provocatively. She appears to dress like most young American women—T-shirts and jeans. Not much difference between American men and women when it comes to dressing. Grace's perky round breasts are probably what enrage other women so. He *has* noticed those. Maybe they think she should show more modesty, hide herself under sweaters and shawls as they do.

"Next thing you know, she'll be after our husbands," the friend says.

"She probably is already working on mine." Then Norinha whispers something that Senhor Estêvão can't hear. The women apparently have finished stacking the pink boxes in one window. "There, let's go see how that looks!" The chime sounds as the door opens. Senhor Estêvão suspects that his wife's motives for stepping out are something other than admiring her window dressings.

"You don't really think your husband would . . ." The friend's voice trails off as they go out.

Senhor Estêvão stands up to stretch. It has never occurred to him that his wife is jealous of Grace. He always attributed her distrust of Grace to the general fear of outsiders so prevalent in the Azores. All the same, Norinha has grounds to distrust him. He has to give her that.

Over the years his indiscretions have been too numerous to count. Everyone in Calheta knows about his infidelities, and they look the other way with a wink. For the most part, the only person who seems bothered is Norinha, and she can't do anything about it. He's a man with needs, needs that she's all too willing to satisfy but can't. Not her fault; she just doesn't do it for him. Partly owing to her inability to satisfy him and partly owing to her "female problems," their marriage ended up childless, a fact that has never troubled Senhor Estêvão the way it does her.

But he is childless only in the eyes of society. He has a son that she doesn't know about. He has made sure that she will never find out. The boy lives with his mother, grandmother, and half sister, and knows nothing of his father. Perhaps the day will come when he will, but then again, perhaps not. Having a son is one thing, and knowing him is quite another. Alas, his son is not well, and with each passing day it seems less likely that Senhor Estêvão will ever have that joy.

He straightens the stacks of documents on his desk, makes sure that each stack aligns perfectly with the next and perfectly with the edge of his desk. Norinha's jealousy awakens him to the possibility of Grace. Until now, he hasn't thought of having an affair with her. He needs her for deeper, more sincere reasons. Now he also wants her from the depths of his being. Oh, her beautiful eyes and silky straight hair. If only he could lie next to her, the smooth whiteness of her skin against his own darker body. He's never been with such a tall woman; it arouses him.

GRACE

Two DAYS HAVE PASSED since Grace received Jake's letter. The weather hasn't let up, and Grace wallows in self-pity. She even cancels Senhor Estêvão's Tuesday English lesson. He seems disproportionately disappointed and tries to get her to commit to another day. She claims herself too busy. Fortunately, he doesn't probe too deeply, because she hasn't yet figured out what she is so busy with.

Today, she decides to get out of bed, at least. After showering, she goes to see if Ângela Maria is home, thinking that talking to her might make her feel better. Ângela Maria genuinely cares for her.

"Hoo hoo!" she calls, poking her head through the door.

"Grace?" Ângela Maria is back in one of the bedrooms. "I'll be right out. Make yourself at home."

Grace walks over to the refrigerator and starts to open it, but she stops herself. She habitually opens the refrigerator at her mom's house, even when she doesn't want something to eat. Instead, she grabs a glass from the cupboard and pours a glass of water.

"Hello!" Ângela Maria sounds a little out of breath. "I was making the bed. I decided to turn the mattress—don't ask me why," she says. "Haven't seen much of you this week. What's going on?"

"Oh, nothing." Grace runs her finger around the top of her glass, causing it to hum. She stops. "I guess I've been feeling a little down in the dumps." She hesitates. "Because Jake isn't coming for Christmas." She hasn't told anyone yet, because she thinks people won't believe that Jake exists if he doesn't come. She worries they might think she lied about being engaged, and rightfully so.

"Oh, you poor thing." Ângela Maria walks over and gets a tissue from a box on the counter. "When did you talk to him?"

"On Monday . . . I didn't talk to him. He sent a letter." Grace accepts the tissue and blows her nose. "I want to go home. I miss my family."

Ângela Maria puts her hand on Grace's shoulder. "It's going to be fine. Everything is going to be fine. You'll see. Things have a way of working out the way they're meant to. I believe that. I do."

It sounds as if Ângela Maria is trying to convince herself. Ângela Maria obviously is worried about things.

"Yes, I am sure, in the end, that everything will turn out the way it is supposed to," Grace agrees half-heartedly. "Everything okay with you?"

"Oh, yeah, yeah." Ângela Maria starts wiping the counter off. Grace notices it isn't dirty. "Miguel is off to Velas today to get the TV fixed, and the kids are at school."

"That doesn't really answer the question I asked—*you*, how are you?"

Ângela Maria collapses into a chair. She twists the rag. "Honestly? Things stink. I know you're already upset, and I don't want to burden you."

Grace sits down across from Ângela Maria, supporting her head with her hand, elbow on the table. "I know you have been wanting to talk to me about something. You might as well get it out."

"Well, Miguel is worried about having you here. He got it into his head that you might bring bad luck. We've had a lot of that." Ângela Maria looks down as she talks. A tear drops onto the table. "I don't believe it, Grace. You're the best thing that's happened to me in a long time." She looks up and reaches over to hold Grace's hand. "But, you know, Miguel has heard things, and then the thing with the police . . . he doesn't believe that it is really about your visa."

Grace feels numb. "But it is! Why else would the police make me get blood tests? That *is* what they told me." Grace pulls her hand away from Ângela Maria. "Does he want me to move out? I can move out. I should move out." Grace stands up. "I'm going to move out right now."

Ângela Maria springs to her feet. "No. You will not, and must not, move out. I won't allow it!" Ângela Maria holds Grace's shoulders. "Please stay. There's more to tell, but I'm not ready, and you're not ready to hear it. I promise I'm going to help you Grace. You'll see. Everything will be fine. I'm so sorry. I shouldn't have said anything to you when you were already upset." Ângela Maria folds Grace into her arms. Grace sobs.

LATER THAT DAY Grace crawls into bed with her notebook. She scribbles furiously and almost illegibly.

December 5, Calheta
Damn it to hell. Damn it. Damn it. Damn it. Fucking shit.
What should I do? I should leave now, give up, go home. How could I have messed everything up already? What did I do wrong? Ângela Maria didn't tell me shit.

Grace stares at the crucifix on the wall. She throws her notebook across the room in rage. Through her tears, she watches as the pages flutter to the ground. She's a fraud. What *is* she doing here anyway? Who's she kidding? She isn't a *real* anthropologist.

She closes her eyes, aware of the afterimage of the cross—the Blackfeet sign of the butterfly, on whose wings dreams fly.

Several hours later she awakens in the dark. Feeling mysteriously renewed, she gets up and makes a cup of tea. She remembers the butterfly sign and chuckles aloud. Funny how one's past, even a rejected one, surfaces when least expected. She hasn't slept on the wings of butterflies since her grandmother's death some fifteen years earlier. She feels like a warrior ready to battle an unknown enemy. First, she needs to find out the truth about her visit from the police.

8

FATHER, SON, AND HOLY GHOST

MAGNUS

MAGNUS SPENDS the day on the *serra*, documenting some active steam vents he discovered when hiking on the previous day. When he finishes he hitches a ride to Topo. Today is not his day, he muses, as a small pickup truck pulls to the side of the road. The cab is full. The driver's a guy Magnus recognizes from the café.

"Hop in, if you don't mind getting a little wet." The driver takes a final drag from his cigarette and throws it on the ground.

"Thanks." Magnus climbs into the back. A starved-looking cattle dog greets him, all too happy to share the ride. Magnus settles down as close to the cab as he can. The dog rests its head on his leg.

Magnus likes dogs. As a boy, growing up on a dairy farm in southern Sweden, he had many dogs. Stroking the wet fur of this dog brings back memories. He was always restless, not one to stick around, much to the disappointment of his father, who had hoped to pass the farm on to his oldest son. Magnus dreamt of adventures in faraway places. The American Wild West and stories of exploration fascinated him. At the age of ten, he drew up elaborate plans to run away to the dark forests of Småland, where he imagined living the life of a storybook character, perhaps joining a band of robbers. He never made it to Småland. His first real adventure came at the age of eighteen, when he crewed a sailboat headed to America. That trip introduced him to the North Atlantic's volcanic gems—the Azores and Iceland.

Magnus is grateful for the warmth of the dog's head on his lap. When the pickup truck pulls over in town, he pats the dog and stiffly climbs over the tailgate.

"Thanks for the ride." He waves good-bye. Time for coffee.

The café owner brings his coffee and *aguardente*, setting them down without a word. He heads back over to his spot behind the counter and resumes the conversation he was having when Magnus entered.

Magnus pulls his notebook from his knapsack and begins working on the notes he took on the *serra*. His hands were so cold that he made only cryptic notations, enough to jog his memory when he got down. As he works, he tries to ignore the conversation at the counter, but he finds himself constantly drawn back to it.

". . . all of the children who have gotten it have recovered except for the boy . . . dialysis . . . doctors don't know what more can be done." Magnus catches snippets. "The American girl doesn't have anything . . ." Why are they talking about Grace in relation to this illness? He thinks about the conversation he had with the café owner a couple of weeks earlier.

Magnus has been thinking about Grace more than he wants to, and has intentionally stayed away from her. When he saw her in Calheta the last time, he felt something stir, and he isn't ready to start anything. He wants a friend, not a lover. The last time this happened it ended in complete heartbreak. A relationship with Grace would surely end the same way. They have their own lives and, more importantly, research, and when they are done with their respective projects, they will go their separate ways; he'll go back to Sweden, and she back to America.

He needs to focus on work. He reviews what he managed to get done and begins working in earnest, this time successfully blocking out everything else, including his own wandering thoughts. When he finishes, he closes his notebook, and orders another coffee.

Tomorrow he'll go to Velas. Perhaps he'll bump into Grace. If he does, he'll ask her about why people in Topo are talking about her, and this time he won't hedge around the issue the way he did the first time. He downs his shot.

GRACE

GRACE JUMPS out of bed on Thursday morning with a sense of urgency. Things are bad, but she might be able to fix them.

Everything is gray. Even the whitewashed walls look gray in this light. She thinks about Dorothy in *The Wizard of Oz* in her black-and-white world and begins humming the tune to "Somewhere Over the Rainbow" as she walks to the bus stop. Funny how things pop into one's brain. She's watched *The Wizard of Oz* every year of her life, until this year. Maybe if she clicks her heels together, she'll go home like Dorothy. She stops, looks down at her black rubber boots, and tries it. Nope. She picks up her pace and whistles the tune to "Follow the Yellow Brick Road." She arrives at the bus stop about ten minutes early.

A white Opal pulls up. She doesn't immediately recognize the driver. The window opens and she sees Zulmira, the nurse from the clinic. "Hi, Grace!" she says. "On your way to Velas?"

"Yeah, off to the archives." Grace tries to sound nonchalant.

"Hop in. I'm on my way there too." Zulmira pushes the passenger-side door open.

"Thanks! Wow, how wonderful not to spend an hour and a half on the bus!"

Zulmira says, "Of course. I have just one condition—that we speak English so I can practice."

"Sounds like a deal," Grace says.

They continue the conversation they began at the clinic about places in the United States. For some reason, Grace is compelled to tell Zulmira about her Native American ancestry, when she hasn't previously mentioned it to anyone, not even to Ângela Maria. Perhaps her heritage is top of mind because of the butterfly image. More likely, she believes it will make her seem more interesting to Zulmira. She needs a friend, an unmarried-woman-her-age friend. Her revelation succeeds at fascinating Zulmira, who shoots one question after another at her, so many questions that she regrets having brought it up.

As they near Velas, Zulmira says, "You know, Grace, I work in Velas every Tuesday and Thursday. I'd be happy to give you a ride down on those days."

"That would be great. Thank you."

"You can wait at the bus stop like today. I always go by at the same time. That way, we won't have to plan ahead," Zulmira says.

"Even better!"

They descend into Velas. "Where do you want me to drop you?" Zulmira asks.

"You can drop me at the square," Grace replies. "I'll probably go to the Café da Ilha for a *galão*. Care to join me?"

"I'd love to, but I have to get to work. Maybe another time? If you want to ride back with me, meet me at the hospital entrance at four thirty. Do you know where the hospital is?"

"Yeah, I know where it is," Grace says. "I'll probably catch the bus. Don't think I can stand staying in the archives that long, but thanks for the offer."

Zulmira pulls over in front of the Café da Ilha. "Here you are. Hope to see you again soon."

"Yeah, me too."

When Grace walks into Café da Ilha, she's pleasantly surprised. Magnus sits at a corner table. He faces the door as if waiting for her. Her heart pounds. "Magnus, I didn't expect to find you here!"

He stands up and pulls a chair out for her. "That's funny." He smiles. " I hoped I might see you."

The owner approaches. "A *galão?*"

"Yes, thank you." Everything feels back to normal. "Actually, I thought I might see you at the archives, but I'm happy you're here instead. This is much more conducive to talking . . . Some strange things have been going on, and I thought you might be able to help."

"And I wanted to ask you about some odd things that I've heard," he says. "You go first."

Grace tells Magnus about her paranoia, her cryptic conversations with Ângela Maria, Miguel's distrust, and finally about the whole thing with the police. "Did you have to do a blood test too?" Grace waits for his response.

He rubs his forehead. "No. I never had to take a blood test, but that might not mean anything. Maybe the visa requirements are different for Americans than for Europeans—you know we *are unified.*"

"Oh yeah, I'd forgotten that." Grace feels of a ray of hope. "Okay, now your turn. What've you heard?"

"Well, snippets of conversation here and there about some illness and sick kids in Topo. The odd thing is that you came up in the same conversation. Why would people in Topo be talking about you in relation to the sick children? So, on the one hand, the visit from the police might be nothing, and on the other hand, it might be something—something related to the illness in Topo."

"How could it be? I've only been there that one day, and on that day I barely got out of my car."

"I know. That's one of the things that puzzles me as well." He shifts his weight. "They think you have something to do with the sick kids, so they ordered blood tests? That's what I'd bet."

"But who are *they?* And why would they test me for AIDS and hepatitis? I obviously didn't pass those diseases to kids that I've never seen, much less touched. That's absurd."

"Are you positive they actually tested you for those things? How would you know?" Magnus asks.

"Well, that's what the officer told me," Grace says. Now that she thinks about it, she hasn't seen the papers herself. The officer kept the paperwork from her. "All I know is they took several vials of blood." She could ask Zulmira.

Magnus reaches across the table and takes hold of Grace's hand. "Grace, I'll help if I can." He lets go, seeming embarrassed. "I just want you to know that you're not alone. I'm here if you need me."

Grace blushes. "Thanks, Magnus. That makes me feel better. It really does."

MAGNUS AND GRACE go to the archives after their morning coffee, and Grace has her first productive day in weeks. Magnus sits beside her, not on the other side of the room. Periodically, they exchange looks. He too combs through old newspapers, only he hunts for references to seismic activity—*rock hard facts*. He kindly passes along articles of interest to Grace, and she does likewise for him. Working together proves vastly superior to working individually; they cover much more ground.

Grace takes notes on calamities that befell São Jorge in the nineteenth century. Inhabitants of São Jorge suffered innumerable disasters: earthquakes, volcanic eruptions, famines, plagues, epidemics, and droughts. They endured more calamities than the people of any other island in the archipelago. Every issue of *O Jorgense* contains some reference to a natural disaster. Grace finds several detailed accounts of people flocking to churches to pray for divine intervention.

One article recounts the story of the 1808 eruption of Pico da Esperança. Huge boulders rained down on Urzelina and Manadas for days on end. Fires burned, lava flowed, ashes fell, and the earth trembled for more than two months. The article illustrates the mercy of the divine Espírito Santo; it could have been so much worse. How terrifying it must have been to people with so little knowledge of the inner workings of the earth. Prayers and promises were their only recourse. No wonder they believed in a god with multiple personalities—the Father, Son, and Holy Ghost —so unpredictable in His ways.

Ângela Maria describes the Father as "unapproachable." When His children want to talk to Him, they have to go through the saints, or the Mother. The Son is "full of love and forgiveness." She describes the Holy Spirit, the person of God most revered by Azoreans, as at once "wrathful and merciful," only appeased through copious prayers, offerings, and fulfillment of promises. Grace understands how a fervent belief in the Holy Ghost came to pass, but she can't imagine believing in something like this herself.

She neither believes nor disbelieves in God. She feels the same about all religions, including the Blackfeet religion. To her way of thinking, all systems of belief are equally valid or invalid; they are, to greater or lesser degrees, consistent with themselves.

She has dreams that speak to her, and at times she prays, but unlike her Blackfeet mother, she's detached from the spirit world. Unlike her doctor father, she's skeptical of science. Facts and truth elude her. There are no simple answers.

AT THE END of the day, Grace can't find Zulmira at the hospital, and the bus is long gone. Fortunately, she sees a taxi and recognizes the driver from Calheta. She and Magnus hung out after finishing at the archives. It was fun. He talked about Sweden, the family farm, and how he had ended up in the Azores. She talked about growing up in Montana, part Indian, mostly white, on and off the reservation. She didn't tell him about Jake. She can't wait to see him again.

9

WHAT PEOPLE SAY

GRACE

THAT NIGHT NOTHING CHANGES. Everything changes. Dreams come on the wings of butterflies. Ângela Maria comes to Grace in the form of a dog, says nothing . . . The dog places her shaggy head on Grace's lap . . . An infusion of warmth and love washes over her . . . She strokes the dog's woolly fur before surfacing momentarily.

Now she climbs down a steep incline . . . She drops something and tries to retrieve it, but can't remember what it is. Something down deep. Rain . . . Raining pebbles. Her feet slip from underneath. Falling . . . Falling rain . . . Tears . . . Tears of stone. The earth cries with a deafening rumble.

Grace bolts upright, heart racing, head throbbing. It's just the sound of the fish vendor's motorcycle. She lies back down, relieved. *Tears of stone.* Makes perfect sense. She'd been reading about the eruption of Pico da Esperança and the boulders. But

Ângela Maria as a dog? A loyal friend perhaps. Grace laughs aloud, thinking that if she had told her mother about these dreams, her mother would have made a big deal of them, would have said they were spirit dreams—even visions. She loves her mother's interpretations of dreams. She loves her mother. She wishes she were here.

Grace gets up. As a girl, shortly after her grandmother died, she experienced a period of strange dreams similar in intensity to what she's having now. In those dreams she flew, floated, soared, and laughed, lifted into flight by an owl-like old woman. Her mother said these were medicine dreams, brought to carry her through hard times. *Strange medicine.*

WHEN SHE WALKS UPSTAIRS, she finds Ângela Maria sitting in the kitchen mending some pants. "Thank God!" Ângela Maria exclaims as she leaps to her feet. "I was so worried about you after the other day. I shouldn't have said anything."

"Nonsense," Grace says. "You helped me. You pushed me into action. I knew Miguel didn't trust me. That's obvious. Knowing and hearing are different things." She recounts her conversation with Magnus about the gossip he'd overheard in Topo. "We suspect that the blood test is related to that; they must think I have a disease that I'm spreading. How I could have done it is another problem altogether."

"Well." Ângela Maria sighs. "I guess I should tell you what I know and have heard. You probably won't believe it. That's okay. You still need to listen, because it is what people are saying."

What people say.

"I'm listening."

"First, you're right about the blood tests. They're related to the illness in Topo." Ângela Maria fills a pan with water. "But not for medical testing."

Feeling a sudden chill, Grace pulls her coat over her shoulders. "Well? What for, then?"

Ângela Maria draws a deep breath. "Magic. Black magic. There's talk of it."

God, what has she stepped into? This is worse than she imagined. She could fight an enemy she believed in.

"I know it sounds strange, and I'm sure you don't believe in magic—Americans don't believe in that sort of thing. You believe there are rational explanations for everything . . ."

Grace's mother filled her childhood with stories of magic: disappearing objects, taken by ghosts, that later reappeared; illnesses sent from beyond; stories of Old Man and Old Woman. Her mother believes in magic, even practices it. Grace *doesn't* believe. Magic is fiction, illusion.

"You need to be careful about whom you talk to, whom you accept gifts from. I'm afraid for you, Grace."

"Why would someone want to hurt me, Ângela Maria? I haven't done anything."

"There's a woman, Nonna Preta, in Topo, who people say is a *bruxa*, a *feiticeira*. Maybe she's a witch, maybe not, but that's what people say. She's the sick boy's grandmother, and people say she wants vengeance. She thinks you're responsible for her grandson's illness. At first, I didn't believe it." Ângela Maria puts some herbs into the teapot and pours the hot water.

"A witch? That's absurd, and besides, how could I be responsible for making someone sick that I've never even seen or been close to?" Maybe she *has* become Dorothy in *The Wizard of Oz* after all.

"The boy's mother claims you gave both her son and daughter *olhado* on the *Espírito Santo* the day you arrived. People say because Nonna Preta is an evil witch she lacks the power to do anything curative, and that's what angers her. The next day, the mother of the children took their clothes to another woman whose name is Tia Carmina. She is a *benzedeira*, what we call a white witch, who lives in Fajã dos Vimes. Tia Carmina said some prayers, washed the clothes in her special teas, and gave the mother some medicine to give to the children. The girl got better right away, but the boy stayed sick and to this day remains in the hospital; they say his kidneys aren't working."

Grace remembers the children from the boat. She remembers writing about them in her notebook. They ate limpets. "I remember them, but I don't recall looking at them any differently than I'm looking at you right now." The mother called the children over to her when Grace tried to talk to them.

Ângela Maria continues, "I don't believe in *olhado*, although I have heard many stories, including one from my own mother." Ângela Maria sets a cup of tea in front of Grace. "Drink, and I'll tell you."

Grace picks up the teacup and inhales its herby fragrance as Ângela Maria begins her story.

"A few years before I was born, the elderly mother of a neighbor, a widow in mourning, had recently moved in. A kind woman who loved children, she cooed over them and gave them sweets. My mother left her three sons, my brothers, with the widow while she went to run errands."

"That night, shortly after retrieving them, they all began to wail. The poor little things got diarrhea like my mother had never seen. She waited until daylight, taking a piece of each child's clothing to the *benzedeira*. The old witch cut swatches from each item and floated them in a mixture of water and olive oil. She observed the movements of the pieces of cloth for some time, in the end proclaiming that it was too late. By the time my mother arrived home, her beautiful sons had dried up. They lay motionless in my father's arms."

"The old widow was *devastada*. She knew she had probably been the one to harm the children, and all because she loved them so much. She didn't want to have the same effect on other children, so she too went to the *benzedeira*. The witch told her there was no cure for the giver of *olhado*, but that she must always be on guard. She must contain her adoration for children and, to be on the safe side, must even protect her own grandchildren from her unwanted power."

"The witch cut a swatch from the old woman's shawl, boiled it in a pot with some herbs, saying an *encantamento* over it, then gave it to the widow, instructing her to give each of her grandchildren a spoonful of the tea each day. When she ran out, she was to return for more. As the story goes, the potion worked."

"So that's my mother's story, and although I don't believe in *olhado*, I have no reason to think that she would lie to me either."

The story serves only to confirm Grace's conviction; magic *is* fiction. "Well, doesn't it seem possible to you that the diarrhea could have been caused by something else, like bad water?"

"I have thought of that, but my mother insists that the water from inside the island has always been good to drink. The thing about *olhado* is that the person who gives it doesn't intend harm. You wouldn't know if you had given it." Ângela Maria goes over to the cupboard and takes some cookies out. "Well, there are others who also claim you gave their children *olhado*."

"Others? What others? This is crazy."

"Children that you've seen on the bus on your various visits to Velas." Ângela Maria puts a plateful of cookies down on the table. "Eat," she says. "We can't know with certainty that you didn't do it, nor can we know if you did."

"That's true enough . . ." It fits her agnosticism perfectly. We can't know anything with certainty. What should she do? What can she do? "But it doesn't make sense to me that the only children I have given *olhado* to would be from Topo. What about the children of Calheta? Urzelina? Norte Pequeno? Rosais? Children from Topo are not the only ones on the bus."

"You're right. The claims have come from several different places, but there are more cases in Topo than elsewhere," Ângela Maria says. She reaches out and holds Grace's hand. "You know, I can help you if you let me. I'm your loyal friend, no matter what comes to pass."

Grace tries to imagine this Nonna Preta. She envisions a haggard and toothless face. Maybe she even has a wart on her nose and green skin like the wicked witch in *The Wizard of Oz*. "What do you think she wants with my blood?"

Ângela Maria squeezes Grace's hand and lets go. "Zoeta, on my behalf, took the liberty of talking to Tia Carmina. Tia Carmina says that in the black practices of magic, one can use substances from a person's body or their belongings to bring them harm. Tia Carmina claims that Nonna Preta has no power. She doubts Nonna Preta is even the person people say she is. All the same, I caution you. Don't trust anyone. You've been fooled once —that we know of. Guard yourself and your things."

Grace thinks about the police officer who took her up to the hospital. She thinks about Zulmira. "You know, I caught a ride to Velas yesterday with a woman named Zulmira—the nurse who drew my blood. Do you think she's in on this?"

"I know who you're talking about. She has always been a good girl. I don't think she would get into something like this, but she *has* people in Topo. I think you best avoid people you don't *know*." Ângela Maria pours more tea into their cups. "One thing, Miguel forbids my involvement. He believes *all* of it. If you decide to let me help you, he can't know. He's afraid that Nonna Preta might bring something bad upon our house."

"Of course." Grace slips into a not-so-brave, not-so-conquer-the-world state. "How can you help me?"

"I'll tell you later. You need to absorb all that I've told you first. When you're sure you want or need my help, I'll be here. Have *faith*. Right now, you're full of doubts. You'll know when the time comes."

Have faith. She has searched for it for most of her life. She attended churches of every branch of Christianity, also synagogues, and for a time became a Buddhist, but she never found faith in anything. As an undergraduate, she read all of the great theological philosophers. She thought she finally felt at peace with its absence, but now circumstances have changed. She wonders where she will find it. If she will find it.

10

OUR LADY OF LIGHT

GRACE

GRACE RETREATS to the comfort and safety of the *loja*. A week passes. She's not sleeping well. The dreams keep coming—always a dog and a pelting rain. In one dream she lies at the bottom of a great crevasse—motionless but not dead—eyes open, staring blankly upward. She's tired. Stones rain down on her, slowly covering her entire body, all but her face. Her white face with her blue eyes shines brightly against the backdrop of black stones, and she begins to cry. The tears burn as they run down the sides of her face. Suddenly, she feels something cool and soft—the dog's tongue; the dog licks away the tears.

During the days, Grace writes in her notebook about nothing in particular. Mostly, she tries to figure out how this all happened. She refuses to believe in this evil eye and magic stuff. There must be a logical explanation. She feels as certain of this as that the Holy Spirit has nothing to do with the havoc wrought upon poor

São Jorge during centuries past. The chaotic and inexplicable laws of nature have everything to do with it.

At the end of a week of inner turmoil, Grace emerges, armed with her powers of observation and analysis. For now, she'll try to handle this on her own. She'll stay on guard, because she's certain there are people in São Jorge who wish her harm, but she'll try to go on doing her research and living her life as if magic does not exist in the world, the way she has always done.

MAGNUS

ON THURSDAY, a week after their shared visit to the archives, Magnus waits for Grace at the Café da Ilha. The prior week they agreed to meet there at ten o'clock. They even joked about Azorean time being the same as Indian time—not too precise. He's been waiting for over an hour and resigns himself to the fact she is not showing up. He tries not to take it personally.

She was fine when he last saw her. Their time together was lovely, at least he thought so. She spoke freely of herself and her family; he wishes he had more of that openness. He's always been reserved when it comes to talking about his personal life. Of course, his life doesn't seem nearly as interesting as hers. She was raised in the heart of the Wild West, an Indian, although she looks more like a Swede.

He proudly told her about his trip to Montana. The year he crewed he had spent three months traveling in the United States while they waited for good sailing weather to return. His goal was to visit all the national parks west of the Mississippi. Glacier National Park, which borders the Blackfeet reservation, fell too far north, and the weather wasn't cooperating, but he managed to visit Yellowstone.

He checks the time. *Why isn't she here?* Finally, he decides to leave; he'll stop in Calheta tomorrow on his way to Topo.

THE NEXT MORNING, a construction worker picks Magnus up before he has reached the outskirts of Velas, and he makes it to Calheta in record time. To avoid arriving too early in the morning, he gets out above Calheta on the main road and walks down an ancient cobblestone trail that remains from pre-automotive days—not all that long ago.

Farmers still use these steep roads to move cattle, oxen, and plows from one terraced plot to another. Although there are no oxen on the path in the middle of winter, he has seen them many times working in the tiny fields. Ingenious how Azoreans discovered the technology best suited to their terrain so long ago. He's seen only one bona fide tractor on the island, and that was up on top, where the fields are larger and more level.

Once down, he walks toward Grace's. Her lights are on. Will she be glad to see him? He sits down across the street on the wall facing seaward and waits still longer—until nine o'clock, a civilized time for calling on her. Gazing across the channel to Pico, he marvels at the phenomenal forces that created that island, pushing it nearly twenty-four hundred meters above sea level. How he would love to have seen Santa Lúcia erupt. *Our Lady of Light.* He has read accounts of her spectacular eruption in the eighteenth century. From where he sits now, he would have had a perfect view of her three flows, just as the people of São Jorge did three centuries earlier. Of course, he'd also have suffered the rain of pea-sized stones. He looks at his watch. Time to go.

As Magnus rounds the house, Ângela Maria greets him. "*Bom dia*, Magnus!" She stands on the stairs hanging wet laundry on a pulley line. That people bother hanging their clothes outside to dry in the winter amuses Magnus. In his experience, clothes don't even dry well here in the summer. "*Bom dia.* Is Grace in?" he asks.

"Yes, yes," Ângela Maria says. She puts her hands on her hips. "She has scarcely left the house the past week. I'm worried about her, but she says she's fine."

"Me too—I'm worried. She was supposed to meet me yesterday in Velas, but she didn't show up." Magnus stoops to pick up a clothespin that dropped. He hands it up to Ângela Maria.

"Well, I hope your visit cheers her up." Ângela Maria goes inside.

Magnus taps on Grace's door. After a few minutes she opens it, smiling. She looks tired but otherwise fine. "Magnus! Come in," she says.

Magnus steps into the tiny *loja*. So ascetic. "I was worried about you when you didn't show up yesterday."

"I know. I'm so sorry. I've been so absorbed in my problems that I forgot about everything else. I should have called. I even missed my lesson with Senhor Estêvão this week. I'm really and truly sorry. Hope you didn't wait too long." The *cafeteira* on the Bunsen burner begins to gurgle. Grace takes it off. "Coffee?"

"I'd love some." Magnus takes off his jacket. He glances around for a place to put it.

"Oh, let me." Grace takes his jacket and drapes it on the end of the bed. "Kind of a simple place, eh?"

"Very nice!" He adds, "For a nun."

"It's all I need. I'm cozy here." Grace pours the coffee into demitasse cups.

"Is that why you haven't come out for a week? Too cozy?" Magnus asks. He looks into her face to read her response and steps closer to put sugar in his coffee. "I like lots of sugar." It's been a long time since he's been this close to a woman. He feels a slight buzz.

"You'll think I am silly if I tell you why I haven't gone anywhere."

"Try me," Magnus says.

"Okay, but let's sit down. Sorry, we have to sit on the bed." Grace plops down on the side of the bed.

Magnus sits down next to her, careful not to spill his coffee, and gives her the right amount of distance. "All right, *shoot*, as they say in your country."

Grace fidgets. "Well, I found out what the blood tests were for and how they're related to the illness in Topo—Ângela Maria told me."

"And?" Magnus fills the pause.

"You aren't going to believe this—I don't really—but she says people say I gave some kids in Topo the evil eye; that's what made them sick. The grandmother of one of them, an alleged witch, contrived to get my blood for purposes of black magic—revenge. They're out to get me."

"Oh, come on!" Magnus says incredulously. "And you are actually worried about this?" He tries not to sound too patronizing.

"Well, I think there could be *something* going on. I believe that somebody wishes me ill, for some reason. Ângela Maria is deeply worried."

"Hmm . . ." Magnus looks intently at the floor, searching for a response that Grace won't find insulting.

"I knew you would think it was stupid, but you asked, and I told you," she says.

He takes his coffee cup over to the little counter. "Well, you know, of course, that I don't believe in any of this evil eye or witch stuff. I have absolutely no doubts whatsoever that the illness has a scientific explanation, and that you have nothing to do with it." Still, he feels bad that this is happening to her.

Grace puts her cup up on the windowsill above the bed. She leans on her pillows against the wooden wall. "I knew you wouldn't. You're one of those people who believe that there is a scientific explanation for everything. That's why I wasn't sure I wanted to tell you. That's why I didn't meet you yesterday. I couldn't bear the thought of getting in a fight with you over this."

Magnus *does* believe that there is a scientific explanation for everything. He sits down on the foot of the bed. "In this case, I absolutely believe it, but I'm not going to fight with you."

"Well," says Grace, "I'm not sure about anything. Ultimately, what you or I believe doesn't matter a rat's ass if everyone else on this island believes something different. I have a problem that needs solving if I'm ever going to get my work done." She crawls under the covers.

Magnus has much to say, but he doesn't say it. Grace is in a vulnerable state, and he knows from experience that caution is warranted. He puts his hand down on the roughly woven bedspread. He can feel Grace's leg beneath. She doesn't pull away. "Well, I would venture to say that few people on this island believe in this stuff. I have been here for over a year and never once encountered it."

He nervously fidgets with the raised knots that form the design of the blanket. Her leg moves underneath his hand, sending a jolt of adrenaline through his body. His heart pounds. There is nothing more he desires in this moment than to hold Grace tightly in his arms, but that seems inappropriate under the circumstances.

"Well, I have an idea," he says. "I sat on a panel yesterday afternoon in Velas, a public health panel, and I met a guy named Dr. Roberto who works at the hospital. I'll talk to him to see what he knows." Magnus, not trusting himself, stands up to signal his departure. "I'm really sorry about all of this Grace. I'm here for you."

"I'm sorry also." Grace crawls out from under the covers, and stands too.

Without thinking, Magnus takes her in his arms. She's trembling. Their eyes meet briefly and he kisses her. She kisses him back. There is definitely something there, but Magnus pulls away, uncertain. Still holding her and looking into her face, he says, "Well, I am glad to see that you aren't mad at me again." They both laugh nervously.

"Nope. I'm not mad at you." Grace now stands with her arms crossed in front of her chest. "I just wish you weren't so damned certain of everything. You know, Magnus, emotions and beliefs are not governed by anything like the laws of physics or science as you define it. You can't just take a few measurements and be done with it; it's considerably more complicated than that. Even if your doctor in Velas tells you the probable cause of the illness, and even if I believe you, I'm still left with the problem of how to move beyond this crisis, how to gain acceptance."

"You have a point," Magnus concedes. "Well, I'll do what I can. In the meantime, take care of yourself, okay?"

"I will." Grace suddenly reaches out to Magnus and wraps him in a firm hug. She buries her face in his neck; he feels her moist warm breath on his skin and smells her hair, a fragrance he can't quite identify, perhaps rosemary, possibly mint. He feels light-headed as he breathes her in. They kiss again. She looks into his eyes. "Thank you for being here."

Although she's a strong woman and stands quite tall, he senses that she might break were he to squeeze her too hard. He wants to make love with her, to hold her and never let go, but he knows today is not the day. No sense in scaring her away. As they separate, he tries to keep his cool. "Well, thanks for the coffee. Let's get together soon. By then I should know more."

"That sounds great. Thank you again, Magnus."

As he leaves, he wants to look back at her, but he doesn't.

GRACE

GRACE HAS MIXED feelings about Magnus leaving. On the one hand, she is drawn to him and she doesn't want to be alone; on the other hand, she is uncomfortable having him in what is essentially her bedroom. Ângela Maria knows he was here. Does she also know that he left? What does she think? What she thinks matters almost as much as *what people say*.

Grace climbs up on her bed to look out the window. She sees Magnus cross the road to the seawall. He climbs up and sits with his back facing her. She wonders what he's thinking. It must be confusing for him too.

Nothing too much has happened between Grace and Magnus yet, but her feelings for him are growing. She needs to tell him about Jake. Then again, maybe she should wait to tell him when and only if he shows a more overt interest in having a real relationship. She always hates it when men jump to the conclusion that she's sexually interested in them because she says something nice, or hugs them, or gives them a kiss. Magnus was being nice to her —that's all. She hugged him and kissed him good-bye—that's all.

ÂNGELA MARIA

ÂNGELA MARIA WATCHES from the kitchen window as Magnus leaves. He seems like a nice enough man, and handsome too. She hopes Grace isn't getting involved with him. It would only make matters worse. People are talking about her enough, and without cause. If they knew that a man was visiting her, their fears about her would grow. Not easy being a single woman at Grace's age here in the islands. Single women are always considered dangerous.

In her twenties, Ângela Maria and a schoolteacher from the continent became good friends—Filomena was her name. They used to sit talking for hours on end. Nobody made her laugh the way Filomena did. She was the most lively and interesting person Ângela Maria had ever met. Filomena introduced her to the world. She wasn't afraid of going anywhere alone or talking to anyone. She was responsible for Ângela Maria's first café visit, which at the time, seemed like such a risqué thing to do, even though they had gone together. Her mother drilled it into her that nice girls didn't go to cafés, period—alone or with other women.

The people of Calheta destroyed Filomena; they gossiped about her terribly. On many occasions, Ângela Maria heard Filomena referred to as a *feiticeira*, and not because she had magical powers, but because people thought she was a bad woman who was stirring up problems. She turned men's heads. It wasn't her fault. Under pressure, the principal at the secondary school asked her to leave.

By the time she left, Filomena was broken. She didn't even want to talk to Ângela Maria about it, except to say that Azoreans were closed-minded. Ângela Maria agreed. She never heard from Filomena again.

She refuses to lose Grace the same way. Fortunately, things have changed; people are much more open these days. But unfortunately, there are still quite a few closed-minded people around, like Miguel.

Shortly after she sees Magnus leave, Ângela Maria cuts a thick slice of caramel cake she made the day before with Grace in mind. She walks downstairs and taps on Grace's door. They have barely spoken since the day Ângela Maria told her about everything. She hasn't pressed the matter; she knows that Grace needs time to think things over. Grace opens the door. "Hi there. I thought you might like to have a little cake?" Ângela Maria holds out her offering.

"Thanks," Grace says, reaching for the cake. "Come on in."

Ângela Maria steps inside. She hates this place. Too dark. "Everything okay?" Grace has dark circles under her eyes, and she looks like she has lost weight.

"Oh yeah, as good as could be expected, I guess." Grace sets the plate down on the counter.

Clearly, Grace doesn't plan to eat the cake. Silly of her to think she can cheer her up with sugary food. Ângela Maria feels useless. "Well, I saw the young man here and wondered . . ."

"Oh, he wanted to know why I didn't show up at the archives yesterday."

"Did you tell him why?" What would it mean if she did tell him? What would her explanation be?

"Yeah, I told him. He doesn't believe any of it." Grace picks at the cake. "He believes in science."

"I certainly understand that." Ângela Maria brushes some crumbs off the counter into her hand. "Sometimes that's easier—not as messy." She takes a fork out and sets it on the plate. "Eat. You're getting too skinny."

"Looks delicious, and I am hungry." Grace sits at the counter. She picks up a piece of chewy caramel with her fingers and pops it into her mouth. "Mmmm . . . this is *maravilhoso!*"

Satisfied with having accomplished her goal, Ângela Maria says, "Okay then, I'll be running along now. Let me know if you need anything."

"I will. Thanks," Grace says, mouth full of cake.

Ângela Maria closes the door behind and heads upstairs. She feels horrible about what is happening and desperately wants to do something to help. Feeding people is what she does best.

As she prepares the noon meal, she comes up with the start of a plan. She will go to Fajã dos Vimes to visit Tia Carmina, tell Miguel she is going to visit her cousin Elisabete, with whom she has been close friends since girlhood. She trusts Elisabete. They'll go together to see Tia Carmina.

11

THE SLEEPING DRAGON

GRACE

To HER PLEASURE, on Monday morning Grace wakes to a slant of sunlight coming through the window. After her ritual coffee and reading, she grabs the opportunity to walk into town to buy a few groceries. As she passes Senhor Estêvão's house, she sees him working in his garden, pulling weeds as usual.

"*Bom dia*, senhor, so glad to run into you. I want to apologize again for missing our lesson last week. I was a bit under the weather."

"Oh, Grace dear, it is wonderful to see you. I am glad you are feeling better. I thought maybe you forgot all about me."

There is something different about him, but Grace can't put her finger on it.

"Of course I haven't forgotten about you. How could I?" She laughs uncomfortably. "I'm feeling much better, thank you. Again, I'm sorry. I should have called."

"No worries, no worries at all," he says.

"Are we on for tomorrow?" she asks.

"Yes, of course! Why don't we go someplace other than my office for our lesson? There is a café in Urzelina that I would love to take you to. It has a nice view."

"Well, okay then, it's a date!" Grace says, feeling a little puzzled by the change of venue.

"Good, I will pick you up at our usual time at your place," says Senhor Estêvão.

As she walks on, she replays their conversation. *Oh, Grace dear, it is wonderful to see you. I thought maybe you forgot all about me,* he gushed. When did Grace become "Grace dear" to him? What happened to Senhora Doutora? She had humored him. *Of course I haven't forgotten about you.* Strange.

Coming out of the market, she sees him again, this time walking down the street, and she notices that he isn't wearing a tie. In fact, each time she has seen him, his formal affect has diminished. Today he wears a white turtleneck with his suit jacket draped over his shoulders like a cape. The empty sleeves dangle, bouncing up and down as he walks. *Superman.*

AT TEN O'CLOCK sharp the next day, Grace waits for Senhor Estêvão on the seawall side of the road. He pulls up in his shiny new Mercedes. Business must be good.

"*Bom dia,* Senhor Estêvão!" Grace hops into the car before he is able to get out to open the door for her, as she knows he plans to do. She hates it when men do that. Do they think women aren't able to open doors for themselves?

During the drive to Urzelina, Grace makes idle chitchat. She feels nervous, unsettled.

When they get to the café, which she has never been to before, he leads her to a corner table with his hand on her back at waist level, takes her jacket, and pulls the chair out for her. Even Grace's father, who she guesses is about the same age as Senhor Estêvão, shed these antiquated practices long ago. Something vaguely creepy is going on. They sit and look at the menu.

"What will you have?" he asks, adding, "It's on me."

"Oh no, I'd like to pay," insists Grace. "I'd just like a little coffee and one of those custard tarts."

"As you wish," he says as he signals the café attendant to come. He places the order for them both. "Now," he says in English, "let me practice to talk to you in English."

Surprising. He has never tried to speak conversationally with her before. He always only reads to her, and then discusses the reading in Portuguese. "So, you can speak English!"

He blushes. "Well, not all that good. But today I think we try."

The café attendant brings their coffees and pastries. He gives Senhor Estêvão a raised eyebrow, and then winks. Grace guesses it has something to do with the English speaking. "No, no, really, you are speaking very well so far."

"Why, thank you, ma'am!" Senhor Estêvão beams.

Happy that Senhor Estêvão wants to talk instead of read, Grace says, "So let's have a real conversation. I'll start." She pauses to think of what they should talk about. "How old are you?" she begins.

Senhor Estêvão thinks for a second, "I have . . . I am sixty years old."

"Really? I would have guessed younger." He actually looks older, but this little lie won't hurt her.

"How old you think I look?" he asks.

Grace fumbles. "Not even fifty, I'd say." She changes the subject. "Do you have any hobbies?"

"Hobbies?" Senhor Estêvão asks.

"Yes, hobbies are things that you do for fun, like reading, collecting things."

"Oh yes! Hobbies . . . I love to garden. I like to learn of medicine plants."

"How did you become interested in that?" She speaks slowly and deliberately, separating the words.

"As a boy. My mother growed them." Senhor Estêvão looks pleased with himself.

"Grew," she corrects.

"Yes, grew."

"Where were you born?"

"I were born in Angola."

"I *was* . . ."

"Yes, I was born in Angola."

"I didn't know that. How did you end up in the Azores?"

He lapses into Portuguese. "You know, when the Blacks made the whites all leave. They killed my whole family. I was lucky to escape with my life."

Grace has wandered into uncomfortable territory. "I'm really sorry. I had no idea." She sips her coffee.

"That's okay. It was a long time ago. I'm not one to live in the past." Senhor Estêvão smiles.

In English she says, "So have you heard about all the trouble I am causing around the island?"

Senhor Estêvão stops smiling. He lowers his voice. "Well, I would not tell the truth if I say no. I hear about it a little in the store. You know women like to talk."

Hard to believe that so many people could be talking about her. "And what do you think?"

Senhor Estêvão slips back into Portuguese. "I think women's talk is silly. That is what I think." He drinks the rest of his coffee. "And how did you come to hear?" he asks.

"Ângela Maria told me . . . because she wants to help me," Grace responds. "And, so, now I'm not sure what to do, because I really don't believe in any of it, you know?"

Senhor Estêvão rubs his chin. "Yes, well, if I were you, I wouldn't spend another minute thinking about it. That stuff going on probably has nothing to do with you. No one in their right mind thinks it does." He reaches across the table and lays his hand over Grace's hand.

Grace responds by pulling her hand away. She pushes the hair out of her face, hoping that Senhor Estêvão won't notice her visceral reaction. The thought that he may be interested in more than English lessons gives her a queasy feeling. "That's what I think too. How could it have anything to do with me, right?"

"Right." Senhor Estêvão checks his watch. "I apologize, Grace, we need to get back to Calheta now. I have to go to rehearsal for os Reis."

Relieved, Grace asks, "What is os Reis?"

Senhor Estêvão approaches to pull out her chair. "os Reis is a tradition here in São Jorge. During the twelve days of Christmas, we go door-to-door singing holiday songs. We are like the kings traveling to Bethlehem. You know the three kings?

"Sure. We have—"

"Great fun. Some households invite us in for a toast. Some have big spreads of food. It is good to show hospitality to help the kings on their long journey. Would you like to join us? We would be delighted to have another voice." Senhor Estêvão helps Grace with her coat.

Grace loves to sing. "I'm not sure. I don't know the songs—"

"Nonsense. You will learn them, and besides we have all the lyrics on paper. That's what rehearsals are for." He urges her to join as he leads her out the door.

"Perhaps not today," she says. "I don't really feel up to it. When and where do you practice, though? I would love to join you another time." In this she is sincere; it will help her get back into the swing of things.

"We're practicing on Tuesdays at one in the afternoon and Thursday evenings from five until six thirty up at the *sociedade*. I would love it if you would join us."

Back in Calheta, he drops her off at her place. It seems like he is in a bit of a hurry. "Well then, until the next time," Grace says, and in a surprising move, he leans toward Grace and kisses her on the cheek. Red welts rise on Graces neck as she hurriedly exits the car.

Grace stands stupidly in front of the house. What just happened? Has she been completely oblivious up until now? Is Senhor Estêvão really interested in her? No, it can't be. For God's sake, he is more than twice her age, even older than her father, and a married man to boot. Perhaps he takes a fatherly interest in her.

Yes, that would make sense. He has no children of his own, and he feels responsible for her.

ESTÊVÃO

Senhor Estêvão feels light on his feet as he bounds up the hill toward the *sociedade* for rehearsal. Yes, he again feels like his former self—Raposinho—a little fox indeed. He felt a certain chemistry between him and Grace. She even confided in him. Her shyness when he touched her hand was so sweet. To think, the year she was born, he was a full-grown married man.

He was taken by surprise when she asked him whether he knew about all the trouble she is causing. If there is gossip to pass, Norinha passes it. Everything is falling into place. He hopes that Grace will join os Reis. What a pleasure it will be for him if she does; they will have twelve glorious drunken nights together.

GRACE

The next day, Ângela Maria knocks on Grace's door.

"Good morning!" she says cheerfully when Grace opens it. "I made arrangements for you to go meet with a cousin of mine in Fajã dos Vimes. She is a weaver, about your age." Ângela Maria has taken on an increasing role as research coordinator. Grace wonders if she is trying to keep her out of trouble.

"Will you be going too?" Grace asks.

"Oh no! This is your work, not mine. I have to babysit. I have arranged for you to take Miguel's car; he doesn't need it."

"Are you sure he doesn't mind? I mean, given how he feels about me . . ."

"As long as you put gas in . . . he'll let anybody use his car if they fill it with gas. It's as good as giving him money."

Shortly afterward, Grace winds her way up the steep grade out of Calheta. The ever-present cloud cover is thin and high, so the Serra do Topo is not socked in. Grace happily gazes out over the treeless expanse. The additional light makes the fields look even greener than usual against the light-gray backdrop; the landscape looks like a colorized photograph—the other side of the rainbow. She marvels at how each day, São Jorge becomes a new place; one day miserable and the next day marvelous. As she nears the turn for Fajã dos Vimes, she looks out over the ocean. Even it is different today—calm. It is good to be working again.

São Jorge *is* a living thing, a sleeping dragon—sleeping for the moment. Grace turns onto the narrow zigzag road leading to the *fajã*. She fumbles for her notebook where she has written directions on how to get to Elisabete's.

ÂNGELA MARIA'S cousin Elisabete is about Grace's age, but she looks considerably younger. She is beautiful. Her hair, jet black and full of tight curls, falls lightly around her perfect face; she resembles a porcelain doll. Must be the pure life she leads in the *fajã*.

They sit at a Formica table in her small indoor kitchen. The room is immaculate.

"Thank you for agreeing to talk to me," Grace says. "I have one of your blankets on my bed at Ângela Maria's."

"Oh yes, that is one of the more modern colorful ones, as I recall," Elisabete says.

"I really love it, it is so warm."

"That is so nice. I figured you might not like it so much,

because it is made of wool. I've heard that most Americans don't like wool."

"I guess I am different," Grace says. "Well, Ângela Maria wanted me to talk to you because she said you are one of the most famous weavers in the Azores."

Elisabete blushes. "She exaggerates. First, there aren't that many weavers left in the Azores. Nobody wants to pay the price for a handwoven blanket when you can buy something from China for practically nothing."

"So, can you tell me how you became a weaver in the first place?"

"Sure, I started when I was just eleven. Most weavers are from weaving families, but that is not my story." She gets up and brings a plate of cake over. "Our neighbor"—she points to the south— "was a celebrated weaver. She was getting older and had no one to pass her trade on to." She cuts the cake and sets a piece in front of Grace. "You see, for most, weaving is a family business. It so happened that I am the only child of a single mother, and so my mother apprenticed me to the neighbor."

"How did you feel about that?" Grace asks.

"Oh, I was happy. I loved the looms, spinning wool, and all of it. I felt special."

"Well, what about school?" Grace asks.

"Oh, I stayed in school to the ninth year, what is required. I had no use for more, because I was weaving."

Elisabete's life seems beautifully simple. As they converse, Grace wishes they could be friends, but she knows the chasm that lies between their worlds is expansive. Elisabete has never left the island; she lives in a world nearly absent of media. After the interview, Elisabete takes Grace on a tour of her family's property, showing her the coffee plants and the banana, citrus, and avocado trees. It really is a little slice of paradise.

An inexplicable feeling of awe overwhelms Grace, a feeling she has felt only one other time in her life, when her Blackfeet grandmother took her to Chief Mountain to camp for several days. What a wonderful experience that was. Grace helped her collect various medicinal herbs and berries, and her grandmother told her countless entertaining stories of Old Man and Old Woman, and of all the ancestor ghosts. Grace felt simultaneously fearful of and drawn to that place, as she does now to Fajã dos Vimes.

Much as she wants to spend the whole day with Elisabete, Grace knows that her time is up. Elisabete is in the middle of working on a commissioned piece for a museum in Rhode Island that is doing a show on Azorean textiles. "Well, I've really enjoyed talking with you. Thank you so much for your generosity of time." Grace kisses Elisabete on both cheeks.

"My pleasure, really. If you write about me, I hope you write something nice."

"Of course I will! Your weaving is wonderful. One day I'd like to have enough money to buy one of your blankets." Grace means every word. "Would it be okay if I leave the car parked here while I explore the *fajã* before I head back?"

"Of course." Elisabete points in the direction of some high-lights: the always-open church, the rocky shore, and the almost-never-open store. "Stop in before you leave. I have some things I'd like to send to Ângela Maria."

"Okay. Thanks again. See you soon." Grace sticks her note-book in the car and switches out the battery in her camera before heading off to the church.

As Grace opens the door to the church, she feels a cold breeze rushing out. No lights on, nor can she see any electric lights anywhere. Fortunately, the windows let in enough light to see. The tiny church is beautifully appointed with colorful gilded vases and images. The vases display greenery and fresh flowers. Clearly, the women of Fajã dos Vimes see to it that the church is kept up. Grace walks toward the front and takes a seat in a pew. She gazes up at Christ on the cross, dripping blood from his crown of thorns. How gruesome. She tries to imagine believing.

God has given us his only begotten son, and this is how he came to his end—tortured upon a wooden cross. It reminds her of accounts of the young men on the reservation who endured the Sun Dance, one of the most revered Blackfeet customs; they danced until their flesh was shredded, until the Sun was pleased. Gods are surely perverse. Although the government long ago outlawed the practice, Grace knows that some of the new traditionalists practice it. She can't fathom why.

The door to the church opens and light floods in. She turns but, blinded by the brightness, can only make out the silhouette of a rather large man. The door squeaks closed. Grace bows her head to say, *Don't bother me. I'm praying.* The man steps into the pew directly behind her. Her heart pounds. Suddenly she feels the firm grip of a large hand on her shoulder. She looks back and sees Magnus grinning.

Bounding to her feet, she says, "Magnus! You scared me to death. What are you doing here?"

"Here specifically? Here generally? Or here existentially?"

"All of them, I suppose!" She is happy to see him. Lately it isn't good for her to be left alone with her thoughts for too long.

"Well, I am in this church, because I saw you come in here. I am in Fajã dos Vimes because I took my boat out for a ride today, and I am here in the world for . . . I haven't figured that out yet."

They walk out together.

"I keep my boat right over there." He points to a shed not far from the beach. "Did I tell you I have a boat?"

"Yeah, you mentioned that once." Grace looks in the direction he pointed. An old man wearing a hooded sweatshirt and a feed cap with "USA" emblazoned across the front waves at them.

"That's Zé, the guy whose shack it is. Nice guy. So what are you doing here? I take it you didn't come here to pray." He pats her on the back, like an old friend.

"No, I was interviewing one of the weavers, and afterward thought I would explore." Grace gestures to her camera. "Taking photos. So beautiful here. Want to walk with me?"

"Yeah." Magnus looks up at the precipice dropping to the *fajã*. "Amazing, isn't it? Sometimes I've thought there is magic in this village, but I don't believe in that stuff, you know." He smiles broadly. He bends over and picks up a rock. "Did you know things grow in this *fajã* that don't grow anywhere else in the Azores? Like coffee, and a number of tropical fruits. A little paradise here."

"And the people, they seem so . . ."

"Innocent?"

"Not exactly innocent, but maybe pure. There's something clean and clear about this place—the light is different." Magnus slips his hand into Grace's. It is warm and dry, comforting. They walk along the rocky beach without a word between them for some time, happy in silence, happy together.

"So, Grace, do you have plans for Christmas Eve?" Magnus asks.

"I do." Working of course. "You know Christmas is a feast, and I have to work through it."

"Of course—don't know what I was thinking. I have a small gift for you and I was thinking of—"

"Why don't you join me for Mass on Christmas Eve? I have something for you too." She doesn't actually have a gift for him, but she will by then.

"Wonderful. I'd love to." Magnus gives her hand a squeeze, and he looks genuinely happy.

They release hands and turn around to head back, again in silence.

Magnus says, "I haven't heard back from my colleague in Velas yet about the stuff up in Topo."

"Well, I can wait. I keep trying to push it out of my mind, thinking it will disappear. Maybe people will forget about it." Grace looks down at her feet.

"Yeah. Well, I hope you aren't spending too much time worrying about it. You know it's nothing, don't you?"

There he goes again, insisting that there is nothing for her to be concerned about. He doesn't understand that unlike his work, which relies on the immutable and persistent laws of nature, her work depends on the goodwill of fickle human beings; it depends on her being liked, trusted, and accepted. Shoving her hands into her pockets and looking into Magnus's face, she says, "Yeah, it's probably nothing." She forces a smile.

When they arrive back at the church, she says, "Good-bye for now, I guess. Great to see you—a nice surprise." She pulls the keys from her pocket. "See you Christmas Eve around four o'clock?"

"Sounds perfect." He leans in for a kiss as she reaches out to shake.

They shake hands a moment too long. Blushing, Grace leans in and gives Magnus a quick peck on the cheek. "See you then."

"See you then." His voice trails after her.

Jake. She needs to tell him about Jake. What will she tell him? She needs to tell Jake too, but what? What is she doing, exactly?

12

THE WHITE WITCH

MAGNUS

MAGNUS WATCHES from a distance as Grace walks toward the car. She must have forgotten something, because she turns suddenly and goes into the house. He remains, watching, waiting. A few minutes later she comes out with a plastic bag. She waves at him as she hops into the car.

He feels conflicted, confused, and a little angry with himself. He wanted so much to embrace her, but he didn't dare. He could kick himself for saying *I take it you didn't come here to pray*. Sometimes he can't avoid being a jackass. So what if she *had* come to pray? Perhaps she had. He might pray if he were in her shoes. As Grace drives off, he turns toward the shed, where he has more work to do with his boat. He is inexplicably heavyhearted.

Magnus's parents are moderately religious people. They say grace at dinner and go to church on Sundays. Otherwise, the family doesn't spend any time talking about God. In fact, his family spends darned little time talking about anything, especially something as deeply personal as one's belief in God. That actually *is* against their religion.

As a boy, Magnus thought no greater man existed than his father, but over the years he has come to think of him as pathetic. Lars Sorenson, a man without a dream, never wanted to go anywhere. He hadn't even been to Stockholm. *Why are you so anxious to leave here, when heaven is right in your backyard?* he used to ask. His heaven was with the cattle, udders heavy with milk, constantly masticating their stringy green mass. Magnus hates cows, and he doesn't believe in God. Ironic that he should end up in a place like this, a place with more cows than people, and more religious fervor than in all of Sweden.

GRACE

Anthropology 101: The rules of gift exchange are central to the understanding of any culture.

THE NEXT MORNING, before reaching the bus stop, Grace faces a dilemma: car or bus. Zulmira's white Opal pulls up next to her. The door swings open, revealing Zulmira's smiling face. "Velas?"

Ângela Maria's words of warning reverberate, but she finds herself drawn to the danger like a proverbial moth to a flame. She has to know. "Sure. Thanks." She hops in.

"It will be good to have company on my drive again," Zulmira says cheerfully as she pulls away from the curb.

"For me too," Grace says. "You know, I came looking for you at the hospital the last time, but you were already gone."

"Oh, yeah, sorry about that. Hope you got home okay." She glances over at Grace uneasily. "One of my mother's friends showed up to visit her son. She took the bus down in the morning and needed a ride back."

Grace holds her breath as Zulmira accelerates to pass a not-so-slow-moving truck on a blind curve.

"But I should be around today if you want a ride back."

"That's okay. I can find my way back on my own, but thanks anyway." Grace looks out the window. The way Zulmira drives, she figures magic is the least of her worries.

"Going to the archives again today?" Zulmira asks.

"Nope, Christmas shopping," Grace says.

"I think you'll be sorely disappointed with the selection."

"So what do people give each other for Christmas around here?" Grace asks.

"Depends on who you are giving a present to. Mostly only immediate family exchange gifts, and then it's more small things. Not like America, you know. People don't go crazy here like there, although anymore it is starting to happen here too. Have you seen all the Barbies this year?"

Zulmira's infectious laugh warms Grace to her in spite of herself. "Yeah! How could I help but see them?" The store windows and stores packed to the ceiling with blinding-pink Barbie boxes astounded her. "Looks like enough Barbies for every girl in São Jorge to have one."

"Or two or three."

Zulmira's driving improves as the conversation grows more relaxed.

"They're cute, don't you think?" Zulmira says.

"Cute? I don't think—"

"And Barbie's husband, Ken, don't you think he's handsome?" Zulmira's mouth drops open in an *oh-my-gawd* expression.

Grace never had a Barbie, let alone a Ken. Her parents began brainwashing her against them at an early age. Although brainwashing was successful insofar as their home wasn't tainted, she secretly played with them at friends' houses. And to the best of her knowledge, Ken and Barbie aren't married. "Are they married?"

"Of course! You don't know that?" Zulmira looks at Grace with disbelief.

"I don't think they're married in America." Grace's disproportionate laughter brings tears to her eyes.

Barbie married. So fundamentally wrong. She's supposed to be the glamorous free-wheeling older sister of Skipper. Married women are anything but glamorous. Definitely not free-wheeling; they don't roll over for anyone but their husbands, and from what Grace has heard, they don't do that too often.

Over the decades, Barbie has gone through many transformations, including rightsizing, breast reduction, pigment alterations, hair color changes, and training for multiple gender-neutral careers. Marriage, however, represents a transformation that the American public would never tolerate; it would make her unappealing to young American girls, therefore reducing Mattel's bottom line. "American Religion: The Bottom Line." That Portuguese Barbie is married points Grace to a key cultural differentiator.

Fortunately, Zulmira laughs as hard as she does, perhaps from nervousness. Collecting herself, Grace asks, "Do many little girls here have Barbies?"

"I'd say most little girls have one or two. They're pretty expensive for many families in Portugal."

They're nearing Velas. So far, so good. Grace checks to ensure all of her belongings are accounted for. She doesn't really believe Zulmira knows anything or is in on the whole thing, if there is a whole thing, but Ângela Maria was so emphatic about not trusting anybody. Grace doesn't see any stray hairs.

"I still don't know what to get for people. Do friends give each other presents at Christmas?"

"Sometimes. They give each other special *lembranças*, you know, little things to be remembered by." Zulmira holds her wrist out. "See this little chain? My closest friend gave it to me."

"Maybe I'll find something like that." Grace hadn't thought of jewelry, but it would be good for Ângela Maria and Ana. The men will be considerably more difficult to buy for.

"It's still early. Want me to drop you off at the café again?" Zulmira asks.

"Yeah, that would be great." Grace hasn't eaten breakfast.

"Zulmira, there is something I want to ask you, and I hope you don't—"

"Go ahead and ask—whatever you like."

"I've been wondering about that blood test, when you drew my blood . . . what sorts of tests were they?" Grace studies Zulmira's face for a reaction.

Perceptibly stiffening, she says, "As I recall . . ." She pauses as if she is having difficulty remembering. "As I recall they were for your visa requirements, so whatever tests they do for that. I don't know exactly. I just draw the blood. Why do you ask?" Zulmira pulls over in front of the café.

"I wondered because I have a friend who is here from Sweden on a residency visa, and blood tests weren't required."

"Hmm, curious. I'm sure everything was on the up and up. My goodness, a police officer escorted you to the clinic; it doesn't get more official than that."

Grace flinches. *It doesn't get more official than that.* Grace didn't suggest that it wasn't official. Only someone who knows that it wasn't would have made that comment. Zulmira and the officer were in on it together. "Yes, of course it was official. I never doubted that." Grace sounds convinced. "Thanks again for the ride." As she gets out, she again checks the seat and floor carefully to make sure she hasn't left anything behind.

"Did you lose something?" Zulmira asks.

"I hope not. I don't think so," says Grace. "Until the next time!" She forces a smile.

"Yes. Until the next time, if God wills it."

Grace closes the door, and Zulmira pulls away from the curb. If the devil wills it, they'll see each other again. She feels betrayed. What has Grace ever done to Zulmira? Finally, Grace believes Ângela Maria that there are people out to get her with dark arts, but she is not ready to accept help, especially if it means getting Ângela Maria in trouble. She can handle this on her own.

The drizzle takes away her Christmas spirit, but she's on a mission. After only a couple of hours, she has gifts for everyone. A pair of pretty earrings for Ângela Maria, a bracelet for Ana, a pocket knife for Miguel, a USA cap for Mário, a book on English verbs for Senhor Estêvão, and a book called *A Ilha de São Jorge* for Magnus. She hopes that he doesn't have it already. It contains topographical information and seems generally like a good reference book. She bought one for herself as well. Anxious to get back to Calheta, she finds a cab. Besides, she doesn't feel like going on the bus or risking exposure to a soul from Topo. She can't well afford more accusations.

ÂNGELA MARIA

ÂNGELA MARIA SELDOM drives if she can avoid it. She got her driver's license in the United States when she was visiting her sister Lúcia three years earlier. Lúcia had insisted. She has become an American through and through.

You may as well be in prison if you don't drive, she said to Ângela Maria. *Just another way for Miguel to keep you in your place.*

Ângela Maria responded, *What good would learning to drive do? There's no place to go in São Jorge.*

Appealing to her "safety first" leanings, her sister convinced her that if Miguel were at sea and there were some emergency, driving could be critical. But it never it occurred to her that she could take an excursion for pleasure. Miguel was surprised when she announced her trip to the *fajã*. He offered to accompany her if she waited until the next day. *No, I need to go today, and it is silly that I don't drive. My sister's right.* Miguel, not suspecting anything, looked at her thoughtfully and said, *Yes, I guess it would be good for you to keep up your driving skills.*

She starts the car. Her palms sweat on the steering wheel as she backs onto the road. As she passes Revelinha, guilt sweeps over her for having lied to Miguel, but it couldn't be helped. Her friend is in need, and she plans to do whatever it takes to help her, even if it means incurring Miguel's wrath. Anymore, he seldom hits her. She knows women who regularly endure brutal beatings from their husbands—that is the way it is. She's lucky. Miguel only hits her sometimes, usually when he's had too much to drink. Fortunately, he doesn't drink much anymore—a glass of wine with meals. The doctor told him to quit or he would ruin his liver. He quit, just like that, one year ago.

Darn. She has just missed the turn for Fajã dos Vimes. She searches for a wide place to make a U-turn and then turns down the steep road leading to the *fajã*, hoping that no one is coming up. She doesn't want to have to back up on this narrow road. Luckily, only one truck comes up, and it's on one of the hairpin curves where there is room for both of them. As she pulls into the driveway at her cousin's house, she sighs with relief.

Elisabete comes running out to greet her. "*A minha prima!* I am so glad to see you." Elisabete helps Ângela Maria out of the car. They exchange kisses. "It's been a long time! Since the Festa de Nossa Senhora do Carmo."

"No, it can't possibly have been that long!" Ângela Maria spent the week of the *festa* in the *fajã*, but it hardly seems like half a year has passed.

Everyone adores Elisabete, especially Ângela Maria, who is like an older sister to Elisabete—an only child who grew up with her mother and grandparents. No one ever talked about why Elisabete's mother never married or about how she got pregnant. It matters. It doesn't matter. In those days many women had children without fathers. Some because their husbands died doing the dangerous work of fishing and whaling; others because their lovers left and never came back.

"Cousin, come in, come in. We have some catching up to do." Elisabete takes Ângela Maria by the hand and pulls her through the back door into the kitchen. "I just roasted some coffee beans. Would you like some fresh coffee?"

"Sounds wonderful."

Ângela Maria never much cared for the smell of coffee beans roasting, but she loves nothing more than the rich taste of coffee made from the freshly roasted beans of the *fajã*. Elisabete dips a small cup into the large metal fishing net float that was refashioned for the purpose of coffee roasting. The beans are still warm. She roasted them the way Ângela Maria likes—dark.

"I enjoyed meeting Grace the other day. She seems like a nice person. A good person."

"She is."

Elisabete turns the crank on the coffee grinder, making a loud grating sound.

"And you know that's why I have come today, don't you?"

"I know."

They often communicate without speaking. Even as young girls they spent much of their time together in silence. Blissful silence. When Ângela Maria's oldest son died, they spent an entire week together without saying a word or shedding a tear, but they knew each other's thoughts, feelings, and needs completely.

"I hope Tia Carmina can help." Elisabete measures out the coffee into the *cafeteira* and puts it on the stove. "She asked me the other day when I thought you would come. I told her soon. She's an old one, but sharp as they come."

"Yes. She is sharp." Wise. Kind. Tia Carmina saved Ângela Maria from the brink of self-destruction after Jaime died. No magic; it was pure compassion. If only it were a matter of magic.

Elisabete gazes softly at Ângela Maria. "Oh come, stop thinking like that!" Elisabete stands over the stove waiting for the gurgle of the *cafeteira*.

"Like what?"

"You know . . ." The coffee maker sputters and hisses. Elisabete quickly turns off the heat. "About Jaime."

"I can't help it. So senseless, and so much my fault." Ângela Maria runs her hands through her hair. "I can't help but wonder if Grace's problems are not somehow related. I never told her about Jaime. She doesn't know about the *loja*."

"It was an accident—nothing more." Elisabete pours the coffee into cups, then sets the cups on the table.

The day Jaime died, Ângela Maria went to the *loja* to fetch some potatoes, but the light had burned out and it was pitch black. She went back upstairs to get a light bulb. Jaime was lying on the couch, where he had been all day, so Ângela Maria asked him to go put the bulb in and fetch her potatoes. He groaned, *Do I have to?* As he stood up, Ângela Maria noticed that his pants were getting too short. At the age of fifteen, his voice had just begun to change, and he had that awkward appearance that one sees only in people who haven't grown into their skin yet.

A few minutes after he went down, the power went out. Not an unusual event given the rain and wind, so Ângela Maria didn't think much about it at first. He had a flashlight. When she noticed that the neighbors' lights were still on, she raced down to the *loja* and found her son lying in an inch of water—the flashlight still in his hand. If she had only known that the *loja* was flooded . . . if she had changed the light bulb herself . . . She would never forget the expression on his face. Electricity changed her life forever.

Elisabete sets a plate of cookies on the table. "Well, let's sit for a few minutes before going to visit Tia Carmina." They drink their coffee and eat their cookies in silence.

ÂNGELA MARIA and Elisabete peek through Tia Carmina's kitchen door. Everything is in perfect order; she isn't there. They smell *incenseiro* burning and so head to the back of her property, where her old kitchen stands. The wonderful and strange smells of Tia Carmina's kitchen intensify as they approach. They hear her voice; she sings a familiar song. Ângela Maria feels at home here, where she and Elisabete spent so many days growing up. She has even memorized the black patterns on the white plaster walls where the smoke rises above the wood oven. She has so many fond memories of life here in the *fajã* before her marriage to Miguel. As they round the corner, Tia Carmina meets them.

"Oh, young people, my children . . . yes . . . I knew you would come today." Tia Carmina's wrinkles deepen with her smile.

"Tia! Good to see you." Ângela Maria kisses her. She smells earthy. "I brought you a cake—your favorite, nutmeg."

"Bless you, but you didn't need to do that." Tia Carmina's hand trembles as she takes the cake and sets it on a small table.

Ângela Maria wonders how old she is. It will be a sad day when they lose her. "What, come empty-handed to see an old witch? I know better than that."

Elisabete kisses Tia Carmina and takes a seat next to the oven without saying a word.

Tia Carmina reaches over and places her hand firmly on Ângela Maria's shoulder, looking her straight in the eye. "Child, you should have come sooner, but it's not too late."

Ângela Maria feels Tia Carmina's breath on her face. It smells of mint, the most powerful herb, she always claims. "Well, Miguel is afraid—"

"Miguel doesn't know what is good for him," Tia Carmina says. "The only thing that boy ever did right was to marry you."

"He doesn't think we should get involved," Ângela Maria says.

"Well, you are involved whether you like it or not. As you know, we seldom have a choice in these matters." Tia Carmina's expression hardens. "Especially when it comes to the likes of Nonna Preta and her progeny."

"Yes, I know, but I don't know what to do." Ângela Maria has only seen Tia Carmina look this serious on the gravest occasions. "I don't know if Grace is willing—"

"She *is* willing," Tia Carmina says. "She comes to me in dreams. She needs to come to me in person if I am going to help her, and you need to bring her. You are linked."

Puzzled, Ângela Maria searches Tia Carmina's face for an answer. "How are we linked?"

"I think you know." Tia Carmina turns to the stove to stir the steaming pots. "You are linked by the boy," she finally says. "He was born the day Jaime died, during that same terrible storm." Her back still to Ângela Maria, she continues, "You'll feel better if you help Grace carry the burden of his mother's tears."

Ângela Maria knows it is true. The sick boy has been on her mind constantly, waking and sleeping. "I'll bring her. Don't think I can make it until the day after Christmas. Is that soon enough?"

"Plenty. There's still time, but this will all take time, and you can count on things worsening before it's over." Tia Carmina ladles a clear brownish liquid into a cup. "Drink this. You look tired."

Ângela Maria sips the tea. So bitter.

"Drink it all," Tia Carmina instructs her.

Elisabete, who until now has remained silent, laughs as Ângela Maria forces the concoction down with a grimace.

"That is awful! What's in it?" she asks.

Tia Carmina plays with the hairs growing out of her chin. "Think I am going to tell you? I would be out of a job if I told everyone my secrets! Nothing more than a couple of bitter roots."

"Very well. Come on, Elisabete, let's get out of here." Ângela Maria takes Elisabete's hand and pulls her toward the door. "See you after Christmas, Tia. Thank you for making me drink that nasty stuff! And Boas Festas!"

Tia Carmina's face wrinkles and her eyes sparkle from beneath her aged eyelids. "You'll be happy you drank it." With a sprig of rosemary as a wand, she mumbles her usual blessing, making the sign of the cross.

As they walk back to Elisabete's, Ângela Maria says, "You know, I am already feeling better."

"Of course you are," says Elisabete. "Has our Tia ever steered us in the wrong direction?"

"No, never."

CHRISTMAS

DECEMBER 25 TO JANUARY 6

13

BABY JESUS'S PEE

GRACE

On Christmas Eve, Grace sits on her bed. Scooting into the warmth of a slanted spot of sunlight that shines through the window, she cuts Christmas shapes from origami paper. She couldn't find wrapping paper she liked and so is making her own. Each of the gifts gets wrapped in a single color, then she glues different shapes on the packages to make them more festive.

On Ângela Maria's she places an angel, for her name. On Magnus's she tapes white stars and makes a ribbon of sorts from a fine colorful paper chain. Looks masculine. On Senhor Estêvão's she pastes the cut-out words *Merry Christmas*. The other three are less well thought out; she's tired and uncomfortable, so she cuts out little snowflakes. When she finishes, she piles the gifts neatly on the counter.

She cleans up her mess and dresses for the festivities. Ângela Maria has invited her and Magnus up for dinner and a gift exchange. Afterward, she and Magnus will go to Mass. On the way, she plans to stop at Senhor Estêvão's to drop his gift off. Grace takes a last look at herself in the mirror and tucks a lock of hair behind her ear. *Good enough.*

She hears a tap at the door but waits a moment to answer. She doesn't want to seem too eager, and yet as she opens the door, she feels a rush of excitement, like a girl on a first date.

Magnus stands there dressed in coat and tie. He has even combed his normally wild hair. Grace scarcely recognizes him.

"Merry Christmas, Magnus!" She kisses him on both cheeks. "You look wonderful! I look pitifully underdressed next to you."

"Well, thank you. And, no, you look perfect, as always." Magnus beams.

"Don't stand there. Come in."

Magnus steps in. He immediately starts digging through his knapsack. "Uh . . . I brought your gift . . . let's see . . . here it is." He pulls a tiny unwrapped box from the depths of his bag and hands it to Grace.

Her heart quickens as she takes the small white box. She has a policy against jewelry as a gift from a man, especially one that she isn't sure she wants to get involved with. Jewelry is the kind of gift that can be laden with obligation. "I have a gift for you as well." She hands him the book. A tiny part of her hopes that Magnus did buy her some simple piece of jewelry to remember him by, a *lembrança* of the sort exchanged by friends.

"Nice wrapping . . ." Magnus holds the book between both hands and moves it up and down as if weighing it, then he shakes it next to his ear. "Hmm . . . I wonder what this is?" He smiles.

"And I wonder what this is?" Grace shakes her little box. "You open yours first."

Magnus carefully detaches the paper chain. "I'm going to keep this—really neat—you must have worked on it for hours." He tears the paper off and reads the title aloud. "Thank you. I don't have this. I've seen it and thought of buying it, but—"

"Well, I don't know if it will be of any use to you, but I think it has some wonderful descriptions of the terrain and history of catastrophes . . ."

Magnus flips through the book. "Oh no, as I said, I have wanted to buy this book, but it was expensive, and I'm on a budget, you know. Thank you so much." He stops and reads the inscription aloud: "'To Magnus, friend of mine, friend of disaster! Thank you for being here. Love, Grace.'"

Grace hurriedly picks up her package, avoiding his eyes. "My turn!" She rips the paper off the box, opens the lid, and lifts the cotton. "A *figa*! I wanted one of these, but the guy in the store told me it's one of those things that you're not allowed to buy for yourself." She runs her fingers over the golden closed fist. She first learned about these from a Brazilian friend at Columbia, and saw the amulets in the store in Velas. She loves it, especially under the circumstances; she might actually need it. She's relieved it isn't something romantic. Or is it?

"You know, of course, that I think this is all silly, but even so, I like it as a piece of jewelry. If it happens to protect you from evil, all the better for me."

Grace puts the amulet back into the box and sets it on the counter. "I would put it on now, but I don't have a chain."

"I know. I forgot about that until I was back in Topo. I'm a little clumsy about these things. I'll get you one next week."

"Don't be silly. I can pick one up myself."

Magnus tucks his book into his knapsack. "Is it all right if I leave my stuff here?"

"Of course!" Grace says as she gathers her gifts to take upstairs.

MUCH TO GRACE'S EMBARRASSMENT, she misunderstood. Ângela Maria didn't expect them for dinner. When she and Magnus arrive, Ângela Maria and Ana are clearing away the dinner dishes; Mário and Miguel lounge in front of the television.

"Come in! Come in! *Boas Festas, amigos.* We're not yet ready for you. I was trying to get everything set up in the *sala*. Come with me." As she leads them to the *sala*, she dries her hands on a towel.

Grace has been in the *sala* only once, the day she arrived; normally, the room is reserved for special occasions and visitors. As they round the hallway into it, Grace is astonished by the transformation.

Ângela Maria looks proudly at Grace. "Well, what do you think of our *presépio*?"

"Wow!" Amazing. Bethlehem replicated, complete with real flowing streams and miniature palms. Ceramic sheep graze on live moss pastures. Buildings, windows illuminated, line the burgeoning streets of the Holy City. Three kings proceed from the east toward the stable, where *o Menino Jesus* lies in the embrace of the Holy Mother. "This is incredible, Ângela Maria! When did you do this?"

"Miguel did most of it with the kids. We haven't done anything like this for about five years. We used to do much more elaborate ones before . . . those times. This year, we plan to make a toast to Os Reis when they come. Now, would you like a little *xixi*?"

Magnus looks confused.

"She means make a Christmas toast," Grace says.

"Oh! I thought *xixi* was a euphemism for urine." Magnus smiles.

"Yeah—the *xixi do Menino Jesus* is good enough to drink." Grace says in English. They all laugh.

Ângela Maria has already poured some sort of clear liquor into small glasses. She holds them out to Grace and Magnus. "This is *anis*." She holds her glass up in the air to make a toast. "To family, friendship, and health during the coming year." She drinks the entire contents of her glass, as does Magnus.

Grace, however, can barely swallow the thick, sweet licorice-flavored liquid.

"Well, make yourselves comfortable while I go get the sweets." Ângela Maria goes to the kitchen, leaving Magnus and Grace alone in the *sala*.

"I'm really sorry, Magnus. I thought we'd been invited for dinner. I must have misunderstood." Grace walks over to inspect a shelf lined with photographs.

Magnus sits down on the couch. "No problem. We'll eat dessert for dinner. People have suffered greater injustices!"

She sees photos of Miguel, Ângela Maria, and their children, organized chronologically from left to right. An austere wedding photo with them, their parents, and their *padrinhos de casamento* begins the sequence. Soon Ângela Maria holds a baby, a boy, and then both she and Miguel each hold a child, another boy, and then a baby girl. Grace is puzzled. Surely, Ângela Maria or someone would have told her they had another child. Grace hears Magnus clear his throat, as if to gain her attention. She turns. Ângela Maria has come into the room with her arms full of cake and *queijadas*. She stops as though something is wrong. Magnus leaps to his feet to help her. He sets the plates on the doilies.

"Thank you. I guess I was trying to carry too many things at once!" Ângela Maria shakes her hands in front of herself as if shaking something off.

Grace says, "These are lovely photographs of your family."

"Yes, well, we were a lot younger in those days," she says. "Let me get the kids so that we can exchange gifts now."

They eat cake and exchange gifts. Miguel comes in long enough to receive his gift from Grace. He barely thanks her before returning to the television. Ângela Maria gives Grace a gold amulet shaped like a horn, and Ana gives her a chain. Ângela Maria helps her put it on. Grace glances over at Magnus. He smiles at her. She feels protected.

ESTÊVÃO

Senhor Estêvão passes the collection basket down the next-to-last row, scooting back to wait for the one arriving from the other direction. He'll be happy to be done with Mass so that he'll no longer have to endure the humiliation of seeing Grace with the Swede.

They stopped at his house unexpectedly before Mass, and anger and jealousy welled up despite his best efforts to keep them at bay. He can't decide what is worse: that she brought him a gift, flaunting their relationship in front of his wife; or that she came to his house latched on the arm of another man. It's definitely the Swede that bothers him the most. Norinha will harp on him endlessly about Grace no matter what she or he does. Adding to the injury, Grace gave him an unsentimental gift—a book of English verbs. The inscription reads, *To Senhor Estêvão, a lover of learning. Your friend and teacher, Grace.*

After Grace and Magnus left the house, Norinha said, *Well, what do you know, looks like there is competition for the little American slut.* Senhor Estêvão replied flatly, *I haven't the slightest idea what you are talking about, Norinha.* He left it at that.

He and the other ushers bring the collection plates forward. Looks like a successful collection—Christmas Eve always is. He catches Grace's eye as he passes. He winks—no harm in that. The choir stops singing, and the ushers return to their seats. Senhor Estêvão sits alone since Norinha is up front singing. He looks toward her. She whispers something to the woman next to her. She never shuts her mouth; everyone knows what she is like. He has come to hate her more with every passing day.

Communion begins. Senhor Estêvão watches as everyone proceeds forward to receive it. Today, he'll pass; he hasn't confessed his sins.

GRACE

GRACE WAKES up on Christmas morning pleasantly refreshed. Today she plans to catch up on her notes from Christmas Eve, and in the afternoon join Ângela Maria and Miguel for dinner. This time, she has been invited. Ângela Maria made a big deal of it the night before, inviting Magnus too. He declined for some reason. Ângela Maria's parents are coming, and she plans to kill a chicken she's fattened for the occasion. She jokingly asked, *Are you ready to learn to kill a chicken?* What a revolting thought. Grace can kill fish and she can kill bugs, but birds and mammals are something else altogether.

More than any other day, today she wishes she were home with her parents. At home, she always sleeps in on Christmas morning until awakened by the smell of frying bacon. She would hear the happy sounds of clinking dishes, her parents waiting for her to get up. After a big breakfast, they gather around the tree to open presents, one by one in turn. She hopes they will at least call today, but she doubts it since they are on vacation in Hawaii, halfway across the globe.

When Grace was growing up, Christmas dinner at the McGuiver house was usually an adventure; the house filled with an unlikely assortment of interesting people. Her parents invited what they called "the refugees" to every holiday gathering. When they lived on the reservation, refugees were people working at the clinic who didn't have family around—usually non-Natives, and when they lived in Billings, refugees were reservation Blackfeet going to school at Eastern Montana University or who worked at the hospital.

Her mother, although raised on the reservation, cooks few Native dishes. She learned to cook from her mother, who learned the art of French cooking in boarding school. Consequently, Grace's mother never developed a taste for some of the native "delicacies" like crow gut or wild head cheese. How fortunate. Even the names of these dishes turn Grace's stomach. She prefers goose or duck, perhaps served with a beef roast, accompanying a variety of tender herbed vegetables and potatoes. The only Blackfeet dish present at every McGuiver feast is a berry pudding made from dried saskatoons and served, of course, with fry bread. Grace's favorite. Her mouth waters just thinking about it. Now a refugee, she is lumped into the category and role of interesting and unusual person at the feast.

eQe

"Can I help?" Grace asks.

"Here"—Ângela Maria hands her the spoon she is using— "You watch over the _caldo verde._ I need to run next door to check on the chicken." Ângela Maria, harried, explains that she ran out of gas so is using the neighbor's oven.

"No problem." Grace stares into the bubbling mass of collard greens and broth. A delicious soup. Other than collards, the only green vegetables she has eaten since arriving are fennel and mint harvested from the roadside. She pushes the collards under the broth. Looks done to her, but she waits for Ângela Maria to get back.

Finally, Ângela Maria appears carrying the chicken—a big one —roasted to perfection. She smiles broadly as she sets it on the counter. "So, what do you think? Looks good, doesn't it?"

"Delicious," Grace agrees, "and it smells good too."

Ângela Maria breaks out into a refrain of "Cheira Bem, Cheira a Lisboa," one of her favorite Lisbon march songs, elaborating on all of the wonderful fragrances filling the streets of Lisbon.

Grace hasn't cultivated a taste for the old popular songs of the continent, nor fado; they remind her of some bygone era better left in the past, but she loves hearing Ângela Maria sing and seeing her so happy and animated. "Bravo!" Grace claps. "Encore! Encore!"

Ângela Maria laughs. "No, no, we don't have time for this silliness. Come help me set the table."

As they spread a handmade lace tablecloth on the dining room table and set the plates and silverware out, Ângela Maria's parents arrive with Miguel. Her mother carries a platter filled with a _carne assada_ cooked in the wood oven. Its aroma fills the house. She also has prepared a cake and several rounds of fresh _bolo de milho._

"_Boas Festas!_" Grace says, kissing Ângela Maria's mother.

"And you too!" Ângela Maria's mother says jovially. Her father, a man of few words, nods his head toward Grace, acknowledging her greeting. Miguel turns on the television and sits on the couch. Mário and Ana emerge from their respective rooms. Festive, but not home.

Grace, feeling awkward and in the way, goes back to the stove and stirs the soup. She pokes the potatoes on the back burner. They are soft—too soft. "Ângela Maria, I think the potatoes might be overdone," Grace says.

Ângela Maria comes over and looks. "No, no, they're perfect." She lifts the large pot and drains it, efficiently transferring the potatoes to a serving dish. "Grace, run and get me the soup bowls, I'll fill them out here."

Happy to have a job, she runs back and forth between the dining room and kitchen.

"Everyone to the table!" Ângela Maria yells.

Grace ends up sitting between Ângela Maria and Ana, for which she is grateful. Miguel wholly ignores her. In recent weeks, he has grown noticeably colder. Ângela Maria's father talks with Miguel about planting. Ana and Mário babble on about who is going to the New Year's dance with whom, and Ângela Maria and her mother discuss a letter Ângela Maria received from her sister Lúcia. Grace eats in silence, moving in and out of the various conversations the best she can. Suddenly she realizes she is being spoken to.

"Graça." Mário tries to get her attention. "Graça, so are you bringing your new boyfriend to the dance? Ana and I have a bet."

The table falls silent. "Mário!" Ângela Maria says sternly. "That is not an appropriate thing to ask our guest."

Grace, recovering from her initial embarrassment, says, "No, no, that's okay, Ângela Maria. I don't mind answering." Grace turns to Mário. "Magnus and I are just friends; we barely know each other. I don't think I'll be going to the dance. So who wins?"

Before Mário can respond, Ana says, "Well, I think we'll have to wait until the dance to know the answer to that!"

Conversation picks up again, and again Grace is out of the loop. She eats her dinner alone, an uninteresting refugee.

When everyone finishes eating, Grace, Ana, and Ângela Maria

clear away the dishes. Ângela Maria's parents go home right away. No sitting around talking. Ângela Maria washes the dishes while Grace dries. Ana disappears.

"Oh good. The coast is finally clear," Ângela Maria says quietly, as if she has a secret to tell.

Grace leans in.

"I was wondering, how you would like to go to Fajã dos Vimes with me and Ana to visit Elisabete tomorrow?" Ângela Maria then adds in an almost inaudible whisper, "And Tia Carmina."

A surge of adrenaline courses through Grace; her heart pounds. "I guess that would be fine. I don't have anything else planned."

"Just for fun. She wants to meet you. Don't worry." Ângela Maria glances over at Miguel, who is seated in front of the television. He's asleep. "Good, then, that settles it."

MAGNUS

ON CHRISTMAS DAY, from the rocky beach of Fajã dos Vimes, Magnus gazes at the glistening whitecaps—too rough to go out in the boat, as it is most of the time in the winter. He remembers the hard lesson of last Christmas Day, when he stupidly took his boat out on a day like this. The boat overturned. Somehow—he never knew how—he made it back to shore safely, cold, wet, and bruised, but otherwise unharmed. The boat was lost, smashed to pieces on the rocks. In honor of the anniversary of his narrow escape, he stops at the *fajã* on his way to Topo from Calheta.

He feels empty; he can't explain it. Perhaps he hoped for more from Grace than she gave him. The gift was fine, and thoughtful enough. It isn't that. More a problem of her not being giving of herself. He didn't expect to be invited to spend the night, but he thought that something would happen between them, and it didn't.

On the walk back from Mass, Magnus put his arm around Grace's shoulder. She pulled away, ever so slightly, enough that he knew she wasn't comfortable with him. He dropped his arm back to his side. When they arrived at her place, they awkwardly said good-bye, pecking each other on the cheek. She didn't even ask him how he would be getting to Topo or whether he had a place to stay. *Maybe she doesn't care. Perhaps she is too self-centered to care.*

His disappointment turns to anger. *Everything is always about her and what happens to her. Of course, why hasn't he seen it before?* Magnus picks up a worn-smooth round gray rock and inspects it. It's about the size of a baseball. He hurls it as hard as he can into the water, seeing but not hearing it splash. He picks up another, and another . . .

"Bom Natal!" Zé's voice booms from behind him.

Magnus startles, turns to see the old guy in his feed cap smiling. *Great. Let's talk about fish.* That is all he and Zé ever talk about. That and the weather. "Yeah, merry Christmas to you too," he musters.

Zé picks up a rock and throws it, even farther than what Magnus accomplished. He doesn't say anything for a while. "So, you aren't planning on taking your boat out today, are you?"

"No, no," says Magnus. "Don't usually make the same mistake twice if I can avoid it." In his head he ends the sentence with, *Except in matters of love.*

"That's good." Zé hurls another rock. "When I saw you here, I wondered." They throw more rocks, then Zé says, "You're pretty dressed up for someone who's come to the *fajã* to throw rocks."

Magnus understands the implicit question; he can answer or not. "Yeah, well, I went to Mass in Calheta last night. Ended up staying at the *residencial*—too tired to go home." Magnus throws another rock—his best throw yet.

"You don't believe in Mary, do you?" Zé has stopped throwing rocks. He forces his hands into the pockets of his hooded sweatshirt.

"I'm not Catholic, if that is what you are asking." Magnus bends over to get another rock.

Zé chuckles. "You're a smart one." He pulls a kerchief out of his pocket and blows his nose. "Doesn't that American girl that was here last week live in Calheta?"

Zé has never taken any interest in anything personal, and now suddenly he is diving into the depths more skillfully than Magnus would have ever imagined him capable. "Yep." Magnus hopes the questions will stop with that.

"Yeah, I thought so." A look of amusement crosses Zé's face. "Well, I best be going. I wanted to make sure you weren't thinking of going out in the boat." He turns to leave.

Good, Magnus thinks.

Then Zé turns around and says with a laugh, "If I were you, I would stay away from the Americana. I've heard that one look from her can dry you up permanently, if you know what I mean. *Adeus.*" Zé waves.

Magnus fails to see the humor.

14

THE OWL WOMAN

ÂNGELA MARIA

"Ana!" Ângela Maria calls down the hall. "Are you ready to leave?"

Ana peeks out of her room. "Mãe, do I have to go?"

"Yes, now come on. We need to be on our way." Ângela Maria told Miguel they were going to the *fajã* so that Ana can visit with Elisabete. True, Elisabete loves the kids and wants to see them, but Ângela Maria is using her as cover to visit Tia Carmina.

Ana drags out of her room. "Is it okay if I bring my novel? I'm almost at the end—"

"Fine, fine, let's get going." Ângela Maria pushes Ana toward the door and down the back steps. Ana always seems to have her nose in a book. "Go ahead and hop in the car. I have to get Grace."

Ana's eyes light up. "You didn't tell me Grace was coming with us!" She sounds much more excited about the prospect of a day in the *fajã* with Grace than one with her mom and second cousin. Ângela Maria doesn't blame her. Ana clearly adores Grace. She told Ângela Maria that she thought one day she would like to be anthropologist like Grace and travel to faraway places. It breaks Ângela Maria's heart to think of losing her daughter that way.

Ângela Maria knocks sharply on Grace's door a couple of times. Grace opens almost instantly. "Are you ready?" Ângela Maria asks.

"Yep! I'm ready," Grace says, grabbing her bag and her coat.

Ângela Maria feels nervous about the day, about deceiving Miguel again, about Ana. She holds the keys out toward Grace. "Do you mind driving? I'm not completely comfortable."

"Not at all!" Grace takes the keys. She pats Ângela Maria on the shoulder. "Are you sure it's a good idea? You know, with Miguel and all?"

Ângela Maria puts her hand on Grace's hand. "Grace, you don't understand this, I know, but I have to do this. It isn't only about you." Ângela Maria wonders when and if she needs to tell Grace about Jaime. Grace must have seen his picture in the *sala* on Christmas Eve. But now isn't the right time. They get into the car.

The drive to the *fajã* goes quickly. Much to Ângela Maria's chagrin, Grace asks Ana to tell her about the novel she is reading. Ana launches off into a hilariously funny retelling of the book. Ângela Maria marvels at her daughter's liveliness and quirky sense of humor. Compared to her, Ana is free. Ana times the retelling of the story to perfectly match their arrival to Fajã dos Vimes. "I am getting close to the end of the book now, and I don't know what happens. You'll have to wait until the drive home." Ana looks pleased with herself.

"What do you want to bet that they live happily ever after and go off in the sunset?" Grace asks. "Those kind of novels always end that way!"

"I'll let you know," Ana says.

ÂNGELA MARIA and Elisabete have devised a plan for the visit in advance. Elisabete takes Ana over to the studio, ostensibly to help with setting up a loom for a special order she received from America. On previous occasions Ana expressed an interest in learning to weave. Ângela Maria is supposed to be showing Grace around the *fajã*, which includes introducing her to a few of the *fajã*'s more colorful characters. As they leave, Ana says, "Give Tia Carmina a kiss from me."

Ângela Maria has not spoken to Ana about what is going on, but she suspects Ana knows. She came home from school one day before Christmas and asked some pointed questions about *olhado* and *feiticeiras*. When Ângela Maria asked her why she wanted to know, she said, *Oh, some girls at school said they heard that Grace might be some kind of witch. We don't believe that, do we, Mãe?*

Ângela Maria has kept talk of witches, ghosts, *olhado*, and other superstitions to a minimum around her children. She prefers raising them without a fear of the same intangibles that darkened her childhood. *No, daughter,* she said to Ana, *we don't believe that; she absolutely is not a witch.*

But do we believe in witches and stuff like that? Ana probed.

I believe there are good people and bad people in the world. Some have more power than others. One day, you'll have to decide for yourself whether they have real or imagined power. You'll have to decide whether imagined power is real. Feeling hypocritical, Ângela Maria dodged the question. She believes in witchcraft and magic.

As she and Grace round the corner, they find Tia Carmina waiting for them. "Finally, you are here." Tia Carmina inspects Grace.

"Good morning, Tia." Ângela Maria kisses her. Gesturing, she says, "This is Grace. Grace, this is . . . you can call her Tia Carmina too. Everyone does. She is everybody's aunt."

"A pleasure to meet you." Grace bends down to exchange kisses with the tiny old woman.

Tia Carmina continues to hold on to Grace's shoulders with her gnarled hands, looking intently into her eyes. "No, no, the pleasure is all mine!" She smiles, revealing several missing teeth.

"Well, can we go in? It is a bit cold out here," says Ângela Maria, worried that Grace might feel uncomfortable in plain view.

"Let's go back to my kitchen. The fire will warm you up." Tia Carmina leads the way along the path to the back of the property. She moves more quickly than one would expect for such an old woman. As she goes, she points out different plants.

Ângela Maria watches Grace's and Tia Carmina's every move. Grace looks comfortable with Tia Carmina, as if she were a long lost acquaintance. What a relief.

Tia Carmina's pots simmer atop the stove, as usual, and the smell of various herbs and roots wafts through the cold air. Ângela Maria and Grace sit in chairs next to the table, and Tia Carmina pours different teas for each of them. Tia Carmina is beginning her work, even without Grace's consent.

After setting out some cake, Tia Carmina joins them at the table. "Well, Grace, I am happy that you have come to meet me in person at last." She looks meaningfully at Grace.

Ângela Maria sips her tea and stares out the window as she listens to Tia Carmina's voice.

GRACE

GRACE LOOKS into the old woman's black eyes. How unusual. A distinctly golden ring encircles her black iris. They know each other. Tia Carmina's words ring in her ears, *You have come to meet me in person at last.* Grace lifts the cup of tea to her lips and sips. What did she mean, *at last?* A strange sensation spills over her tongue; simultaneously sweet and bitter. Intensely sweet and bitter. Suddenly, she remembers where she saw Tia Carmina. Not possible. Grace's tongue feels thick as she speaks. "Yes. I'm glad too," she says. She floats, as in a dream. Grace looks over at Ângela Maria. She sits placidly looking out the window, not noticing. Grace turns to Tia Carmina. "My mother said I would see you again, but I didn't believe her."

Tia Carmina laughs warmly. "You haven't needed me much, a little here and there in a dream or two."

"I don't understand how . . . how it is that you—"

Tia Carmina puts her hand over Grace's. "How could I have been there and here?"

Grace nods. Talking requires too much effort.

"Only my body remains here. This is where it was born, and this is where it will die. My spirit goes where it wants, where it's needed, to those for whom I am a guide and help, to people in the world like you. Those who have seen me leave my body say that I take flight as an owl. I'm not aware. We all take different outer forms, but know only our inner selves."

Grace is completely immobilized. A tug, something lifts her upward. She looks down to see herself, her body, sitting across from Ângela Maria's—apparently asleep. Tia Carmina's body stands in front of the stove as if frozen in time. Grace rises higher. The soft wing of an owl brushes against her. She sees the dog from her dreams running below her, jumping and barking. She feels exhilarated. If this is a dream, she doesn't want it to end.

Her euphoria quickly vanishes, giving way to panic. What if this is real? She plummets, opening her eyes just before hitting the ground. *What the fuck?*

Tia Carmina stirs something on the stove. Grace looks over to where Ângela Maria was sitting. She's gone. Good thing she doesn't know how to swear in Portuguese.

"Did you have nice nap?" Tia Carmina asks without looking.

Grace struggles to sit up straight. "Wow, I must have been really tired!"

Tia Carmina chuckles as she brings Grace another cup of something.

"Thanks, but no thanks," Grace says emphatically. The first tea was more than enough.

"It's coffee, coffee from the *fajã*." Tia Carmina sets the cup down in front of Grace. "Don't worry. It isn't more of my special tea." She chuckles again as she shuffles over and takes a shawl down from a hook.

"Where did Ângela Maria go?" Grace asks, trying not to look overly concerned.

"Oh, she'll be back soon. That husband of hers showed up— all in a rage about her being here." Tia Carmina sits down. "He'll get over it." She clicks her tongue. "So, what should we do about your situation?"

Grace suddenly begins to regret having let Ângela Maria bring her here. She doesn't belong here. "Well, I guess I should avoid Topo—that's been working for me pretty well so far." She knows she hasn't given the correct answer, but she doesn't plan to let this crazy old woman get under her skin with drug-induced magic. Just as she thought. Smoke and mirrors. Illusion.

"That would be fine if it were about you, but it's about so much more. You'll have to do better if you hope to succeed."

Tia Carmina knows her. Drugs or not, she has wriggled under Grace's skin and deep into her pores.

Tia Carmina gets up to tend the stove. "When you figure things out, and you understand that you are but one small piece of a puzzle, come back. Then I can help you."

Dismissed. "Thank you. I'm sure I'll be back." Amazingly refreshed, lighter than she was when she arrived, she rises to her feet. "It really has been a pleasure meeting you." An unpleasant pleasure.

"As always," says Tia Carmina. "By the way, you should know that Nonna Preta is the least of your worries; you have darker things lurking on your path."

Great. What could be darker?

Tia Carmina clutches a sprig of rosemary. She kisses Grace on both cheeks. As she leaves, she hears Tia Carmina mutter something. Grace turns to see she's praying.

THEY NEVER LEARN how the novel Ana is reading ends; Miguel drives home. Grace sits in back with Ana, who buries herself in her book. Grace stares silently toward Pico. How she wishes to be anywhere but in this car, silenced by anger. Miguel went to Fajã de São João with his brother to help deliver a table saw. On their way back they stopped in Fajã dos Vimes to see when Ana and Ângela Maria planned to return.

Although Grace didn't have an opportunity to talk to Ângela Maria about what happened, Ana, at one point, whispered, "He's mad that she took you to see Tia Carmina." Grace understands; she too is angry with Ângela Maria for taking her there.

Could the owl woman in her girlhood dreams have been Tia Carmina, or did the hallucinogen in the tea awaken her desire to return to simpler times, tapping into her subconscious? She wrestles with whether to tell Ângela Maria. No, she doesn't need to know. Besides, Grace herself is unsure what happened, whether anything happened. Perhaps she *had* just dozed.

Finally, Calheta. Grace breaks the silence. "Miguel, would you mind dropping me off at the post office?"

GRACE GOES into the phone booth at the post office, the only one in town now that everybody has a mobile phone. She punches in her for-emergencies-only calling-card number, then dials her parents' cell phone number. They're still in Hawaii, so they might be up. She hopes they are. She waits impatiently for the connection to go through. It's ringing.

Finally, her mother answers.

"Hi, Mom, it's me." A knot forms in her throat; she starts to cry.

"Are you okay, sweetie?"

"Yeah, I'm okay. I wish I were there . . . I wanted to tell you I think I met the owl woman from the dreams I had when Grandmother died."

Silence.

"Mom? Are you there?"

"Yeah, I'm here . . . things must be pretty bad there if you met her." Silence. "Why didn't you tell me that things were so bad?"

Grace chokes back tears. "Mom, I can't really talk about it right now . . . People listen." She sniffs. "I'll send you an email from the firehouse later." She hates that it is so hard to get an internet connection, but at least she can go there.

They stay on the phone talking for a long time about how they spent their respective Christmases. Her parents, although ostensibly on vacation, were on duty at a free clinic offered for Native Hawaiians and barely had time to think about Christmas. Grace feels a little sad about that. Her dad has already taken off for his shift so she doesn't have to talk to him. Small blessing.

As their conversation approaches its end, her mother says, "I want you to promise me something."

"What?" Grace waits.

"I want you to promise me that you will listen to the owl woman. I know how you feel about this spiritual stuff, but it's extremely important that you open your heart to it now. Will you promise?"

Grace feels ambivalent about making such a promise. If she makes it, she will have to keep it. "I'll try."

"Trying isn't enough. I'm not letting you go until you promise." Silence.

"I promise," she says. How can she make such a promise and keep it? She plans on staying as far away from Tia Carmina as possible.

"Okay then. I'm waiting for your email." Her mother says with finality.

"Okay. And, Mom, don't tell Dad about this."

"Don't worry. I won't. He'd laugh at me."

"Thanks, Mom. I love you. Give Dad a hug and a kiss from me."

"I will. I love you too. Bye."

"Bye, Mom."

Grace enters her calling-card number again and dials Jake.

"Hi, you've reached Jake's answering machine . . ." She waits for the beep and leaves him a message wishing him a belated merry Christmas and a happy new year. She doesn't say *I love you*. Just as well. She isn't in the mood to talk to him.

15

THE KINGS' JOURNEY

GRACE

THAT NIGHT, the cold night air and the brisk walk toward the *sociedade* wake her up. Late, as usual. Under the streetlamp ahead, she sees the silhouettes of the group of singers, some with instruments slung over their shoulders. They move toward her, and she quickens her pace. Finally, their faces come into focus.

Senhor Estêvão leads the group. *"Boa noite!"* His voice rings out.

"Boa noite!" Grace responds. "Sorry I'm late."

One of the women in the group, whom Grace doesn't know well, says, "Americana, don't worry about it. Come on, come on, you're our only alto tonight."

Wonderful. No one to follow. This should be entertaining.

Senhor Estêvão moves closer. "You see, it is no problem at all." His voice is full of condescension and honey. "We planned to begin singing in your neighborhood anyway." Addressing the group,

"Everybody feel ready to begin?" He turns onto a path leading to the house of someone Grace doesn't know.

They sing two songs. The first song is the rough equivalent of "We Wish You a Merry Christmas," and the second song, sung as a thank-you for the white envelope handed to Senhor Estêvão, is a blessing for the new year. They go to two more houses before coming to Ângela Maria's house.

Senhor Estêvão turns to a woman named Delfina. "We haven't sung here for the last few years. What do you think?"

Delfina says, "I don't know. Grace, you live here, don't you? Should we sing here?"

Grace is puzzled. She thought they sang at everyone's house. "Of course, why wouldn't we? Ângela Maria is expecting us. She wants to make a toast."

"Well then, we must sing!" Senhor Estêvão says as he heads toward the front door.

Grace has never seen this side of Senhor Estêvão: the jolly side.

They begin to sing. The front door opens. Ângela Maria looks delighted, tears in her eyes. Miguel and the kids come up behind her.

Grace feels inexplicably proud for being a part of this scene. After they sing their first song, Ângela Maria invites them in for the toast. Her *sala* has been prepared for the kings' arrival with a festive spread of cakes, cookies, figs, nuts, some hot hors d'oeuvres, and plenty of alcohol. They stay for about twenty minutes, eating and drinking shots of *aguardente* and *angelica* and finishing the visit off by singing their thank-you song, envelope in hand.

Ângela Maria has never looked happier, and even Miguel is somewhat cordial, in spite of the events earlier in the day.

As they walk up the hill to the next house, Grace hurries to catch up to Delfina. *"A senhora."* She tries to get her attention.

Delfina turns and slows. "Yes? Were you talking to me?" Her round face shines under the streetlights.

"Yeah," says Grace, out of breath from the pace. "I wanted to ask you why you weren't sure about singing there."

"We never sing at houses where people are in mourning," she says.

Obviously, common knowledge. Grace has managed to live there for three months without knowing. "I didn't realize . . ."

Delfina pats Grace's shoulder. "It's okay. It has been a long time. They aren't in mourning anymore. That's why we sang there." She smiles at Grace reassuringly. They arrive at the next house, and Delfina says, "We have to sing again."

After they sing and begin walking again, Grace asks Delfina, "But who died?" By now, Grace has figured it out—the other son. She hopes Delfina will give her the story.

Delfina's expression changes. "A terrible, terrible thing. They lost their son Jaime in an accident. A mother's worst nightmare."

Grace walks along without saying anything, waiting for Delfina to say more.

"I'm surprised you didn't know about it, living there and all." Delfina walks quickly for someone with such short legs. "Well, here we are again!"

They sing. Nobody comes to the door, and no one looks out the window—no second song. They continue on their journey.

"Well, yes . . ." Grace picks up the conversation where they left off. "You'd think I would have known something. How did he, did he . . ."

"Die? By electrocution." Delfina tells Grace about the storm, the potatoes, the water, the light bulb, and finally the funeral. "Ângela Maria practically vanished from the earth. She was completely devastated. And poor Miguel. Left taking care of the two younger ones. For him, it was as if he lost a wife and a son."

"You women, hurry up!" Senhor Estêvão says from ahead. "We're cold and ready to go to the next toast." He sounds irritated.

Grace and Delfina fell behind without realizing it. They run to catch up.

Grace feels sick. Ângela Maria's son died in the *loja* where she now lives. No wonder no one ever told her about it. She struggles to maintain a cheerful demeanor. How will she make it through the rest of the evening?

Os Reis sings at twelve more houses and receives toasts at three. Fatigue weighs on Grace; she desperately needs to sleep. She hurries ahead of the group, wanting nothing more than to end this miserable day.

From behind she hears Senhor Estêvão say in English, "Hey, beautiful woman, wait for me." No doubt thinking no one but she would understand him. He grabs her arm and hooks elbows.

"*Ó senhor!*" Grace pulls away. What has got into him?

"What? You don't like my compliment?"

He's not himself at all, at least not the person she thinks he is. Maybe he's had too much to drink. "It's not appropriate," Grace says in Portuguese. She slows down, looking back. "Senhora Delfina!" she calls. "I have more questions for you." Grace moves next to Delfina, leaving Senhor Estêvão walking solo in the lead.

AT THE NEW Year's dance, strobe lights flash, and a large mirrored ball spins in the center of the *sociedade* ballroom, casting bright reflections around the room. A mother-and-two-daughters band, accompanied by a canned pop soundtrack, provide loud entertainment. New Year's Eve celebrants, dressed in their best clothes, move about the dance floor laughing.

Grace has entered the twilight zone. Catapulted into the past. Too young to have experienced the discos of the seventies personally, having only seen them in movies, she imagines them to have been something like this.

Ângela Maria asked Grace to chaperone Ana and Mário. At first she declined, but Ana and Mário convinced her to go. *Come on! It'll be fun, and we'll hang out with you.* Ana went on, *It's the least you can do, on account of my losing that bet about you and the Swede.* Yep. She lost the bet. Real life, unlike novels, seldom has a happy ending.

In theory, the three of them are there together, but Ana and Mário both disappear into the throbbing mass of dancers immediately upon arrival. Grace attempts invisibility, hiding behind her notebook at a table in the corner of the room. Like a photographer's camera, her notebook gives her social distance. A barrier that says, *I'm busy with very important things. Don't talk to me.* Illusion.

She draws a diagram of the room, illustrates the relative positions of the stage, the dance floor, the tables, the bars, and so forth. Next, she documents the people who are there. She describes their clothes, their ages, where and with whom they sit, whether they are talking, drinking, and what they eat. Interesting. Senhor Estêvão and his wife sit with a couple Grace recognizes from Os Reis. They both wave at her. Grace has successfully dodged Senhor Estêvão during the last week. She buries her face in her notebook, exaggerating her enterprise. She can't deal with him tonight. As if deep in thought, she looks up, biting the cap of her ballpoint. Where has he gone?

"*Boa noite, a senhora!* May I have the honor of this dance?" Senhor Estêvão stands behind her, holding his arm out for her. A gentleman tonight. He looks handsome in his tuxedo.

The humiliation of her last dance with him at the *baile de* Santa Catarina looms large. No, can't do it. She thinks also of his comment to her on the first night of Os Reis. "Thanks, but I really shouldn't. Perhaps your wife would like to dance?" Gesturing toward her notebook, she says, "I am in the middle of documenting."

"Nonsense. You have plenty of time to do that! Almost an hour remains before the new year, and the rest of the night beyond that." Senhor Estêvão juts his elbow out again to say, *Take my arm.*

"Honestly, Senhor Estêvão, I don't feel right about it . . . your wife."

"*Pois!* My wife suggested it! She feels sorry for you here alone with your notebook."

Grace glances over to their table. Norinha isn't paying any attention to them; she's talking to the other couple. Perhaps it would be all right.

"Well then . . ." Grace closes her notebook and sticks it in her bag. "I guess it would be okay." She slowly rises to dance.

The song ends just as they reach the dance floor. Grace stands uncomfortably across from Senhor Estêvão, whose eyes remain fixed on her face. She fights the urge to flee. His intentions are clear—not fatherly. The music begins to play; a slow dance. Senhor Estêvão places his right hand firmly on the small of Grace's back, and takes her right hand with his left. Grace feels his breath on her ear as he begins swaying gently with the music.

She glances over at Norinha, whose face she will never forget. The couple seated with her look almost as disturbed as she does. Grace pulls away. "I really can't do this." Without looking back or over at Norinha again, she hurries to her table, gathers her belongings, and begins searching for Ana and Mário, but she doesn't see them.

Not able to leave without them, she climbs the stairs to the mezzanine to the overflow seating. Empty, thank God. She sits where she can see but not be seen. How could she have been so naive about Senhor Estêvão? She feels like a fucking idiot. He's been giving her signs for weeks. Has she inadvertently invited it? It is finished now. No more Os Reis. English lessons are out of the question. Blindness.

ESTÊVÃO

FOR A BRIEF MOMENT, Senhor Estêvão revels in triumph. With her body against his, he held his face close to hers, breathing in the essence of her being. Everything was perfect. What happened? Norinha herself suggested they dance. Was it a test? Of course. It *was* a test. Norinha never felt sorry for Grace. *Estêvão, why don't you dance with the poor girl?* A joke. He gained the upper hand. Serves her right. As for the girl, his time will come.

16

SOMETIMES VOLCANOES ERUPT

GRACE

GRACE PUSHES THE DOOR OPEN. She hasn't been to the Café da Ilha since before Christmas. She misses talking to Magnus. So much to tell him. Perhaps he doesn't want to see her. He hasn't called or texted. On Christmas Eve, when they parted, she could tell that he was hurt and angry with her for pushing him away. It's time to tell him about Jake. She looks around, but he isn't there.

After drinking her *galão*, she walks to the archives. She's not motivated to do research, but what else is she here for? She greets the archivist and puts her things down in her usual spot, then hunts in the stacks for something to read. The musty-smelling room is cold and empty. As she rounds a bookshelf, she run smack into Magnus.

"Magnus! I was hoping to run into you, but not this way!" Grace laughs.

"Ha, ha," he says. "I guess I hoped to see you too." His voice sounds cold and flat.

"You guess? You sound unsure about it." She tries to sound upbeat.

"I think we need to talk, Grace."

Her neck warms. The dreaded welts. "Yeah, we really do, but here?"

"No. Let's go to my place."

ON THE WAY, Grace fills Magnus in on all that has happened since they last saw one another. She doesn't tell him about the connection she has with Tia Carmina from earlier in her life. A little too bizarre. He seems to listen to her story with guarded interest. He's probably still upset about being rejected.

"Well," he says, "sounds like your life is full of drama and as fascinating as ever."

She notes his sarcasm.

"Here we are." They walk around to the back of the house. Magnus holds the door open, and she steps into a dark hallway. "All the way upstairs," he says.

His rented room, more of a rented floor, opens at the top of the stairs. The attic space has been converted to a lovely studio apartment. Magnificent compared with her place. A large window looks out over red tiled rooftops, with a backdrop of the port. Grace imagines that on a clear day one can see both Pico and Faial. "Nice view!"

"Yeah, I like it."

He shows no emotion. What is he thinking? What will he say? Perhaps he'll declare his love for her. Romantic stuff. No. He doesn't seem to be in that frame of mind.

Clearing away some books and papers from a small table, he asks, "Tea?"

"Sure." Grace sits down. "I'll take my tea plain, no drugs please." Grace laughs nervously. He doesn't smile.

Magnus fills a small pan and puts it on a Bunsen burner to heat up. "Well, Grace . . ." He walks behind her and squeezes her shoulders firmly.

She wishes he would keep going forever. She didn't realize how tight her muscles were until he touched them.

"What's going on? I mean, with us? I guess I'm confused." He stops massaging her shoulders and sits down.

She meets his hard stare. "Well . . . ," Grace begins, "I really do like you . . . I mean, I am really attracted to you . . . It is—"

"Someone else?" Magnus interrupts.

"Sort of . . . Well, I'm not even sure . . ." Grace launches into telling Magnus about Jake. She ends with, "And now, I am so confused. I just don't think it is fair to anyone, least of all you . . ." She watches Magnus, immovable. She wants him. Her heart feels like it might explode.

He stands up without saying anything and pours water into the cups. With his back to her, he says, "I guess not."

He turns and sets the tea down in front of her. She watches the steam curl up out of the cup. She yawns with anxiety.

"You could have said something sooner, Grace. Before I fell flat on my face in love with you."

She stares blankly at the teacup; Magnus's eyes would burn a hole through her if she were to look at him. "I planned to, but . . ." Why hasn't she? *He loves me.*

"But you think the world, with all of its little dramas, revolves around you," Magnus says bitterly.

Grace's eyes swell with tears. Her natural inclination is to fight back, but she doesn't. He's right. She has been completely self-absorbed. A tear drops onto the table.

Magnus hands her a clean white handkerchief. Just another thing she likes about him. He uses handkerchiefs and always has a clean one handy.

"I'm really sorry, Magnus. I really am."

"So am I." He reaches across the table and takes her hand.

They sit for some time not saying anything. Then Magnus says,

"So now I know. Not what I hoped to hear, but the truth is better than an imagined reality." He lets go of her hand and stands up. "At least, that is what I have always believed."

"Do you think we can be friends?" Grace asks.

"Of course, what's the alternative?"

MAGNUS

Friends. How many times has he heard the phrase *We can be friends?* Magnus envies Grace's easy tears.

"I don't want you to feel like I am kicking you out. You are welcome to stay as long as you like, *friend* . . ." Perhaps he emphasized the word too much. "But I have a meeting over at the hospital." He gathers papers for the public health panel's monthly meeting. Today he will present a paper on the dangers posed by volcanic gases. *Sometimes volcanoes erupt.*

"Lock up when you leave." Magnus exits just like that, leaving Grace to sit alone in his empty place.

In spite of his anger, he can't help feeling sorry for Grace. The fact that she may or may not be involved with someone else doesn't change his feelings for her, and he cares what happens to her. True, she has experienced an unusual run of events, but then, he thinks, perhaps she *has* brought some of them on herself. Yes, that must certainly be the case. Undoubtedly, she gave Senhor Estêvão subtle cues, just as she has given him.

And all the silly business with the evil eye and the alleged witches in Topo and Fajã dos Vimes—she has fallen prey to her own desire to find something mysterious, inexplicable, and romantic in an otherwise dreary old-world European culture. She told him once that what she does is not science, but *art*. She would ultimately write fiction, not fact. How true. Some people, like her, seek complication, are drawn so much to it that they create it where none exists.

At the hospital, the man from the agriculture department drones on. "In conclusion, the anti-Brucellosis advertising campaign targeted at dairy farmers has proven effective. Brucellosis is on the decline in the Azores, and in Portugal in general. Nevertheless, it still poses a significant health risk . . ."

Magnus has barely heard a word of what has been said. The meeting is over. He stands up stiffly. His part went well enough.

"*Boa tarde*, Senhor Doutor Sorenson."

Magnus turns toward the voice. Doctor Roberto. "*Boa tarde, senhor.*"

"I found your presentation most interesting," says Doctor Roberto. "You know, it really could explain many of the respiratory illnesses we have seen, but then there are so many things that can cause those . . ."

"Yes, yes, of course," Magnus says. "Did you get my message from a few weeks ago? I had some questions for you about that illness up in Topo?" Magnus moves toward the door as he speaks.

Doctor Roberto looks puzzled. "No . . . I didn't have a message from you. Are you sure you reached my office?"

"Most certain," Magnus replies. "I spoke with your secretary." They enter a large room where cake and coffee are served.

"What do you want to know? I'm not aware of any major recent outbreaks in Topo."

"Well, I heard about an outbreak of what sounded like dysentery to me, that one boy remains hospitalized because of it." Magnus steps in line for coffee.

"Oh yes, that. Not what I would call an outbreak. A few children came down with bad cases of diarrhea—probably unrelated cases—a lot of things could have caused that," says Doctor Roberto, as he pours his coffee. "Why are you so interested?"

"A friend of mine thinks she might be responsible somehow."

Magnus takes a piece of cake and heads toward an empty table. Doctor Roberto follows.

"*Pois é.* This friend wouldn't happen to be the Americana?" Doctor Roberto chuckles, as if he finds humor in something.

Magnus sees that the doctor knows exactly where the conversation is headed. Word travels. "Well, yes. You have no doubt heard the absurd talk about *olhado?* The problem is, she half believes all this stuff and has even gone so far as to visit a so-called witch."

Doctor Roberto lets out a real laugh. "Unbelievable! Who would think that an educated American could fall prey to peasant superstitions that way?"

"I know, it seems improbable, doesn't it? Anyway, I hoped you could give me something concrete to pass on to her to try to convince her that she has nothing to do with any of this."

Doctor Roberto smooths his hand over his tie. "Of course . . . concrete . . . *pois,* we didn't isolate a specific organism, nor did we try; may well have been viral. As a precaution we treated the children with antibiotics, and within days all but the boy recovered. Not too concrete."

"So you're saying that you don't know the precise cause?" Magnus asks.

"It could be one of many different things or multiple things." Doctor Roberto turns his wedding ring around on his finger. "No identifiable pattern."

Disappointing. No hard data. Magnus hoped to find incontrovertible evidence that neither the evil eye nor witchcraft played any part in these illnesses. "Well, surely, you must have some idea about why the boy remains so ill."

Doctor Roberto clears his throat. "Absolutely. Kidney failure, likely the result of damage by the organism that caused the initial gastroenteritis." Doctor Roberto takes a sip of coffee. "You see, Doctor Sorenson, we don't have the expertise or diagnostic facilities here on the island. The boy *really* needs to be flown to Lisbon, but he is not strong enough for the trip. He isn't even strong enough for the trip to Terceira."

Magnus swallows the last of his coffee and rises to his feet. Extending his hand, he says, "Thank you so much for your time."

Doctor Roberto stands and shakes hands with Magnus. "Well, I'm sorry that I can't give you more definitive answers. I think you should be able to assure your friend with confidence that she is not responsible for any of this." He chuckles again.

Magnus cannot fathom why Doctor Roberto finds the whole situation so amusing. It's true: The situation is absurd. Grace could not be at fault for any of this. Magnus, at least, understands how she came to think that she might be. His anger at her has already begun to subside.

GRACE

GRACE NEEDS to make things right with Magnus and is in no hurry to get back to her cursed *loja*. She lingers at his place in hopes he will return home as soon as his meeting is over, but to her disappointment he doesn't come right back, and if she doesn't leave now, she will miss the last bus. Against her better judgment, she decides to stay and wait. She calls Ângela Maria.

"*Está?* Hello?"

"Hi, Grace here." Grace has rehearsed her phone etiquette.

"Is everything okay?" Ângela Maria asks. Granted, it's unusual for Grace to call.

"Yeah, everything's fine," she lies. "I'm going to stay the night in Velas. I missed the last bus and decided I'm just gonna have a nice restaurant meal and stay at the *residencial* tonight. Kind of a mini vacation."

"Oh, okay, what about the Day of the Kings? You won't want to miss the procession."

"Yeah, yeah, I'll be there. I'll either take the early bus or catch a ride."

"Well then, okay . . . I guess I'll see you in the morning, then," Ângela Maria says. "And, Grace, thank you for calling. You know how much I worry."

"Yes, exactly my thoughts! I'll see you in the morning."

MAGNUS

AFTER THE MEETING, Magnus decides to go looking for Grace. He was a little meaner than he intended to be. He heads to the Café de Ilha first.

"The usual?" the owner asks as he enters.

"No, actually, I am wondering if you have seen the American woman?"

"Nope, not since this morning."

"Thanks." Magnus heads to the archives, but when he gets there, the doors are locked.

He thinks Grace undoubtedly has hightailed it back to Calheta after he left her sitting in his apartment. Needing a drink, he pops into the bar down at the port.

It's full of guys just off work, and the air smells of cigarette smoke—*I wish I hadn't quit*. He steps up to the bar.

"What'll it be?" the bartender asks.

"I'll have a Sagres and a shot of *aguardente*."

Magnus downs them. Orders another round. Just the thing he needs. He heads home, pleasantly but not too drunk.

GRACE

As the apartment darkens, Grace gets sleepy and moves to a more comfortable chair in the sitting area. She turns on a lamp and pretends to read a book in Swedish that is on the side table. At some point, she dozes off. The sound of footsteps on the stairs awakens her. Other than the reading lamp, the room is dark, and she feels disoriented for a moment, but now she remembers why she is sitting there. Magnus is finally home. Her heart pounds as the door opens and he flips on the light switch, flooding the room with warm light. She leaps to her feet.

When he sees Grace standing in the middle of the room, his face brightens. Grace can't quite read his expression. He isn't unhappy, which is a good start.

Unsure of what to say or do next, she feels her legs trembling beneath her.

"Grace! Am I ever glad to see you. I figured you would never want to see me again after my little fit." He approaches her. "I'm sorry I left you like that." Now holding her shoulders, no doubt emboldened by the alcohol she smells on his breath, he says, "It's just that I can't be *just friends* with you. I *love* you, Grace . . . I want us to be more."

Through tears, she says, "I'm sorry, Magnus. I shouldn't have said what I did either. I love you too, I do . . . I am just afraid." Magnus pulls her in and strokes her hair as she sobs. "I'm sorry, I'm so sorry . . ."

"Shhhh . . . ," he whispers. "Everything is going to be okay." They begin kissing each other, frantically at first and then slowing to a more gentle exploration of each other's face, eyes, and mouth.

Magnus takes her by the hand and leads her to his bed, which is covered in a lofty Scandinavian down duvet. He turns toward her, looks her disarmingly in the eyes, and slowly begins to pull her T-shirt off over her head. Her nipples are hard. Electricity vibrates throughout her body. He is patient, not greedy. Gentle. Grace tentatively reaches out and begins unbuttoning the dress shirt he wears. They stand before one another, each half-nude and vulnerable.

They kiss slowly and tenderly while exploring the contours of each other's bodies. Magnus guides her firmly down onto the bed and, never taking his eyes off hers, slips his hand into the front of her unzipped jeans and gently slides them off. He stands and removes his own pants. Grace is near anguish with desire as she watches and waits for him. He is torturing her. She pulls him toward her. She wants all of him, invites him in, and they make love into the wee hours of the morning, when they finally fall asleep in each other's arms.

17

EPIPHANY

GRACE

In her dream, Grace and Magnus climb the steep path up to Pico da Esperança. She likes following his confident steps. Sure-footed best describes him. As they near the top, she loses sight of him. She hurries to catch up, but he has vanished. She panics; her heart races and sweat runs down her face, stinging her eyes. She looks frantically in all directions and suddenly finds herself engulfed in silent flames that ebb and flow around her, as if she were a rock in a river of fire. The surrounding air becomes so hot that she thinks she will surely die the next moment. Suddenly something sharp grabs her arms, plucks her from the earth, and carries her upward. She fills with calm and lightness. From high above the island, she sees the full length of the dragon with its scintillating eyes . . .

GRACE AWAKENS DRENCHED. *What time is it? Oh, shit.* Magnus sleeps peacefully next to her. What a night. She leans over and gently kisses his face. His eyes open, and he smiles sweetly.

"Am I dreaming?"

"No, Magnus, I'm really here, but I have to go. I need to get to Calheta before ten o'clock. I promised to be at the procession."

He looks disappointed.

"I'll call you later, okay?"

"You better." He starts to kiss her like he means it.

"You have to let me go now," Grace chides him, pulling away and getting out of bed. She feels him watching her as she walks across the room in naked splendor to the bathroom.

Grace hurriedly takes a quick shower to wash off the night, grabs her bag, and runs to the bus stop just in time to catch the bus.

THE *CATEQUISTAS*, in white dresses, queue up in front of the fire department, bearing shiny cellophane-wrapped cakes and breads for the Dia de Reis auction. Grace snaps photos along the route to the church but stops about a block away. No Mass for her today; she doesn't want to risk seeing Senhor Estêvão and his wife, and she's exhausted. She turns back toward home in need of coffee.

As she rounds the back of the house, she sees Ângela Maria feeding the chickens. They cluck merrily around her feet. She speaks to them in her usual gentle voice. "Oh, come on, let that one in . . . you've had enough . . ." She clicks her tongue.

"*Bom dia*, Ângela Maria!" Grace waits for her to look up; she doesn't want to scare her. "I'm surprised to see you. I thought you would have gone to Mass."

"Not today. My Miguel is not feeling so well. Thought I'd better stay here." She tosses the rest of the food on the ground and comes toward Grace. "And you, did you make it back from Velas to see the *meninas*?"

"Oh yes." Grace holds her camera up. "I got a lot of pictures of the little cuties."

Ângela Maria lets herself out of the chicken yard. "Why don't you join me for a little coffee, then?"

"Thank you. I think I will," Grace says as she follows Ângela Maria up the stairs.

Ângela Maria makes the coffee and sets out *papo-secos*, cheese, and fig preserves. Before they begin enjoying the spread, a loud knocking from the *loja* startles them. *What on earth?* Grace dreads the thought that it might be Magnus, especially after last night. "I'll go see who it could be," she says.

"Okay. Whoever it is . . . invite *him* or her to join us!"

From the sounds of it, Ângela Maria thinks it is Magnus too. Grace hurries down the stairs as she calls, "We're up here!" When she reaches the bottom step and can finally see, her heart nearly stops.

Norinha, face bursting with anger, turns toward her, looking like a wild animal ready to strike.

"A Senhora Norinha . . . ," Grace begins, "how nice to see you."

"This isn't a social call," Norinha hisses.

The bitterness in her voice makes Grace shudder. "Well, why have you come, then?"

Norinha trembles. She points her finger at Grace as she screams, "I want you to stay away, far away, from my husband!"

Grace tries to reason. "You have it all wrong, senhora!"

"Oh, I don't think so." Her voice rattles, coming from a dark place inside. "You must think I'm blind, but I am not the one here with an eye problem. Everyone knows it's you. First the children, and now, God help us, you have set your sights on our men, my husband. You have sucked him dry with your icy eyes. I see him lusting . . ."

"That's just it . . ." Grace tries to defend herself, but Norinha keeps screaming at her, getting more and more out of control. *He lusts, not she.* It isn't her fault that Norinha's husband is a creep.

"You are nothing but a witch, a horrible, putrid little whore of a witch who . . ." She looks beyond Grace, bursts into tears, turns and runs. Before disappearing around the corner, she looks back and says, "If you don't stay away, you'll be sorry you ever showed your evil face on this island."

Grace remains fixed. She turns and looks at Ângela Maria, who has apparently driven Norinha away. Ângela Maria stares at Grace in question. Grace averts her tear-filled eyes, says, "I have to go." Without a word more, she turns and retreats into the *loja*.

Grace finally stops sobbing. Is this an evil force at work? Nonna Preta's curse? One of the "darker things lurking on her path"? No, not magic. Bad luck, maybe. Wrong place at the wrong time. Poor Norinha. What an unhappy woman. A cursed woman. Cursed with the misfortune of having married a vile and lecherous man. All the same, the situation remains dire for Grace. Her world has suddenly become much smaller than it was. Not only does she have to avoid Topo, but now she also has to avoid Senhor Estêvão and his wife, which means keeping clear of the center of town. Her research will suffer.

ÂNGELA MARIA

Ângela Maria sits down at the table she laid for Grace's and her breakfast. The coffee is cold. Fortunately, Norinha's screaming hasn't awakened Miguel. Ângela Maria has heard people talk about Norinha's concerns, but she knows for a fact that Senhor Estêvão is last on the list of Grace's romantic interests. She hasn't taken the gossip too seriously; little more than idle gossip, but then again, that is what had driven her friend Filomena out of town— idle gossip. She fooled herself into thinking that things have changed. Never again will she think of gossip as idle.

She should have anticipated this. All along she was more concerned about what people would think about Grace's relationship with the Swede. Still, what could have driven Norinha to make such a scene? Something sent her over the edge. Ângela Maria couldn't help feeling responsible. She introduced Grace to Senhor Estêvão. She had heard about his numerous indiscretions. Everyone knows about them. Still, he seems like such a nice, responsible man. He has always been kind to her. She had no way of knowing that things would have ended up like this.

ORDINARY TIME

EPIPHANY UNTIL LENT

18

THE WITCH'S THIMBLE

GRACE

GRACE CAN'T STAND BEING in the *loja*. The bare incandescent bulb that once comforted and warmed her now seems like a sinister instrument of death. The sun is out, so she leaves and crosses over to the seawall to stare out at Pico. Today, a lenticular cloud sits like a hat atop the peak. Magnus told her that is a sure sign that bad weather is coming. She takes out her mobile phone, checks her minutes. Still good. She dials Magnus.

"Hey," she says when he answers.

"Hey, how'd it go? Did you make it on time?"

"Yeah, it was fine." Her voice wobbles a little.

"What's wrong? You sound upset."

"Yeah, well, being called a whoring home-wrecking witch has that effect on me, I guess. Norinha stopped over to give me a piece of her mind about an hour ago."

Silence. "I'm so sorry, sweet girl. What can I do? Do you want me to come there? Do you want to come stay with me?" His voice is full of genuine concern.

"I do, Magnus, I really want to run straight into your arms and to stay there forever, but I don't think that is the best idea right now." Grace is trembling. "I am so fucking confused about everything. I need to break things off with Jake, and I need to sort out whatever is going on here, and I can't do that if I hide out with you, much as I want to. I won't be good for you in my current state."

"I get it." Magnus sounds disappointed. "When can we see each other?"

"Soon, I promise . . . next week."

"Okay, I'm here if you need me."

"I'll call," Grace says. "And, Magnus, thank you for giving me your love last night. I can't survive without it. I'll be thinking of you too much."

"Likewise. If you have trouble reaching me, keep trying. I might be up on the *serra* working. I miss you already. I love you."

"I love you too." After Grace hangs up the phone, his words reverberate, *I love you.* She takes comfort in knowing that someone on this island does.

GRACE HAS BEEN UP since four o'clock. She hasn't been sleeping well, and she's been afraid to leave the house. Today is the first day she'll set foot in town in the week since Norinha's visit. She needs to get a few groceries and also to make good on her promise to Magnus to settle things with Jake.

She stops at the market first. She makes it quick. God, she hopes she doesn't see anybody she knows. The shopkeeper treats her with her usual polite disinterest, and nobody else is in the store, to her relief. Next stop, the phone booth at the post office. Good, the phone booth is empty. She makes a beeline for it, forgoing her usual pleasantries with Senhor Silva.

She feels safer sealed inside the booth. She dials. Waits . . . waits . . . finally, he picks up.

"Hiya, Jake," Grace says, suppressing her dread of this conversation. She has always been the one broken up with. She doesn't know how to make a graceful exit.

"You woke me up." Jake's gravelly morning voice. "What's up?" He doesn't even sound the least bit happy or surprised to hear from her.

"Yeah, sorry about that. I figured you'd be up by now." He's usually up early.

"Yeah, well, we went to see Chris Isaak last night at the Bottom Line."

"Cool, that sounds fun. We . . . ? Who else went?"

"Jack and Susie . . . and this other girl you haven't met."

Grace thinks she hears a muffled voice in the background. *This other girl.* "Huh . . ." Grace stalls, weighing what to say next. "So is she there now?"

Complete silence.

"Well, okay then." Grace's welts have risen. "Guess you have just made this conversation super easy for me."

"Hey, Gracie, come on! I didn't mean for anything to happen. I miss you, baby." He sounds pathetic. His new friend must have left the room, because he goes on, "I just bought my tickets to come visit you for spring break."

Grace is fuming. "That's too bad, Jake, I hope they're refundable. But knowing how cheap you are, I am pretty sure they aren't!"

"Please, Gracie. You *know* I love you. You can't just throw away what we have. *Please*, I'm begging you to give me a chance."

"That's the thing, Jake. We don't have anything. Just so you know, I think I'm in love with someone else," she says with an air of finality. "I gotta go now because I *really* can't afford this phone call. Have a good life." Grace doesn't wait for Jake's response before hanging up.

Grace comes out of the post office knowing she has been betrayed and that she is a betrayer—not the best feeling, but she feels lighter knowing that the truth has been spoken and that she is free to follow her heart. She crosses to the promenade on the seawall side of the road and dials Magnus to let him know she will be coming to Velas tomorrow.

GRACE SIPS HER *GALÃO*, licks the residual foam from her lips. The sweet, milky coffee tastes good; it's comforting. She has missed the routine she established before everything fell apart. She pulls her notebook from her bag and begins to write. She doesn't know what else to do. Grace sits staring at the mostly blank page. Blather. Pure dreck. She has nothing intelligent or insightful to say. She begins doodling across the page in pretend writing, when suddenly she realizes she isn't alone. She looks up. Magnus smiles at her from across the table. How long has he been there? Her heart skips a few beats.

"I didn't want to disturb you." He reaches over and places his hand on the corner of her notebook as if to steal a peek. "You looked like you were doing something terribly important."

"Ha, very funny." She slams the notebook shut. "Not really. Did you see what I was writing?"

"No. I didn't see anything."

Magnus's voice is gentle. She's incredibly happy to see him. "Good, because it was drivel."

Magnus orders an espresso and another *galão* for Grace. "I've missed you," he says. "I came looking for you last week, but you never showed up, and under the circumstances . . . and under the circumstances, well, I didn't think it would be right to stop by your place. I mean, you were pretty clear that you had some things to deal with."

Grace shrugs. "Well, it would have been fine—I would have liked it." She smiles coyly, flirtatiously. "I missed you too, but like you said, I had to work out some shit, namely with Jake."

"And?"

"It's done. I'm free, I guess." She smiles broadly.

He takes a sip of coffee. "You have no idea how happy that makes me." He raises his eyebrows. "Want to come to my house?"

"Right now?" So much for patience. "What about work?"

"Work can wait, but I can't." He stands up and offers his hand.

MAGNUS

GRACE AND MAGNUS spend most of the day in bed enjoying each other's bodies. Magnus has not felt this happy in a very long time. Grace is on her side, fully nude, stretched out alongside Magnus, who is on his back. She drapes one leg over his legs and is dragging her fingertips across his hairless chest ever so lightly, stopping occasionally to encircle his rosy nipples.

He doesn't want to spoil the moment, but he realizes that in the heat of their first passionate encounter he had forgotten to share the information that he received from Doctor Roberto.

"Umm, there is something I forgot to tell you the last time you were here."

Grace stops her stroking, props her head in her hand. "Really? What?"

"Well, I wanted to tell you that I talked with my colleague Doctor Roberto about the boy from Topo and the other children."

"What did he say?" asks Grace. She is now sitting up.

"He assured me that the illnesses up there are completely unrelated to one another, probably different organisms, and possibly even viral—nothing definitive, but—"

"What about the boy?" Grace asks.

"He has some sort of organ damage from the initial infection; they're struggling to keep him alive. Doesn't look so good for him." Magnus gets up and pulls on his jeans.

"So I guess I couldn't have had anything to do with it?" Grace asks, now on standing and putting on her T-shirt and jeans.

"Well, not unless you are able to cast bacteria from your eyes!" Magnus laughs. "No, seriously, how could you realistically have anything to do with this? Doctor Roberto said the causes of these sorts of illnesses are endemic here: contaminated seafood, shellfish, beef, water—you name it, and they have it."

"Hmm . . ." Grace says. Magnus watches as she ponders this last comment. "Well, even so, you have to admit I still have some serious problems brewing. It doesn't really make a difference."

Magnus sighs. "You could say 'Thank you, Magnus, for looking into that for me,' but instead you launch into the drama. Really, Grace, sometimes it seems like you don't think about anyone but yourself. I realized something the other day when we were fighting . . . You *never* ask me anything about how my life or work is going. You aren't the only person in the world, even if you are the center of mine."

Grace falls silent for a moment. "Funny you should say that. Tia Carmina said something similar—that everything doesn't revolve around me," Grace says, "You're right . . . I'm being selfish, and I'm sorry. To tell you the truth, I have had a problem with that for most of my life, and I'm working on it. It stung a little when Tia Carmina said it, but hearing you say it actually hurts."

Magnus's expression softens. "I'm sorry I blurted it out that way. It's—"

"Don't worry about it. I had it coming." They sit quietly for a couple of minutes. "So, tell me about your life—what's going on?"

"Nothing—nothing whatsoever, especially since you haven't been around!" Magnus laughs. "I guess my conversations with pumice and steam vents probably aren't as interesting as human interactions."

"I don't know about that. I'd rather talk to stones sometimes. At least they don't threaten your life, do they?" Grace says, laughing.

"Depends on what you say to them and whether they are coming out of an erupting volcano," he says. "Did someone *really* threaten your life?"

"Norinha. I don't take her threat all that seriously, which is why I didn't mention it before. I'm more worried about everyone in

Calheta thinking I'm a man-eating slut, and everyone in Topo thinking that I carry the evil-eye gene. Not sure how I can do my work if nobody trusts me."

"But are you sure that *everyone* really thinks those things?" Magnus asks.

"No. I'm positive that many people don't, but how do I know who does and doesn't? I can't really go up and ask, 'Do you think I'm a *puta*?' or 'Do you believe that I'm the one responsible for the sick kids around the island?' There are plenty of people who don't know about any of this stuff and wouldn't care if they did."

Magnus puts his arms around Grace. "Okay, you want to know what I think you should do?"

"Okay."

"First, you can't give up. But you may have to change your life." He sits back. "What I mean is, lie low—."

"I can hardly lie any lower than I have been—"

"Let me finish. I don't mean vanish. For a while you should spend time with different women in Calheta, learning about women's lives and gaining their trust. Much as I hate to say this, you need to avoid the company of men, except for perhaps priests, and me, of course."

"But how will I gain any understanding of the male perspective if I don't spend time with men?"

Magnus laughs. "So you think you can understand the male perspective? You think Azorean men will share that with you? They only know one way to share with women, and it isn't what you're looking for. Grace, wake up! You're not behaving properly by Azorean standards. I'm not a trained observer like you are, but have you ever looked around the café? Have you ever seen any lone woman? Other than yourself, have you ever seen any woman without a man or, minimally, another female companion?"

Grace's face is turning red. "Well, no, but I'm an American, and I assume that most Azoreans give me more license because they know American women have more freedom." Grace turns her face away momentarily. Turning back, "You don't have to be such a fucking *mansplainer*."

He continues, "Look, I'm not trying to make you feel bad. What you've been doing hasn't worked."

Grace says, "Yep. You're right about that." There are tears in her eyes.

"On the up side, they treat you as one of their own, holding you to Azorean standards."

Grace rubs a tear from her cheek. "I guess, or they think I'm a total freak. You know, my advisor said this might happen. I didn't believe him. Everything that has happened is my fault for thinking I could barge into town and lead my life as myself." Grace lets out an awkward laugh.

"Please, don't be mad at me. I want to help." Magnus smiles. "You know where to find me Wednesday through Friday—I'm always here. I'm here for you."

Anthropological Field Methods 101: One of the most difficult tasks of the neophyte anthropologist is to find her point of entry into a foreign culture's social structure. To be successful at fieldwork, and to have a positive experience, one must genuinely *enter*, hence the term *participant-observation*.

ESTÊVÃO

Senhor Estêvão's hands, covered in wet black soil, move quickly around the bases of the various perennial herbs and flowers that adorn his garden. Weeds. He can't tolerate the sight of them. With each weed successfully pulled, root intact, he feels a cleansing of his soul. As a boy in Angola, he often spent long days in the garden, primarily to escape the constant bickering between his parents. In the garden he befriended the family gardener, an African Angolan known to him as Cricket. Cricket taught him all that he knows about plants. Although not an educated man, Cricket knew everything about the plant world: which plants were good to eat, what they tasted like, which had curative properties, and which were poisonous.

Senhor Estêvão inhales the aromatic fragrance of rosemary and thyme as he moves into the herb garden. Somehow the piney smell of the rosemary brings thoughts of Grace, what she might be doing, whether she is with the Swede. A surge of jealousy swells, and he digs the tines of his rake deep into the soil, loosening the roots of a tenacious weed that has grown up undetected next to a mustard plant. The wet weather has given start to so many weeds. Senhor Estêvão attacks them vengefully.

He is bitter, not only about Grace, but about all that has passed in his life. He has never known happiness. Sure, there were moments, but mostly his has been a life without joy or love, and now the latest developments with Norinha . . . she seems to be losing her mind. After New Year's Eve, things have not been the same with her.

She came to him for several nights following New Year's, each night progressively more scantily clad, hoping to elicit some response from him—any response at all. He felt nothing, and his flaccid body told her that. Finally, on the last night, she snapped at him as she left the bed frustrated again. *You think that I don't know, but I do.* He didn't flinch—after all, what did she really know about him? Not much.

He hid his considerable surprise when she continued. *You have always taken me for an idiot. I have loved you and been a good wife to you, even though I have always known about your women, and even your bastard child.* How does she know? Gossip no doubt. Perhaps gossip would serve *his* needs this one time.

For some reason, in her mind, his infatuation with Grace is so much worse than his other sins. Perhaps he hasn't done enough to hide his feelings. He could have tried harder for the sake of Norinha's pride. He has moved beyond that. He no longer cares. She doesn't understand. This has nothing to do with her. Nothing to do with Grace. Everything to do with future generations.

Ah . . . tender green shoots of fennel. They will be ready for soup soon. He pinches off the top and slips it into his mouth. The sweet licorice flavor spreads over his tongue.

Senhor Estêvão goes into his *loja* and finds his pruning shears. Spring is not far off; time to rid the garden of old growth to make way for new. He refuses to let Norinha take everything away from him. Perhaps her family owned the store since the turn of century, but he has turned it into a profitable business. He worries what she might do; she could ruin his plans. She could ruin his life. Using his shears, he carefully prunes the witches' thimble, always one of his favorite flowers.

19

CARNIVAL

GRACE

FAT TUESDAY COMES, and Grace feels fat. She makes the mistake of stepping onto the scale in Ângela Maria's bathroom and is shocked to see that since coming to São Jorge, she has gained seven kilos; that's around fifteen pounds. Women spend a lot of time cooking and tasting. Everywhere she goes she eats and drinks. This week is no different. In preparation for Lent she has been learning about the fine art of making baked and fried *filhós*. Baked *filhós* are similar to popovers filled with custard, and fried *filhós* are pretty much the same thing as Indian fry bread. Both are favorites.

THAT AFTERNOON, Grace steps out of the torrential rain onto the covered porch of the rectory. She knocks on the heavy wooden door.

A small severe-looking woman answers; it is Father João's secretary. Her expression betrays neither joy nor dissatisfaction. "Please, do come in," she says. "The padre expects you." She directs Grace to a large sitting room. "Can I get you some tea while you wait?"

"No, thanks. I'm fine," says Grace.

The woman leaves. The room exudes opulence, the opulence of a universal church. Antiques from different periods and various cultures furnish the room: a Chinese vase, a Queen Anne drop-leaf table, a heavy-looking Spanish colonial-style desk. Persian rugs, woven in intricate patterns, cover all but the edges of the hardwood floor. Ornately carved mahogany moldings frame the door and fireplace mantle. Grace has never seen a home as grand as this. Hanging on the wall, aside from the requisite crucifix, are a couple of old-looking paintings in the Flemish style. One of them is of the Virgin Mary. In this depiction a blue-eyed Mary gazes wistfully through a window.

"Isn't it something?" Padre João's voice booms out of thin air.

Grace jumps. She didn't hear him come in. She shakes hands with him. "Yes," Grace says, "And good afternoon to you as well, o Senhor Padre!" Padre João, a man of sixty-some years, is one of those men who feels compelled to cover his bald spot by combing his hair across his scalp, drawing more attention to his hair loss. Vanity. Isn't that a sin?

"Sorry if I startled you. Please, have a seat." He waits for Grace to sit before taking a seat across from her. "So you like the painting?"

Grace looks up at it. "Yes, I like it very much. She looks sad, though, and I was wondering . . ."

"Why she is so sad?" The padre stands up and walks toward the painting. "Yes, odd, isn't it? Not every mother gets to be the Mother of God. One would think she would be the happiest mother on earth." He puts his hands in his pockets and turns to Grace, smiling in a patronizing way. "I suppose she must have felt the pain that every mother feels when their sons die, don't you?"

Grace feels like an idiot. "Yes, of course." Now she understands, at least she thinks she does.

Padre João seems nervous. Perhaps it's his nature. He returns to his seat. "Well, I'm happy that after all this time we have found time to meet. I apologize again for standing you up in Topo back in . . . in—"

"November—just before the Festa de Santa Catarina," Grace says. That was the day she met Magnus, a day forever planted in her memory.

"November! How time flies, as they say. Here we are with Lent already upon us."

"Oh, no, no, don't worry about it. You undoubtedly had something more important to do that day." Perhaps he will tell her what it was.

He puts his palms together in prayer position in front of his chest. "Yes, so what can I help you with today? I already know you are not Catholic, so I gather we are not meeting for spiritual purposes?"

Grace smiles uncomfortably. "Well, no. I wanted to talk to you about the Festa do Espírito Santo. Everyone has said that you know all—"

"That I know all there is to know about it?" The padre, hands still in prayer position, rises to his feet and begins walking slowly around the room. "I hardly know everything, but I have written some articles on it—you know the church's perspective on it." He walks over to the desk and pulls out some papers. "Here they are. I think that should do it, then. Anything else?" He hands Grace the stack. "If you really want to know about it, you'll have to speak to a lay preacher. Most of what Azoreans call Espírito Santo has little to do with the church."

"Thanks so much." Grace glances through the articles. *Thanks for nothing.* Not exactly forthcoming. Why did everyone insist she talk to him? Perhaps he feels uncomfortable revealing anything but the official church line. "Well, actually, there is one more thing I wanted to ask you about."

"I thought so," the padre says. He continues pacing.

Grace clears her throat. "What can you tell me about *olhado*? I've heard through the grapevine that people think I am guilty of it."

He stops. "Of course. I have heard this too. A man in my position can't help but hear things." He turns toward her. "Let me begin by saying you have behaved remarkably well under some unusual circumstances." The padre walks to the door and closes it, presumably so his secretary does not hear what he is going to say. "The day I was to meet you in Topo I was with one of the families who claim cases of *olhado*."

Grace thinks of the boy who tapped on the window, wrapped head to toe. Of course, he must have been terrified of her. What if the Americana were to work her evil on him like she had the others?

"I make a monthly call on that family; they are poor. The boy is very sick and the grandmother elderly. That was the first I heard. I couldn't very well meet with you on that day out of respect for them. I assure you that *olhado* has nothing to do with these illnesses; it *is* the will of God. Moreover, the boy who remains ill is in God's hands. His salvation will come through prayer," he says with fervor as he crosses himself and bows his head.

Grace flushes with embarrassment at this display of religiosity. She remains perfectly still until he finishes. "I have wondered at times if—"

"If everyone in São Jorge is against you?"

She bristles at his interruption. "No, actually, I was going to say I have wondered at times if I *do* have something to do with it, especially—"

"Since Senhora Norinha visited you? Again, not your fault, I assure you. I have known her since her youth. She makes mountains out of mole hills—has a real knack for creating drama where none exists. Surely, you know people like that?" He looks at her pointedly. "As for her husband, he has a reputation. I assure you he is harmless, not a bad man."

Grace sits stone-faced. She didn't anticipate this turn in the conversation. She hoped to lead to a discussion of witchcraft, but clearly he controls the conversation and not she. Her neck burns. How does he know so much? Who is she kidding? Everyone on this blasted island knows everything.

The padre pauses before saying, "Forgive me, I think I've said too much. What I am trying to say is: all that has happened to you is less about you and more about the individual people you have encountered. People in the Azores are not all like *these* people. There are many good, decent people here in São Jorge, and I hope you don't leave with the impression that we are all like the superstitious and crazy people you have gotten involved with."

"Oh, believe me. I have met many more good people than bad!" exclaims Grace.

"Good, then. I hope, as a student of science, you will represent our culture with fairness and objectivity, if you understand what I am saying."

Grace understands it too well. "Of course. I certainly will try to be as objective as is humanly possible."

Not objective at all. Clearly, she can't generalize about Azorean culture based upon her experience of it, which has included a series of obviously unusual events on one island. She can conclude that some people, however few, believe in and practice black and white magic, and that a belief in the evil eye, though somewhat hidden, is still prevalent among certain people. As for Senhor Estêvão and his wife, she isn't sure how their story will wind its way into her monograph.

"No need to worry, Father, your culture is in safe hands."

"I know," he says, crossing himself.

His culture is in the hands of God. "I want to thank you for being so generous with your time." Scarcely a half hour has passed. She reaches out to shake hands. His cold and limp hand rests in hers.

GRACE FACEUP, eyes open, on her bed. The walls of the *loja* appear to be closing in on her as the light from outside dims. Illusion. She just finished reading a few of Padre João's articles. The papers are of little use from an anthropological perspective. Intended for an ecumenical audience, they provide guidance to priests about appropriate involvement in Espírito Santo festivities, including possible topics for sermons during the festival period.

It's too dark to keep reading. Grace rolls off the bed and onto her feet to turn on the light. The yellow light of death illuminates the room. Ângela Maria still has never told Grace of her son. Unlikely she ever will.

Ângela Maria's and her friendship is stagnant these days. Their conversations with one another are impersonal and strained. Is it the thing with Tia Carmina? Or is it related to the day Norinha showed up? Is it that Ângela Maria caught wind of her indiscretions with Magnus? Maybe Ângela Maria has finally become afraid to associate with her. Maybe Miguel has gotten under her skin, or worse, maybe he has threatened her. They need to talk about so many things. Spontaneously, she decides that the time to talk is now.

Rain pelts her as she hurries up the stairs and pushes the backdoor open. "Hoo! Hoo!" she calls.

Ângela Maria stands over the sink peeling potatoes. "Come in, come in, and close that door! It is terrible out there. Terrible!" She still has her back to Grace. "And how are you?"

Perhaps this is not the right time to talk. "Oh, fine. I interviewed the padre today, so that's good." Hardly an interview.

Ângela Maria glances at her. "So, what did you learn?"

"Honestly? Not a whole lot." Grace peers over Ângela Maria's shoulder, watching her hands quickly peel and clean the eyes out of the potatoes. "Can I help with something?" she asks.

Handing Grace the knife, Ângela Maria says, "Sure, you can peel the rest of the potatoes while I get the *couves* ready. I'm making *caldo verde*."

Grace, adept at peeling with a knife now, gets straight to work. One good thing has come of time spent with Azorean women;

Grace's kitchen skills have improved dramatically. "So what's up with you?"

"Not much." Ângela Maria stacks the giant collard leaves and rolls them into something resembling a massive cigar. Then she begins the laborious process of cutting them into paper-thin slices. "Just worked on Ana's and Mário's costumes for the party tonight —are you planning to go?" Ângela Maria asks.

"No. Don't think it's such a good idea, do you?" Grace studies Ângela Maria's face for a response.

She continues slicing. "Probably not," Ângela Maria says quietly. "Such a shame."

"It's okay. Really." Having experienced several dances, Grace doesn't feel like she will be missing a critical event. The costumes would have been fun to see, and probably culturally relevant. Nothing like the lavish celebrations in Brazil or New Orleans, though. One person described Azorean Carnival to her as being like an American Halloween party with no scary costumes. She can afford to miss that. She peels the last potato.

"Great. Thank you for helping," Ângela Maria says as she picks up the potatoes and puts them in a large aluminum pot.

"Think nothing of it," Grace says. "My pleasure."

"I'd invite you to stay for dinner, but Miguel's family is having us over—"

"Don't worry about it. I came up here because I miss talking to you . . . and, well, there is something I've wanted to tell you . . . having to do with Tia Carmina." Grace watches Ângela Maria compulsively wipe down the counter.

"Really?" Ângela Maria works diligently without looking up.

"Yeah." Grace takes a deep breath. "I've known her for a long time."

"What are you talking about?"

"It's a long story—do you have time for it?"

"Of course. I have nothing but time." Ângela Maria drops into a chair, still holding the wet towel.

"Before I tell you how I know her, you should know something about me," Grace begins. She tells Ângela Maria about her Black-feet ancestry: the Blackfeet religion, that her mother is a gifted healer, and about her rejection of it all. Finally, she tells of her childhood dreams and the owl woman who helped her transcend her grief over her grandmother's death. "I should have told you before. I've felt a chasm between us, a rift that has grown wider with each passing day. I want you to know I appreciate your taking me to see Tia Carmina. I'm still wrestling with what to do. To tell you the truth, it scares me to death. I've spent so much of my life denying that part of myself, convincing myself that it doesn't exist . . . and yet, here it is."

"Thank you, Grace. I've been sure since that day in Fajã dos Vimes that you thought I was nuts for taking you there." Ângela Maria checks the potatoes. "I am crazy, but that aside . . ." She returns to her seat across from Grace. "We also know Tia Carmina as Coruja Branca, and many bird-watchers have come to the Azores in search of our elusive white owl." She chuckles.

The potato water sizzles as it boils over. Ângela Maria turns the burner down. As she sits again, she says, "And, my friend, I have something to tell you, something that I have kept from you." She looks at her hands as she speaks. She tells Grace in detail of Jaime's horrible death. They both cry.

Grace gets up and wraps her arms around Ângela Maria to comfort her.

"We finished the *loja* to hide evidence of the dark place where Jaime died." She blots her face. "Having you living there has made it a brighter place for me, but I should have told you—"

"It's okay. You have told me now," Grace reassures her.

"There is something that Tia Carmina said that I've been puzzled about. Maybe you have an idea about it . . . She says the two of us are in this thing together. It'll take both of us to carry the burden of a mother's tears—do you know what she means?"

Grace thinks of the weight of the stones in her dreams—tears of stone, the burden of a mother's tears. It still doesn't make sense. What does this all have to do with Ângela Maria and her? "I have no idea. I'm not a mother—"

"No, but I am, and I'm responsible for Jaime's death, just as you could be responsible for that boy's—"

"Has he died?" *Please don't be dead.*

"No, I was going to say, just as you could be responsible for that boy's *life*. He has a mother in pain; think of her. If we work on this together, there may be hope for both of us—redemption."

Ângela Maria, with tear-filled eyes, gets up and goes to the stove. She pulls out her *máquina mágica* and sticks it into the pot with the potatoes and begins to purée them.

Grace almost has to scream to be heard over the loud whirring of the stick blender. "I guess I have to get to the point where I think I need some sort of redemption." Frustrated, she says, "And to the point where I believe that there is such a thing as redemption. I'm not at that point yet."

Ângela Maria pushes the mountains of finely shredded collards into the large pot of potato broth. She adds an enormous amount of olive oil and salt and turns up the flame. Turning to Grace, she says, "I know you are not at that point. I'm worried about what has to happen before you get there. Will someone have to die?" She walks up behind Grace and wraps her arms around her. "I'll wait."

20

SAINT VALENTINE

GRACE

GRACE AWAKENS on Valentine's Day with a vague sense of impending doom. She hasn't had any dreams, at least that she remembers, and she's slept soundly. Valentine's Day has always been one of her favorite holidays—a holiday of love—a simple holiday requiring only the exchange of cards. This year she'll spend it alone or, if she's lucky, with Magnus, but she has mostly been keeping her distance. Normally she labors over making cards for all of her friends. This year she doesn't bother. It's too much work to find the materials she needs. The only person who would've cared is Jake, but he's no longer a factor. Perhaps her sense of doom is a sense of guilt.

MAGNUS

MAGNUS SITS at a corner table trying to tune out the conversations around him at the Café da Ilha. He's been coming here religiously on Thursdays, hoping Grace will show up. Maybe he made a mistake in pointing out to her that she is the only woman he's ever seen there unaccompanied. Maybe he shouldn't have given her the idea to seek the company of women. Maybe she's mad at him for being a pompous ass. He's texted her and called her repeatedly, but she hasn't responded. She must have taken his advice to avoid men seriously. He misses her, and not just the sex—the conversation, the friendship. He wonders how things are going. In the absence of information, he assumes things are okay.

He digs into his knapsack and pulls out a stack of mail. He stopped at the post office and was surprised to see so many letters. The postmaster said they were held up at the sorting station in Lisbon for some reason. *It happens sometimes.* Magnus flips through the envelopes. The postmarks span a period of about eight weeks. He opens the one from his mother first.

> *Dear Magnus,*
>
> *I hope this letter finds you in good health. Things here are more or less fine, but I thought you should know that your father has had some problems with his heart . . .*

Magnus looks at the postmark—she sent it four weeks ago. *Damn it.* He should have called, but he hates to talk on the phone. He hates the expectation of communication imposed on one by the mere existence of phones. He returns to reading the letter.

No need for alarm. On February 7 he will be having surgery to replace a bad valve. He doesn't want you to come home . . . doctors say the outlook is positive . . .

That's good, since I didn't get this until now, he thinks. *Shit, that means he had surgery almost two weeks ago.* He imagines their disappointment. He hasn't even called to wish his father well, and undoubtedly, although his father said he didn't want him to come home, he really did. Magnus's throat tightens. He's been a failure as a son in his parents' eyes. Lucky they have their *good* son to fall back on. His brother has made it known to Magnus on many occasions that he feels like Magnus has abandoned the family and burdened him with their aging parents. Magnus quickly reads the rest of the letter, which is full of newsy tidbits about Magnus's nephews, nieces, cousins, aunts and uncles. When he finishes, he shoves the whole pile in his pack and heads out the door. He has to call to see how things went for his father.

MAGNUS FIDGETS as he waits for the call to connect.

"*Hallå?*" His mother's familiar singsong voice.

"*Hej*, Mamma, it's me—"

"Oh, Magnus, I have been so worried that we haven't heard from you with all that has been going on here . . ."

He hears her voice quaver. "Oh, Mamma, I'm so sorry, your letter just arrived today! I feel just terrible . . ."

"Everything is fine. The surgery went well," she says.

"Maybe I should come home for a bit," Magnus suggests, "help out with some of the chores around the farm."

"No, no, that isn't necessary. You have your work, and your brother has things under control."

Your brother has things under control. "*Ja*, Mamma, I really would like to help. I wish you had called me instead of writing a letter.

Please, Mamma, call me on my mobile number if anything changes." He also gives her Grace's number in case he's out of range.

After hanging up, he feels empty. What if his father dies while he is here? Is his research that important? He decides then that he needs to go home. It's the right thing. He'll go home for a few weeks, until he feels satisfied that his father is going to make it. Before leaving, though, there's much to do. First, he needs to stop at the travel agency. Next, he needs to go up to Topo and collect some of his belonging, and finally, he needs to talk to Grace.

GRACE

GRACE SHIFTS the car into low gear. Wonderful to leave Calheta for a change. She and Ângela Maria head to Zoeta's house in Topo to make loaves of *folar*, special sweet Easter bread. Grace glances over at Ângela Maria, who stares out the passenger-side window deep in thought.

Spring pours into Grace's soul, giving relief from the weight of the winter. It only rains intermittently now, and the cold edge is gone from the wind. On some days, like today, the sun shines almost the entire day, and she can see the length of Pico extended languidly on the other side of the channel. A single lenticular cloud perches above the nipple of Pico like a flying saucer, blemishing an otherwise perfect sky.

As the car climbs the steep road to the top of the island, they pass several tidily planted vegetable gardens full of onions, collards, and potatoes. Grace has scarcely been aware that people have been planting; these abundant gardens seem to have sprung up miraculously overnight. *Like magic.*

The verdant pastures dotted with black-and-white cows remind her of pictures she has seen of Switzerland. Hydrangea hedges bud with new life, and the black stone walls bordering the road appear especially black against the backdrop of the bright-green fields.

"You'll take the next left," Ângela Maria instructs her.

They pass the place where Grace dropped Magnus off the day she met him. She turns to see his house, spying nothing but hedges and a path. What is he up to these days? Does he miss her? She misses him terribly. But she can't go running to him now. So many times she has thought about the possibility of living with him in Velas. If only the timing were different. She veers left onto an unpaved road.

"It's up there. You can turn in at the end of that white wall," Ângela Maria says.

Ângela Maria has been too quiet. Maybe she feels nervous about bringing Grace to Topo. Maybe she is afraid of Nonna Preta. Grace isn't, not after what Tia Carmina said. She's more worried about the "darker things lurking on her path," whatever they might be. Grace pulls into the driveway.

From outside, Zoeta's house appears tiny, almost like something from a fairy tale. The house is white, as most houses in São Jorge are, with a traditional terra-cotta roof. Bright-blue paint frames all of the windows and doors. More protection. Round white stepping stones wind their way through a picturesque garden.

Unlike most of the gardens Grace has seen in São Jorge, this garden, although obviously planned, looks disorganized. Collards are planted with an eye to ornamentation rather than sustenance, and onions grouped in clusters like naturalized bulbs. From every nook and cranny of Zoeta's yard, something wonderful grows. Thyme spills from cracks in a wall; nasturtiums fill in the blanks. Carefully, staying on the stone path, Ângela Maria and Grace walk to the back of the house, which is much larger than it appears from the front. Ângela Maria coos through the back door as she leads the way into the kitchen.

Zoeta rushes toward them. "*Bom dia*, you two! I'm so delighted to have your help. I'm far behind for some reason this year." She kisses Ângela Maria quickly on both cheeks, then takes Grace by the shoulders and looks into her face. "You are

Graça!" She pulls her forcefully to her and kisses her firmly on each cheek. Zoeta's hair smells of a wood fire, and as she pulls away, the smell lingers behind. "Come, come, and take your coats off."

"It's nice to finally meet you," Grace says. "Ângela Maria has told me so much about you."

"I bet she has!" Zoeta, a good six feet tall, towers over the two of them. Her light-brown hair and blue eyes distinguish her from other Azorean women Grace has met; apparently a Jorgense of Flemish descent. Grace assumed she would be a *morena*, like her darker-skinned cousin.

Taking their coats, Zoeta says, "I'm going to throw them in this room over here so they don't get covered with bread dust." She disappears. She smiles broadly when she comes back. "So, we are going to put you to work making *folar*." She claps her hands together.

"Yes! Ângela Maria explained to me that you supply half of the island for Easter, which is why you start so soon," Grace say.

"Well, my cousin exaggerates a little," Zoeta says. "But, it is true that I have a lot of orders to fill. I've been working on it already for weeks."

The kitchen reminds Grace of old farm kitchens in the United States. A long heavy plank table fills the center of the room, benches serve as seats. The table can easily seat twelve. White Formica countertops surround the room on the outer wall. At the far end hangs a large iron door. From the black marks above it, Grace surmises it's a wood oven, although she hasn't seen one like it before.

"Graça, since you are the youngest and strongest, go get that big sack of flour and put it up on the table for me. Ângela Maria, run and fetch the starter—you know where it is."

Grace lifts the burlap sack, but it's much heavier than she anticipates. She loses her balance, and the bag slips out of her hands and lands with a thump back on the floor. A plume of flour rises out of the open top into her face.

Zoeta laughs as she points at Grace, who is covered in white flour. "You look like a giant *boneca de pão*!" she says.

Grace feels embarrassed but can't help laughing. Zoeta's laugh is infectious. "Very funny."

Ângela Maria comes back into the room and, upon seeing Grace's white face, also cracks up. She sets down the crock she's carrying. "Maybe we should put you in the oven! Some little girl would love to have a bread doll like you!" She hands Grace a damp cloth to wipe her face and collapses into a chair. "I'm sorry, Grace. I can't stop crying . . . I mean laughing." Tears stream down Ângela Maria's face. "Zoeta's laugh has always done this to me."

"Yes, it is true, and you, *a minha prima* Ângelinha, have always had that effect on me as well!" When Zoeta finally stops laughing, she says, "She always got me in trouble in church!"

Zoeta then effortlessly picks up the sack of flour and sets it on the table. She walks over to the iron door and opens it. Grace sees flames kick up as Zoeta adds more *lenha*.

"So much for youth," Ângela Maria says, as she gives Grace a pat on the shoulder.

ZOETA KNEADS the enormous bowl of sticky dough rhythmically. Grace and Ângela Maria, supposedly there to help, sit and watch as Zoeta does the work.

"My *folar* is different than other people's. I have a secret ingredient," Zoeta says proudly.

"Oh really? Are you going to tell me what it is?" Grace asks.

"Well, it isn't really a secret, and now some others have started doing it too. Used to be that people cooked a whole egg in the shell into the *folar*—some still do. But because I make so many loaves ahead of time and have to freeze them, I can't put the egg in. So, to make it so the bread still has surprises in it, I started adding candied almonds." She breathes heavily as she speaks. Beads of sweat form on her brow and lip.

"Here, let me have a turn," says Ângela Maria. She stands up and pushes Zoeta out of the way. "She thinks she is the only one who can do this part."

Zoeta wipes her hands clean and sits down next to Grace as Ângela Maria goes to work on the enormous lump of dough.

"Mmmm . . . that sounds good." In her notebook, Grace writes *Zoeta's secret: candied almonds.*

"I have volunteered to sponsor a *coroação* in praise of o Divino Espírito Santo, *a prima*," Zoeta says.

"Really?" Ângela Maria looks up from the bowl. "That seems like a rather sudden turn of events. Has something good happened that I don't know about?"

"Well, yes, you know how things happen. I'm not doing it on my own, no need to worry about that," Zoeta says.

Grace perks up. "A *coroação*? Isn't that when someone has a promise to fulfill?"

Zoeta puts her hand on top of Grace's forearm and squeezes. "Yes. I made a promise some time ago and now it is time for me to repay the Holy Ghost for his gift to me."

"Well, aren't you going to tell us what the promise is?"

Zoeta says mischievously, "When the time comes, you will both know what it is."

Ângela Maria looks puzzled. "May I ask who you are doing it with?"

Zoeta laughs. "Nope. You'll find that out soon enough."

AT HALF PAST FIVE, Grace and Ângela Maria pull into the driveway at home. Magnus, to their surprise, sits across from the house on the seawall, an enormous backpack leaned up beside him. He looks like he's going someplace. Upon their arrival, he leaps to his feet and crosses the road to greet them.

"*Boa tarde, senhoras!*" he says somewhat formally.

"Magnus! What a surprise!" Grace says. Perhaps too exuberant, but she can barely contain her happiness at seeing him.

Ângela Maria greets him warmly and quickly excuses herself to go into the house to make dinner, leaving them out front alone.

"I'm glad you finally showed up. I thought I might have to leave before seeing you." He takes Grace's hand. "I've really missed you."

"Me too." Grace looks down at the ground. "I mean, I have missed you too. " She laughs nervously. It isn't *all* about her.

Magnus lets go, putting both hands in his pockets. He looks out toward the channel. "I have to go home to Sweden. My father is sick—heart problems—and I didn't want to leave without saying good-bye, in case—"

"In case you don't come back?" Grace feels sick. The thought of being here without him is frightening.

"No, no, I'll be back, probably in a couple of weeks, but it could be longer. Given how things were going for you the last time we saw each other, I thought there might be a chance you would be gone by the time I returned," he says. "Anyway, I want to give you my phone number in Sweden and my parents' address and also my email address. Of course I will call and text you while I am there. I just want you to know that if you need to talk to me . . . you have many ways to reach me." He closes her hand around a piece of paper.

Grace can't look at him. She knows she will fall apart. "Thanks. I hope your dad'll be okay."

He wraps his arms around her and kisses her on top of the head. Then he looks into her eyes, and they kiss each other as if it might be their last kiss ever. *Who cares who sees them? What does it matter? He is leaving.*

Magnus pulls back. "You'll be fine. I'll see you really soon. Besides, it's better if you don't have me in the way of your work."

Grace begins to sob, not because Magnus is leaving, but because she's afraid she will never see him again.

Magnus strokes her hair. His hands are strong and loving. How Grace wishes she had done things differently.

Holding her face in his hands and looking directly into her eyes, Magnus says, "Well, I have to go. I'm heading out on SATA for Terceira tonight. Can't miss my plane." He pulls a clean handkerchief from his pocket and hands it to Grace. "You can return it when I get back."

"I'm sorry, Magnus. I'm sorry about everything." Grace blows her nose. "I hope you have a safe trip and that you're back soon." She hugs him and gives him one last kiss on the cheek. He turns just in time to meet her lips instead.

LENT

BEGINS 46 DAYS BEFORE EASTER

21

MIRACLE OF THE ISLET OF TOPO

GRACE

MAGNUS'S DEPARTURE is quite a blow to Grace. Even though she has been keeping her distance, she takes great comfort in knowing that he is there. She feels empty and vulnerable now, but she also has a lot of work to do. Festival season is just beginning. No time to wallow.

While at Zoeta's, she nearly filled a whole notebook with recipes, anecdotes and stories, and sits at her counter in the *loja* reviewing them. Translating them to English and transcribing them is painstaking work that requires moving back and forth between her notes, her recordings, and her dictionaries. She needs to send a new batch of notes by email to her advisor who is storing them on backup drives for safekeeping in New York.

Today she focuses her attention on a classic story Zoeta told while they cooked, one that encapsulates so much of what *Jorgenses* believe about the Holy Ghost, a story she has heard repeatedly in many different forms.

Fieldnotes, February 23, Lent, Topo

Milagre do Ilhéu do Topo, as told by Zoeta, transcribed and translated.

A gente [people] say this is true, and I believe that it is.

A long time ago, during the year that followed Mandado do Deus [Literally "Sent by God"—refers to the events of July 9 to 11 in 1757 when terrible earthquakes hit the island], there was a man here in Topo. His son was very sick, and had been sickly during his entire life. With each passing day, he took a step closer to the doors of death. The man only had this one son left. God had taken the rest of his family in the earthquake, along with many hundreds of other Topenses. Those were terrible times. The man decided one day that he could take no more, and he decided to give a bodo in praise of o Divino Espírito Santo in hopes that his son would survive.

In preparation for his sacrifice, he took a cow out to the Ilhéu do Topo [an islet just offshore from Topo] to fatten him on the sweet wheat grasses that grow there. You know, it doesn't look like much from the shore; it looks only like a large rock sticking out of the sea, but it's more than it appears to be, like many stones, like many things. The time of Espírito Santo arrived and the week of his jantar [ceremonial dinner] was near, and the man readied himself to retrieve his now fat and healthy cow from the Ilhéu. The sea suddenly became wild with a storm that raged for days, and it was too rough for the man to contemplate the short voyage to retrieve his cow. The man was not despondent like some would be, but maintained faith through the storm.

Finally, the day of the sacrifice arrived, and the sea was still boiling and angry, but even this did not shake the man's faith. He and three other men went to the place where they planned to sacrifice the cow, xopa [special knife for killing the cow] in hand. They sat down and waited. The three other men thought their friend crazy, mind you, but they waited with him—for what, they did not know.

Suddenly, a miracle, the man's cow came walking toward the group of men, the very cow he had put out on the ilhéu to fatten. The cow had swum across the channel through the fierce waters, and had arrived to give her own life in sacrifice on this day.

A gente say that the son of the man was miraculously cured, and that he lived to help his father through old age. A gente say this, and I think it is true.

Note: Several people have told me this or a related story, and I have read a similar story about the Ilhéu da Praia on the island of Graciosa.

ÂNGELA MARIA

ÂNGELA MARIA IS WORRIED about Grace. She has been withdrawn, and isn't eating well. Maybe she's sick or, even worse, in love with that Swede. He's been gone for a couple of weeks. Ângela Maria pounds on the door to the *loja*. Grace hasn't mentioned her fiancé much lately, and it seems like he was supposed to be visiting sometime this month. It's hard to believe that March is already under way. In any event, it is probably a good thing that Magnus is gone. Grace finally opens the door. She's wearing pajamas, and her uncombed hair hangs limply around her face. "You *malandra*! Were you still in bed? Lazy bones!"

"I was awake. Just sitting in bed reading a novel that my mom sent." Grace holds out the book: a paperback with an orange cover.

Ângela Maria takes the book, reads the title aloud, "*The Sto-ry-tell-er.*"

"That's pretty good! I didn't know you could read English," Grace says.

"I can sound it out, but not read it. I have no idea what it means."

"A storyteller is a person who tells stories," Grace explains. "Fascinating novel. I can't put it down. I relate in some ways to the main character; he transforms himself into something that he was not at the beginning." Grace fans through the pages nervously. "If it were written in Portuguese, I would give it to you. Wonder if there's a translation?"

"Doesn't matter. I don't have time to read." She runs her hand across the inviting cover of the paperback. Ângela Maria loves reading, always has. As a girl she read constantly, borrowed books from whoever would lend them. She especially loves reading novels, but her reading bothers Miguel, maybe because he isn't a good reader. He only completed the seventh year of school. She was lucky enough to get through the tenth year. Her father had gone to America to work for a few years, and she, her mother, and sisters went to live with an uncle in São Miguel, where she could continue on in school. Perhaps Miguel felt shut out when she read. So she stopped; stopping was easier than putting up with his anger.

Ângela Maria hands the book back to Grace. "I was wondering if you could do a favor for me. I have to watch the little ones this afternoon, and I won't have time to go out. Would you mind taking these letters to the post office?"

"Sure. I don't mind at all. Do you need anything from the *minimercado*?" Grace asks.

"No, not that I can think of." Her plan to get Grace out of the house looks like it will work. "On second thought, would you mind picking up a box of milk? I've run out of fresh, and I'll need some for the children."

"No problem," Grace says.

Ângela Maria says good-bye and goes back up to her kitchen.

Grace sounded cheerful enough. Better than expected. Months have gone by since the blood collection incident without consequence—probably nothing to it. Alternatively, as Tia Carmina said, Nonna Preta didn't have any real power to begin with. Then, of course, there was the threat from Norinha, and nothing came of that either. Ângela Maria hasn't seen her anywhere lately—not at church or in her garden. In fact it seems like she's dropped off the face of the planet.

This constant worrying needs to stop. What good does it do anyway?

GRACE

GRACE WALKS alongside the seawall toward the post office. She runs her hand over the tops of the black stones, feeling the roughness. The sun sparkles on the water. The sky rises upward in endless blue, beginning at the ocean almost white and continuing overhead to a saturated turquoise. How Grace wishes she could capture some of it, any of it. There's neither a camera lens wide enough, nor a pen broad enough to represent the vastness of her experience.

How does that saying go about the month of March that Ângela Maria used when they were at Zoeta's? It was something like *Março, Marçagão . . . de manhã, inverno . . . de tarde, verão.* Kind of related to "In like a lion, out like a lamb." Winter's not over. There'll be more storms. March came in like a lamb—*a sacrificial lamb*, she thinks. She crosses the street to the post office, pulls Ângela Maria's letters out of her bag, and slips them through the mail slot—letters to her sisters in America. She catches Senhor Silva's eye. He signals that she has mail, so she steps in line behind a woman she doesn't know.

When she arrives at the counter, he hands her a letter. "From New York," he says, as if he knows from whom it has come.

Is nothing private? Postmasters and priests, both communication conduits, hold tremendous power in a place like this. "Thanks." Grace hurriedly takes the letter and turns to leave, in the process bumping into the person behind her. "Oh, excuse me—"

"No problem at all, senhora," Senhor Estêvão says.

"Forgive me. I didn't know you were there." Grace hasn't seen him since the New Year's dance. "And how are things going with you?" He has returned to his former formal self, no attempts at being mod. His arms are in his sleeves. *Thank God.* A sign that he is over his infatuation? She hopes so.

"Things are going well! Thank you, a Senhora Doutora . . . Listen . . . can you wait for a minute? There is something I would like to talk to you about." Senhor Estêvão steps up to the counter. He hands the postmaster a small package, then turns back to her. He steers her through the door outside. In a hushed voice he says, "I want to apologize about everything that has happened." He pauses.

Grace doesn't know how to react, so she says, "For what?"

"Well, a couple of things . . . my behavior for one—too much to drink, eh?" He smiles.

He looks sincere enough, but it doesn't keep her from the desire to run away as fast as she can. "Okay." She can't wait to hear the rest.

"I also understand that my wife paid you a little visit—she told me." Senhor Estêvão turns to greet a man stepping into the post office, and then continues, "I apologize on her behalf. She has not been well for some time, and her condition is getting worse each day, I'm afraid. Some sort of progressive dementia that predisposes her to paranoia. Thanks to God, she's taking her medicine now. I thought you should know. I apologize again."

"Apology accepted . . . on both counts," Grace says awkwardly. "I'm sorry to hear about your wife. I hope she gets better."

Senhor Estêvão's eyes fill with tears. "Yes . . . well . . . not much hope of that I'm afraid."

"Well, I have to get going. Ângela Maria needs me to fetch some milk. But do take care of yourself." Grace turns toward the *minimercado* before finishing her sentence.

"Oh, I will! *Adeus, senhora.*"

Senhor Estêvão's voice rings in Grace's ears from behind. She doesn't want to look back. The image of him in her mind is bad enough—what a pathetic human being.

She clutches the letter from Jake in her hand. Should she read it now? No, no doubt it will upset her. Maybe she will never read it. She tucks it into her bag and enters the *minimercado* to buy milk. She hurries back to Ângela Maria's to tell her about her conversation with Senhor Estêvão.

"POOR MAN. I really do feel sorry for him," Grace says. "He seems so pitiful. He even had tears in his eyes."

Ângela Maria walks over and turns down the television. The kids are watching cartoons. "Yes. I feel sorry for him too. I had no idea. I guess that explains why I haven't seen Norinha around lately." Ângela Maria comes back into the kitchen, pours some milk into a pan, and begins to heat it up to make the kids their midafternoon snack of hot cereal.

"Not to change the subject, but I received a letter from Jake today," Grace says.

Ângela Maria stirs some cream of wheat into the hot milk. "When does he arrive again? Seems like it should be soon now."

Grace hasn't told her about her call with Jake back in February. She hasn't told her she is in love with Magnus. Maybe she knows it, but if she does, she has never indicated it. She doesn't know how to talk to her about any of this—that Jake is sleeping with someone else would imply that they too had slept together. Although Ângela Maria has never said so directly, Grace knows that she doesn't approve of premarital sex. She tells too many stories about girls who have "gotten into trouble," and girls who are "loose."

"He isn't coming . . . period . . . ever . . . We've broken it off." She leaves it at that. Ângela Maria coddles her a bit, but doesn't press her for more information. Grace wishes she had told her sooner.

Jake's letter sits unopened, leaned up against the wall on the counter. A week has passed since she received it. Grace stares at the red, white, and blue border and studies Jake's loopy handwriting. What does it say about him that he writes so neatly? *Like a girl.* Grace takes a deep breath as she reaches toward the envelope. She opens it and begins to read.

> *Dear Grace,*
>
> *Well, what can I say? I am so sorry. I do love you, you know. The thing with Nancy surprised me as much as it did you. I have been lonely, and I guess it made me more vulnerable . . .*

Grace puts the letter back in the envelope. Nope, can't read this. Don't want to hear it. She seriously doubts he was as surprised as she was. But who is she to point fingers? She had slept with Magnus by then. *Nancy? Really?* He told her it was someone she doesn't know. Double whammy. Losing two friends at the same time is tough.

Just then, Grace hears male voices outside her door and then a knock. Upon opening it, she fills with dread. The policeman who took her up to the clinic for the blood test and one of his colleagues stand in front of her looking very official. *What on earth?* Come to kick her out of the country, no doubt.

"*Bom dia.* Are you here for my fingernails this time?" she says, meaning to be funny.

The two men don't smile, nor does Ângela Maria, who is standing on the stairs above looking upset.

"I'm sorry," she says. "I can see that wasn't the right thing to say."

"Senhora, we have come with some bad news, and we would like to ask you a few questions if you don't mind," says one of the officers.

"Of course. Come in."

Ângela Maria comes down farther on the steps. "Why don't you all come up here where it is more comfortable?"

Grace's heart beats wildly. She feels like she might faint. Hurriedly, she slips on her shoes and follows the others up to Ângela Maria's kitchen. Ângela Maria scurries around putting water on to boil and arranging chairs at the table.

When everyone sits down, the officer that Grace doesn't know says, "Senhora, someone died. The person who died is someone you know, and well, we need to ask you a few questions . . . we don't believe there was foul play, but we're investigating to rule it out completely."

Magnus. Could Magnus be back? Would he have come back without telling her? Her mind races. Did Magnus die? Grace chokes up, imagining the worst-case scenario. Maybe he fell into a steam vent. People say that happens. "Who . . . who . . . ?" she stutters.

"Senhora Norinha. Her husband discovered her early this morning in their garden."

Grace covers her mouth as if to suppress a scream, but she feels more relief than anything else. Of course, it *is* terrible and sad, but at least it's not Magnus. "My God! That poor woman! I'm so sorry. But I don't know how I can help you?"

"As I said, we believe that her death was accidental, but we need to rule out other possibilities, and we understand that the two of you had an altercation back in January. Can you tell us what that was about?"

Ângela Maria sets out a pot of tea with some cups on the table, and then busies herself with something else.

"Well, yes . . ." Grace wonders if she really can tell them what that was about. It happened so long ago that it isn't all that fresh in her memory, and even immediately following, the event seemed so unreal. "Senhora Norinha believed that I stole her husband's affections, so to speak."

The officer writes something in his notebook. "And did you?" he asks. His affect is flat as he studies her face.

"I absolutely had no interest in him, if that's what you are asking!" Grace says emphatically. "I can't speak for him."

"And how did you respond to her accusations?" the officer asks.

"Well, I guess I didn't. I tried . . ." Grace struggles to remember exactly what happened.

Ângela Maria comes up and stands behind Grace, placing her hands reassuringly on her shoulders. "Grace couldn't get a word in edgewise. I was there. Senhora Norinha was screaming all sorts of accusations at her."

The officer looks up at Ângela Maria. "Then you witnessed the whole thing?"

"How could I help it?" Ângela Maria gestures to her back porch. "She was crazy. As she left, she even threatened harm to Grace. She said something like, 'If I ever see you anywhere near my husband, you'll be sorry you came to this wretched island!'"

The officer doesn't flinch. He hurriedly writes more notes. Looking back at Grace, he asks, "And when was the last time you saw Senhora Norinha?"

"That was the last time," Grace says.

"And when was the last time you saw her husband?"

A knot forms in her stomach. "Last week at the post office."

"Did you speak to each other?"

"Yes, Senhor Estêvão apologized to me for all that happened, and he told me that his wife has been ill." Grace now regrets that she spoke to him. What if his story to the police isn't the same as her story? No, she's being paranoid.

"Hmm . . ." the officer says. "And finally, where were you last night between ten and six this morning?"

"Here." Grace points down. "In the *loja*, asleep most of the time."

The officer looks up at Ângela Maria. "Can you verify that?"

Of course Ângela Maria can't. Grace feels sick.

Ângela Maria says, "Yes, she was here the whole night as far as I know."

The officer makes a few other notes and closes his notebook.

"That's all for now. We might have more questions, depending on what the investigation turns up."

Grace perspires profusely. "Excuse me. Can you tell us how she died?"

"A stone . . . she hit her head on a stone. They think it was an accident, but one of her friends said we should speak to you." The officers stand up. "Thank you, senhoras."

Grace rises as the officers go out the door. She and Ângela Maria stand silently together. How she wishes to feel the rush of an owl's wings or the touch of a dog's tongue now. If only she could get this unbearable weight off her chest. Perhaps she will wake from this dream soon. Maybe she has unknowingly played a role in Norinha's death. If Grace hadn't come to the island, would all of this have happened? Would the boy be sick? Norinha dead?

GRACE DEBATES CALLING MAGNUS. He insisted that she call him if she needed him, and she does. She digs through her bag for the folded up paper Magnus passed to her when he left two weeks before. He said it was his parents' contact information in case she failed to reach him on his mobile. He wrote it on graph paper, of course. When she unfolds the paper, the page greets her with a sweet love letter written in a messy scrawl. Her first from him, or anybody for that matter. At the bottom, he wrote his parents' address and phone number. "Call me, please! I miss you already. You are the light of my life." Her heart is full.

She hurries down to the post office phone booth, pulls out her calling card, and nervously dials Magnus's mobile number. No answer. Next, she tries his parents' phone number. A message system picks up. She leaves a message in English. She doesn't even know if his parents speak English.

"Hello, my name is Grace McGuiver. I'm a friend of Magnus's. Please let him know that I called, and please ask him to call me back as soon as possible. Thank you. He has my number."

22

SACRIFICE

GRACE

ON HER TWELFTH BIRTHDAY, Grace combed her dead grandmother's long white hair. When her grandmother died that day, she had been holding Grace's hand. Her grandmother was old, perhaps ninety-eight, but nobody knew for sure. Even now, Grace can hear the final rough breaths that escaped after she left, and she can smell the odor of death that filled her grandmother's house, and see how relaxed her grandmother's body suddenly became, how her jaw hung slack, her eyelids half-closed as a person drifting to sleep.

Grace's mother, aunt, and one of her grandmother's neighbors immediately rushed into motion. They tied her grandmother's mouth shut to hold her jaw in a closed position and bound her hands and legs together. When rigor mortis set in and the ties were removed, she appeared to be a woman in relaxed repose, peacefully sleeping. Nobody cried; there was too much to do. Later, they wailed mournfully as their mothers had done for their grandmothers. Her grandmother's hair was beautiful.

THE DAY of Norinha's death seems interminable. Ângela Maria insists that Grace accompany her to Senhor Estêvão's house to pay respects. "If you don't, it will seem like you're avoiding it for a reason," she argues. Grace sees her point. Viewing Norinha's corpse is the last thing she wants or needs to do. Although curious about Azorean funerary practices, she would have preferred learning about them under different circumstances.

As she and Ângela Maria ascend the walkway at Senhor Estêvão's house, Grace marvels at the beauty of his garden. The variety is astounding. "What a wonderful garden!" Grace says. Perhaps an inappropriate time to admire the garden, just when someone has died in it.

Ângela Maria nods in agreement. "Senhor Estêvão is known for his green thumb." Ângela Maria gestures up behind the house. "He even has a greenhouse so that he can grow tomatoes the whole year long."

The open front door signals that Senhor Estêvão is accepting mourners. His house buzzes with mourners talking in hushed tones. No one takes special notice of Ângela Maria's and her arrival, for which Grace is grateful. News of her police visit that morning has no doubt spread through Calheta like wildfire. Do people think she had something to do with Senhora Norinha's death? Nothing she can do about it if they do.

Grace finally catches sight of Senhor Estêvão. He looks terrible. A crowd of people hang around him waiting to give their condolences. Ângela Maria steers Grace in his direction. They silently wait their turn. Beyond the place where Senhor Estêvão stands, Grace sees the coffin, lid open. A number of people sit on folding chairs placed around it. How can she avoid looking? Death seems too personal.

When they move to the front of the line, Ângela Maria goes first. "Senhor, I'm so sorry for your loss. Please let me know if I can do anything to help you. What a *terrible* thing."

"Oh, thank you, Dona Ângela Maria. Thank you for coming," he says as he holds and pats her hand. Ângela Maria then moves past him into the dining room.

A wave of nausea surges through Grace. She looks down at the floor as she approaches Senhor Estêvão. "I am so sorry for your loss. I can't imagine what—"

Senhor Estêvão takes Grace's hand and with his other hand tips her face up to look at him. "I know you can't, but I'm going to be fine. Thank you for coming. You don't know what it means to me." He pats her hand, the way he patted Ângela Maria's. He gives it an extra squeeze before letting go. Grace steps into the room behind him, relieved to be done with that. She feels sullied by his touch.

Ângela Maria sits on one of the chairs, head bowed, eyes closed, apparently praying. Grace isn't sure what she's supposed to do, so she takes a seat next to Ângela Maria. She bows her head as if in prayer for a few minutes, then sits quietly observing. The casket is beautiful; it appears to be made of walnut, but Grace can't be sure. Senhora Norinha looks better than she did in life. Death has taken her angst away. She wears a turquoise-blue dress, and someone has placed a rosary in her hands. At each corner of the casket stands a vase filled with flowers and greenery from the garden. Grace examines the flowers—one appears to be white foxglove, one of her favorites. Must have come from the greenhouse, she thinks. She has seen many flowers in bloom, but even for the Azores, it's too early for foxglove.

THE NEXT MORNING, dressed in dark clothing, Grace, Ângela Maria, Miguel, Ana, and Mário walk down to Senhor Estêvão's house. Although it's Tuesday, the town is quiet. No scooters buzz down the street; it feels like a holiday. A hearse is parked in front of the house, and a large crowd of people mill about, waiting for the procession to the cemetery to begin. Grace's black sweater soaks up the sun, making her too warm. Miguel has gone off to talk to his brother, and Ana and Mário have joined friends of theirs. People speak quietly with one another as they wait.

Padre João pulls up in his black Opal with his perpetually expressionless secretary. She remains in the car as he gets out and hurriedly puts on vestments. Without so much as a greeting, he rushes into the house.

"Won't be long now," Ângela Maria says to Grace.

Grace moves closer to Ângela Maria and asks quietly, "Do this many people go to all of the funerals?" To her, it seems the entire town has shown up.

"Not usually," Ângela Maria says. "You know, Norinha's family goes back a long way in Calheta . . . a well-respected, and well-to-do, family."

"Of course." Grace knows that. She studies the crowd and sees the two officers that questioned her the day before. They stand in front of the hearse smoking cigarettes and talking jovially as if this were any old parade.

After perhaps ten minutes, the padre comes out of the house with Senhor Estêvão, who looks weak and sad. The casket comes next. Four of Senhor Estêvão's friends, men Grace knows from os Reis, carry it to the hearse. The pallbearers betray no emotion. When the hearse's door slams shut, the crowd organically falls into place behind it, forming two lines. They have been on this march before. The officers, now somber, enter their car, turn on their lights, and pull slowly away from the curb.

As the procession moves rhythmically toward the cemetery, Grace suddenly becomes acutely aware of how out of place she is. She towers above all of the women and most of the men. How strange she must seem to these people. No wonder they pay such close attention to her every move, her every glance. How can they avoid seeing her? No matter how she might try, she will never blend in. She will always be viewed suspiciously and hated by some people simply because she is different.

She should have understood this sooner. São Jorge is no different than the reservation, where as a child she was ostracized for her differences. Kids said that she wasn't a true Piegan. Her response then was to reject her Indian-ness altogether and to become the blond, blue-eyed Ivy League white girl that she is. She sees now, as she rocks back and forth in this sea of shorter, darker, curly-haired people, that her only way out is to embrace them, to embrace her other half.

AFTER THE FUNERAL, Grace hears Miguel tell Ângela Maria that the police ruled Norinha's death accidental. They found no evidence to indicate anything else; she simply slipped and fell. Grace feels inexplicably responsible nonetheless. She can't help but think that if she hadn't come to São Jorge, this would never have happened. Her being here completely upset the rhythm of life. She is a stone thrown into a pond; concentric waves emanate out from her, bringing destruction in their wake. She believes this. *I am the stone.*

That night, Grace welcomes the afterimage of the crucifix; she welcomes the sleep that comes on the wings of butterflies. She flies high above the island of São Jorge, allowing the strength of the White Owl Woman to enter her. She's not afraid.

GRACE GAZES at the black patterns burned into the wall as Tia Carmina hunches over the stove crumbling leaves of various herbs into different pots. Steam rises up from several kettles on the stove. The air, thick with smells of herbs and roots, transports Grace home to her childhood on the reservation. Tia Carmina pours cups of tea from separate pots through separate strainers for her and Ângela Maria.

"There," she says as she sets the cups down. "Grace, yours is a little bitter, but you have to drink it all."

Grace takes her first sip. More than a little bitter. She puckers her face.

"Go ahead," Tia Carmina instructs her. "And don't worry. This tea will not take you away like the other that I gave you. You needed that tea then to get your eyes and heart more open—to wake you up."

"It worked." Grace laughs.

"Only works if the person drinking the tea wants it to," says Tia Carmina. "Now go ahead."

Grace guzzles the tea without breathing to minimize the taste. "There." She sets the cup down. "That stuff is terrible!"

Ângela Maria laughs. "Nobody makes worse-tasting tea than Tia Carmina!"

"Terrible and good at the same time . . . just like people, just like o Divino Espírito Santo." Tia Carmina chuckles as she picks up the empty cup and fills it with more tea. "This is peppermint. Good for your stomach and will leave a good flavor in your mouth." She sits down at the table, interlacing her gnarled arthritic fingers.

Grace and Ângela Maria wait for Tia Carmina to say something more, but she doesn't. She fixes her gaze at some point halfway between them. Ângela Maria signals to Grace to keep quiet.

They sit this way for about five minutes. Suddenly, Tia Carmina turns toward Grace. "Do you know why you are here?"

The question surprises Grace. "Because you're the only one who can help me. I think one person has already died because of me, and I don't want that boy to die," says Grace. "I promise to do whatever I can to make things better."

"Hmm . . . so I have heard." Tia Carmina closes her eyes. "It requires faith . . . I'm not sure that you have that."

Grace isn't sure either, but she feels a lot closer to having it than she ever has before. What explanation could there possibly be for her strange dreams and the events since her arrival? She needs to try. "I have faith."

Tia Carmina's eyes light up. "Ah . . . down deep . . . buried . . . Perhaps if you help carry Ângela Maria's burden, you will find something to believe in." She turns to Ângela Maria. "And you, you help Grace carry her burden." She spreads her arms wide. "And it will take both of you to bring that boy the rest of the way to safety. After you do this, things will fall into place, but it must be done in faith."

Grace looks inquisitively at Ângela Maria, whose face betrays little of what she is thinking.

"Grace, you have made a promise to the Holy Ghost for the recovery of the boy and Norinha's safe passage into the other world," says Tia Carmina. "I believe He has already come some of the way for you."

Grace is uncomfortable at the mere mention of the Holy Ghost. True, after Norinha's death she half-heartedly made a promise to Espírito Santo, more out of desperation than anything else. She can't remember the promise exactly. Blood rushes into her face. And how does Tia Carmina know that He has come through for her? Who is this woman anyway? God's right-hand woman?

Tia Carmina continues, as if she hears Grace's doubts. "You promised to do anything that you can to make things better, didn't you? Isn't that what you promised when you spoke to o Divino? If it helps you find your faith, think of the Holy Spirit as the Sun or as Old Man, or any power that you sincerely believe in. Believe in yourself and you will find Him. The Holy Spirit has many names and appears to people in many forms."

Grace touches her face as if checking to see if she is really herself. "Okay. I can do that."

"You must pay your promise in Topo, and I think you know that I have already made arrangements for that." Tia Carmina looks back at Ângela Maria. "You will help her complete her promise in payment of yours."

Ângela Maria looks surprised. "Can it really be?" Tears well in her eyes.

Tia Carmina's eyes twinkle as she smiles. "Jaime needs you to let him go—the time has come. His spirit must move on." She stands up and stirs a pot on the stove. "Zoeta also has a promise to pay and, to ensure that everything is done with the utmost care, she will contribute her most excellent services to your and Grace's efforts, and she has also offered to lodge both of you, so that you don't have to spend so much time ferrying between Calheta and Topo." Tia Carmina turns back to Grace. "Grace, you should know that payment of a promise requires sacrifice, self-sacrifice, and I know how difficult that can be for you."

23

MAUNDY THURSDAY

Now that I, your Lord and Teacher, have washed your feet, you also should wash one another's feet. I have set you an example that you should do as I have done for you.

—*JOHN 13:14-15*

GRACE

AFTER GRACE GETS home from Palm Sunday Mass, she changes her clothes. Why hasn't Magnus returned her calls? She has made several attempts on both his mobile phone and his parents' phone. Surely, he must know she's been calling him. Maybe there is someone else back home. He's mentioned a woman named Adriana. The crisis that prompted her initial call to him has passed—the police ruled Norinha's death accidental—and Grace doesn't feel as desperate. Now she simply feels rejected.

Just as she slips into a morass of self-pity, her mobile phone rings. It's Magnus. He's coming home on Tuesday.

MAGNUS

THE SATA PUDDLE jumper taxies onto the runway at the airport in Terceira, its propellers turn and the engines roar. Magnus crumples into one of the seats, leans his head up against the cool window. He contemplated not returning to São Jorge, and probably wouldn't have if it weren't for all the loose ends, not to mention the thousands of dollars of equipment on loan to him from the Volcanological Institute. He's in no shape to work, but one other thing holds him captive in São Jorge—Grace. He can't quite imagine letting her go. He needs to find out what the possibilities are with her.

His trip home to Sweden was more difficult than he ever imagined. He was neither prepared for the death of his father, nor the sight of his mother who has aged considerably during his two years away. It was hard to leave her there looking so frail and sad, and yet it was impossible to stay.

Magnus gazes down on *his* island, *his* volcanoes. He strains to see his laboratory in Topo. He can make out a few of the landmarks he knows so well from the ground and by sea. There's the lighthouse and the *ilhéu*. He finds the road, but he can't see his little house.

He'll spend the next three months putting everything in order. He needs to sell his boat, return the seismological equipment, get rid of the few pieces of furniture he has acquired over the past two years, and pack up his books. How will he tell Grace that he is going back to take care of his mother? Will she even care that he's leaving? Of course she will, but will she understand?

When he spoke to Grace on Sunday, she was overwhelmed

with joy at the news of his return. She didn't question his explanation for not returning her calls: his father had died the day of her first call. The message box on the phone had filled up with sympathy calls, and her calls were lost in the mix. He'd turned off his mobile phone because he lacked the fortitude to respond to all of the sympathy being offered. He'd been subsumed with unexpected grief. After that, Magnus didn't have the heart to tell her that he is going to return to Sweden. Of course, he knows she won't be staying on São Jorge too much longer either. Her year will be up at the end of September. Then what? Then where? His heart feels heavy at the thought of their parting ways.

The plane passes by Fajã dos Vimes. Magnus can see the houses and the little road snaking its way up to the top of the island. And there is Calheta. Is she there now, or has she gone to Velas to meet him? She said she was going to try.

The plane hugs slightly closer to the island as it passes over Manadas, Fajã das Almas, Urzelina, and then it lands. He sees her waiting on the tarmac.

THE SUN SHINES BRIGHTLY. A few large cumulus clouds billow upward in the blue sky. The taxi descends into Velas. Magnus holds Grace's hand and can't stop looking at her. She *actually* showed up. She's even more beautiful in person than in his mind's eye. He can't wait to get home.

He's been gone little more than a month and yet Velas looks foreign to him again, the way it did when he first arrived. He sees people streaming out of the church. Why would so many people be there on a Tuesday? *Of course, it's Easter week.* Religion puzzles him. How do so many people put faith in deities? If there were a god, who was anything like that posited by Judeo-Christian religions, then surely there wouldn't be chaos, and of all of the facts that Magnus is the most sure of it is the fact that chaos exists.

Chaos is God, a god that demands humans create order through Science. His musings end as the taxi pulls up to the house.

In his hasty departure, he left quite a mess. The bed is unmade, and dirty breakfast dishes from that day remain in the sink. "Sorry about the mess . . ."

Grace turns to him. "Do you *really* think I care?" She kisses him, and they tumble into bed.

GRACE

A COUPLE of days after Magnus's return, Grace finds herself back in Velas for the third day in a row. Her eyes ache as she emerges into the bright sunlight from the church. The foot-washing ceremony, Maundy Thursday Mass, is over. Ângela Maria asked Grace to attend with her, but in the end couldn't go. Grace jumped at the opportunity to go by herself for an excuse to see Magnus again.

Other than the last two days with Magnus, she hasn't been to Velas since before he left. The day Magnus pointed out to her that she was the only lone female ever at the café was her last time being there alone. How did she fail to notice? She likely has made many worse social blunders than sitting in a café alone. Even so, Magnus was on to something. Spending more time with the women of Calheta and beyond has been good for her. She's learned much more than she ever learned from transcribing articles at the archives.

Walking aimlessly toward the café after Mass, she passes a store that she's never seen and steps inside. It's an exceedingly small grocery store; perhaps only ten feet by ten feet. The proprietor sits behind a long counter reading *Expresso*, a weekly newspaper journal from Lisbon.

He looks over the top of the newspaper. "Can I help you?" he asks.

"Not really. I'm just looking."

"Okay then, let me know if you need something."

The place is chock-full of food items that Grace hasn't seen anywhere else on the island, mostly imports from the United States. The counter is full of fresh fruit for sale at exorbitant prices, something she also hasn't seen for a long time. She scans the shelves. *Oreos . . . mmm . . . Cheetos . . .* On the top shelf, among multiple bottles of scotch, gin and rum, stands a solitary dusty bottle with a label that reads "Four Roses Straight Bourbon Whiskey." Grace thought she knew all of the bourbons. Jake considered himself a bourbon expert, and he loved passing on bourbon lore. She learned a lot about it from him. *Bourbon is an American original,* he said. *Gotta be made in Kentuck-uh tuh git called bourbon.*

"Excuse me." Grace waits for the proprietor to look up. "How much is that bottle of bourbon?"

"Fifty-two euros," he says without lowering the newspaper.

Wow. More than she expects. Grace digs around in her bag for her wallet and counts out the bills. "I'll take it . . . and a package of Oreos . . . and a bag of Cheetos."

The man finally puts his newspaper down. He pulls a ladder over to where the bourbon is. "Last bottle," he says. "And from the looks of it, it's been here a long time. Folks here prefer Scotch." Without saying anything else, he gets the Oreos and Cheetos off the shelf and sets them on the only available spot on the counter.

Grace hands him the money. She's really splurging—not much of a Lenten thing to do. Well, she isn't Catholic anyway. She takes the bag and walks back onto the street. It'll be fun to share these treats with Ângela Maria.

She walks toward the café slowly. As she opens the heavy door, her heart pounds a little with expectation. Two woman sit at one table, and a man at the bar, but Magnus isn't there. She doesn't really expect him to be. He's spending the day at home getting some matters in order. She told him she'd stop by before heading back to Calheta. As if for safety's sake, Grace takes the table next to the two women. She reaches into her bag and takes out her notebook. Without having taken her order, the owner brings her a *galão*. She's happy to be back here.

"It has been a long time, *Lourinha*," he says warmly as he sets down the cup.

Grace smiles up at him. "I've been busy up on the other end of the island."

"So I've heard." He smiles back, with a wink. The door opens and the owner looks up. "Ah! I think someone is here to see you."

Grace looks over to see Magnus walking toward her table with a sack of groceries in hand. "Magnus, I didn't think I'd see you here," she exclaims.

Magnus smiles at her, as he settles in across from her. "Hey, fancy meeting you here. Nice to see that you don't always take my advice." He reaches across the table and squeezes her hand. "I hope you're as happy to see me as I am you."

"Definitely." Grace blushes. They've spent the last two days together, so it's bit of a ruse for the benefit of the audience at the next table over who seem to have a keen interest in them.

MAGNUS

MAGNUS STILL HASN'T TOLD Grace that he plans to return to Sweden. In fact, he hasn't told her much of anything about his trip home. The time they've spent together has been filled mostly with lovemaking. Grace tried a time or two to get him to talk about his trip, about his father, but he always found a way to redirect the conversation to something less fraught with emotion, like talking about her work. She seems lighter now, more hopeful, less dramatic.

"Hey, how about we get out of here? There are some things I want to talk to you about, and I need to get some of this stuff in the refrigerator." His eyes rove to the table next to them.

"Yeah, let's." She finishes the last of her coffee and gathers her belongings.

GRACE

As THEY WALK toward Magnus's place, he looks rather serious.

"You've probably noticed that I haven't wanted to talk much about my trip home." Magnus kicks a stone along the sidewalk. After a long pause, he continues, "It's good that I went." He pulls out a handkerchief and blows his nose. "At least I got to spend a week with my father before it happened." His voice catches.

Magnus goes on to tell her all about the time he spent with his brother and his brother's children on the farm, and how his mother has aged. "So, the bad news is I've decided to go back." He pauses. "I've already arranged for a research position at the university in Lund." They ascend the stairs at his apartment silently.

Grace doesn't know what to say. So unexpected. "Well . . . that's wonderful!" She tries to sound enthusiastic, but her enormous disappointment comes through anyway. "When will you be leaving?" Now she is dangerously close to crying.

"In three months, give or take . . ."

"Wow. I really thought we had more time . . ."

Magnus takes Grace in his arms, pulls her in for a hug. "Well, three months is something; it's enough time to figure out what we are, if we are . . . anything."

Grace looks at the floor; she can't look him in the eye for fear of falling apart. She has begun to imagine that Magnus might be "the one." Now she's confused, a little angry. "Yeah . . . I'm gonna be really busy. I won't have a lot of free time . . . I haven't told you everything about my life either." She moves away from him. "While you were gone, I went to visit Tia Carmina in Fajã dos Vimes. She told me that I need to perform an act of sacrifice and faith to remedy things." She laughs uncomfortably. "I know, it's a little weird." Grace studies Magnus's face to gauge his response, but he just looks like someone who's listening carefully. No judgment. "So I made a promise . . . I'll be giving a feast in honor of the Holy Spirit the fourth week of Easter. That means distributing *esmolas* to twenty-four families of my choosing, and on the fifth Sunday of Easter I will feed twenty-four children in Topo . . . Ângela Maria and Zoeta will help me."

Magnus looks at her softly. "And me? Can I help too? I'll have time."

"Will you still be here?"

"Yeah, at least until the end of May."

"I figured you'd think it was silly. That I'm a nutcase. I know you don't put much stock in magic or religion." She pushes a lock of hair behind her ear.

"You know what I think?" he says, looking down at his feet. "We're all trying to do our best in this crazy, fucked-up world . . . And you know what else I think? I think I love you, and I want to spend as much time as possible with you between now and when I leave."

"I'd like that too," Grace says, and gives him a hug.

"Just let me know what to do."

"I will."

24

GOOD FRIDAY

GRACE

ON HER RETURN FROM VELAS, Grace stops at the post office to check for mail. She doesn't have any. She sent her mother a long letter about everything as instructed and has been updating her by telephone regularly. As for Jake, Grace hasn't bothered to finish reading his last letter, and he hasn't sent another.

Outside the post office, she sees Senhor Estêvão approaching on the street. *"Boa tarde!"* Grace waves to him.

He waves back. *"Boa tarde,"* he says, smiling broadly. Perhaps too broadly.

He looks much better than he did the last time she saw him. In fact, he isn't even wearing mourning clothes, as is customary for a prolonged period after one loses a spouse. She will have to ask someone about that.

"Nice to see you," Grace says, "I know this must be a difficult time for you. How are you doing?"

"Oh, things are much better, thank you." Senhor Estêvão puts his hands behind his back. "As good as can be expected, under the circumstances," he adds.

"Of course. Well, I have to run. I borrowed the car today and need to get it back." Grace starts toward the car. Though she empathizes with Senhor Estêvão, something about his demeanor continues to discomfort her, and given her history with him, it is better to be cautious.

"A Senhora Doutora . . ."

She stops. "Yes?"

Senhor Estêvão holds his hands out in a giving gesture. "I have a book that I have been meaning to give you concerning Festas do Divino Espírito Santo nos Açores. Maybe you could stop by one of these days and pick it up? I gather from word about town that you will be needing it."

"Of course—how thoughtful of you, but perhaps you should only loan it to me." Gifts from certain types of men come with too many obligations.

"As you wish." Senhor Estêvão pretends to tip a nonexistent hat.

Grace smiles politely at his antics. "It would be my pleasure . . . Should I stop by the store?" Grace asks.

"Oh no, I haven't had the heart to reopen it yet . . . you know how it is," he says. "Please, stop by the house anytime that's convenient for you. See you then." He waves and turns toward home.

ÂNGELA MARIA

ÂNGELA MARIA's fingers are sore from all of the sewing she's been doing. Ana needs a new Easter outfit, and Elisabete asked her to make a skirt. As usual, she's working hard, but for the first time in ages she can go about her work lightheartedly. Finally, Jaime will leave her dreams and move into heaven to be with our Lord, where he belongs. "Ouch!" She pricks her finger. She slips her thimble over her thumb as someone stomps up the stairs. Maybe Grace. She's happy for her too. All of this bad stuff will soon be gone. She looks up as the door opens.

"Hello, Grace! How did it go? Did you like it?" The questions fly out. She's been waiting all afternoon for Grace to return from the foot-washing ceremony. Too much work to be done for Ângela Maria to go, much as she wanted to.

"It was beautiful!" Grace says.

"Oh, I'm glad you got to see it. One of the more uplifting parts of Easter—such a sad time, and yet . . ." Ângela Maria clicks her tongue as she lays her sewing on the table and rises to her feet. "Looks like you also did some shopping while you were down there." She peers nosily at Grace's bag.

"Yeah!" Grace sets it on the table and takes out three items. "I found a fun little store in Velas that sells a lot of imported foods. These are some of my favorite American things—I thought we could have some right now."

Before Ângela Maria has a chance to respond, Grace tears open the orange bag. "Well, that sounds very nice." Ângela Maria goes to the cupboard and takes down some plates.

Grace says, "Get us a couple of little shot glasses too. I'm gonna treat you to some *aguardente da minha terra!*"

"Okay." Ângela Maria does as instructed. Grace seems extraordinarily full of herself and happy, something she hasn't been for a while. Perhaps the foot-washing ceremony helped her. After setting the dishes on the table, Ângela Maria picks up the bottle of bourbon and inspects it. "Is it strong?"

"You'll see." Grace, smiling, takes the bottle and opens it. She pours each of them a shot glass full and hands one to Ângela Maria. "Cheers! As we say in my land, *Down the hatch!*"

Ângela Maria tries to repeat her, but it comes out wrong. They both laugh and take sips of their shots. "Whew! This is really strong, but I like it." Ângela Maria downs the shot. Next she tries a Cheeto. She carefully takes one out and inspects it. "It's an unnatural color," she comments, and takes a bite. As she chews, she nods her approval. Following Grace's lead, she dips her hand into the bag for a handful. "Delicious!"

"And now for dessert . . ." Grace opens the Oreos and holds the package toward Ângela Maria, who eagerly snatches one and takes a bite.

Still chewing, she says, "Now *this* is *really* good! No wonder you Americans are all so fat!"

"Hey! So you think I'm fat?" Grace asks.

"No, not you, but all the other Americans." She's treaded too close to one of Grace's sensitive spots. "At least the ones I've seen on television." She examines the bright-orange residue left on her fingers from the Cheetos. "Those things are messy!" she says as she grabs the paper napkins and sets them on the table. "So, what kept you in Velas so long? It didn't take you all afternoon to buy those things." She points at the stuff on the table. Ângela Maria thinks she detects a blush.

"Well, I went to the Café da Ilha for a *galão*," Grace says. "I met Magnus . . . he's back . . ."

"Ah-ha, I see, and . . . ?"

"Afterward we walked and talked," Grace says. "His father died while he was home, and he really needed someone to talk to."

"Such a shame. Well, he is lucky to have a friend like you."

"And I am lucky to have a friend like him . . ." Grace looks at her hands. "He's going back to Sweden soon to take care of his mother."

"Oh, Grace, I am so sorry. I know you must feel sad about that." Ângela Maria's suspicions about Grace's feelings for Magnus have been more or less confirmed. Her multiple trips to Velas this week make more sense now.

"Well, he'll be here through the end of May, so at least we have that."

Ângela Maria reaches out and pats Grace's hand. "Well, that is something," she says reassuringly.

"I told him about the *jantar*, and he's offered to help us in whatever way he can."

"Good. Because with this short notice we're going to need all the help we can get! We have less than four weeks to get ready, and there's a lot of planning and buying to do," Ângela Maria says. "You know, Grace, this is going to be expensive and difficult to accomplish, given the time."

"Yeah, I've been wondering about that . . . How much *is* it going to cost?" Grace asks.

"Depends. The biggest expense is going to be the cow, and they range in price, depending on how old, how big, and so on. There are lots of expenses that add up. I'm guessing that for twenty-four *esmolas* and the *jantar* we're going to spend three to four thousand dollars, probably more." Ângela Maria can see that Grace hasn't worked all of this through. "You know, you don't have to do this—"

"No, I am doing it. I don't have any *extra* money. I'll just have to leave a few months sooner, that's all." Grace looks a little sad.

Ângela Maria touches her on the shoulder. "Things'll work out fine—you'll see. They always do."

Grace stands up and readies to leave. "Oh, I almost forgot, I ran into Senhor Estêvão, and he has a book to loan me. I was wondering if you would mind going over to his house with me?"

"Absolutely, I won't allow you to go alone, after all that has happened." Also, Ângela Maria has a nagging feeling about him. She has seen him about town, and he seems unreasonably happy, given his wife's sudden death. He hasn't even been wearing the clothes of *luto*; it's as if he were deliberately mocking tradition.

GRACE

GRACE THOUGHT she understood what Tia Carmina meant by making a sacrifice for others, but the enormity of the sacrifice did not fully hit her until she sat in the kitchen with Ângela Maria the previous afternoon. The financial sacrifice is nothing compared to the personal sacrifice. She'll have to return home several months earlier than planned, missing the entire summer, the season in which the vast majority of *festas* take place. Her dissertation down the tubes, and all for what? Too late to change course now. Something pushes her onward—she must fulfill her promise.

As she prepares to go to Senhor Estêvão's house, she hears someone descending the stairs outside. Probably Ângela Maria. Grace opens the door before she can knock, "I'm ready to go." She and Ângela Maria head down the road toward the center of town.

Grace and Ângela Maria wind their way through Senhor Estêvão's garden to the back of the house. Although Grace appreciated the beauty of the garden before, she didn't really have an opportunity to take in the details on the day Norinha died.

"Look at that beautiful flower!" Grace exclaims, pointing to an iridescent blue flower that grows out of a crack in the black stone wall. "Do you know what that is called?"

Ângela Maria steps over to take a closer look. "No idea. He has a lot of exotic flowers here, some from Africa, I know that."

As they move over the stone path, Grace can't help but think of Norinha, poor misguided soul. How did it happen? Did she step out to collect eggs early in the morning and slip on a dew-covered stone? Did she hear a noise in the night? Did she call for help? A chill runs down Grace's spine.

When they reach the door, Grace knocks, and Senhor Estêvão opens it almost immediately, as if he were waiting. Perhaps he saw them coming.

"Good morning, senhoras! And Dona Ângela Maria too—what an unexpected pleasure. Please come in."

Ângela Maria speaks first. "So sorry to horn in on the invitation, senhor, but I wanted to bring you this loaf of *folar*, so when Grace told me she was coming to see you . . ."

Grace suppresses her amusement at the formality of the exchange. She's seen Ângela Maria and Senhor Estêvão exchange pleasantries after church on a number of occasions, and they've never been quite like this.

"Don't be silly, Dona, always a pleasure to have your company, invited or not." Senhor Estêvão takes the loaf. "And thank you. I can always use another loaf of my favorite Azorean bread." He smiles, revealing a mouthful of gold teeth.

"Come in, and I'll get the book." He leads them into what appears to be a study. Built-in bookshelves, overflowing with books, fill two whole walls. "How about a little tea?" he asks.

Grace exchanges looks with Ângela Maria. "Sure, that sounds good."

"Perfect, I have some newly harvested mint—do you like mint?"

Ângela Maria and Grace both say they like mint, and Senhor Estêvão excuses himself to the kitchen, leaving them alone in the study.

Grace takes a seat in a chair next to a side table piled high with books; all books about plants. She picks up one from the top of the pile called *Plantas Medicinais*. A bookmark holds a spot in the book. Grace opens it to the marked spot. On the left-hand page is an etching of a plant. The caption reads: *Tab. XXX: Digitalis purpurea. Common names: Dedaleira, Witch's Thimble, Our Lady's Gloves.* It is the flower Grace knows as foxglove, the one she'd noticed in the vases by Norinha's casket. She looks at the text—someone has under-lined a paragraph:

Digitalis, if taken in nontherapeutic doses can cause paranoia, dizziness, confusion, nausea, vomiting, and in severe cases even death. Extreme caution should be used when using the plant form of this drug because it can be diffi-cult to control the dosage, and there is little difference between a therapeutic dose and a toxic one.

When Grace hears Senhor Estêvão coming, she slips the book-mark back into the book and turns to a different page.

"Oh, I see you have found some reading!" he says, oozing enthusiasm. "You can see that I don't have a shortage of books. What is that?" He gestures at the book sitting open on Grace's lap.

She closes it and turns the book around so he can see the title. "Interesting book. I've always been fascinated by the medicinal uses of plants. I'd forgotten that it was an interest of yours . . . your *hobby*."

Senhor Estêvão takes the book from Grace as he says, "Yes, yes, well, I've been interested in botany my entire life. If it were a more lucrative vocation, I probably would've followed that path instead of the one I did."

Grace suddenly feels extremely uneasy. She certainly isn't inclined to drink tea that Senhor Estêvão has brewed. If only she can prevent Ângela Maria from drinking it. She lifts the teacup to her lips and pretends to drink. "Delicious," she comments. Illusion. No doubt paranoia. He affects women that way, apparently.

Ângela Maria picks up her teacup, smells the tea. "This is very fragrant. I usually make mine a bit weaker, I think."

"Yes, yes, that is the Azorean way, isn't it? Weak tea and strong coffee." Senhor Estêvão sits down. "I like my tea strong, I suppose, but then, as you know, I'm not from here."

"Americans like strong tea too," Grace offers, attempting to make small talk. "And most Americans take their coffee pretty weak."

Ângela Maria laughs. "Yes, that's why my sisters call American coffee *chá-fé*, coffee the strength of Azorean tea, *chá*."

An uncomfortable silence follows their laughter. Grace can't wait to leave. The small talk continues for an agonizing ten minutes more.

Senhor Estêvão picks up the teapot. "More tea?" He looks at their almost-full cups. "Why, you have hardly touched it. Is there something wrong with it?"

Ângela Maria quickly says, "No, no, I wasn't in as much the mood for tea as I thought, and honestly, it *is* a little too strong for my tastes."

Evading the question about the tea, Grace looks at her watch and says, "Well, we have to be going now. Almost time for Mass! You know . . . Good Friday?"

"Of course." Senhor Estêvão sets the pot on the tray. "Here's the book I promised you." He walks over to the bookshelf, pulls out a book with a green binding, and hands it to Grace.

"Thank you so much. I'm sure it'll come in handy," Grace says. "And I'll return it before I go back to America."

Senhor Estêvão waves his hand toward her and says, "No, no, that won't be necessary."

ÂNGELA MARIA and Grace hurry down the path and out onto the street without saying a word. Grace glances back at Senhor Estêvão's house and notices him standing at the window watching. She smiles and waves casually one last time. They walk silently until they are a fair distance away.

"Ângela Maria, why didn't *you* drink the tea?" Grace asks.

"Well, mostly because it *was* too strong—not to my liking, but also I don't trust the man. A man in mourning doesn't dress or act the way he does."

"Mmmm . . . I wondered about that." They walk a bit further. Finally, Grace says, "I think he might have murdered his wife."

Ângela Maria stops. Turning to Grace, she says, "The same thought has crossed my mind more than once. What makes you think so?"

Grace tells Ângela Maria about the *dedaleira* entry in the book. "That's why I didn't drink my tea. Thank God he made it too strong for your tastes!"

Ângela Maria starts forward again. "I can't for the life of me figure out why he would do something like that. This island is too small. People don't murder other people here."

Grace hesitates before saying, "Maybe it was because of me . . . maybe in his warped mind he thought if she were out of the way, he could have me."

"No, this isn't about you. Men here have affairs and lust after other women all the time. No need to murder your wife to have an affair—otherwise most all of us would be dead!" She laughs. "Norinha was nuts with jealousy, but there was nothing she could do about it. That's the way life is—"

"That's it! She could . . . and that's why he killed her. She must have had something on him, something to ruin him with, but what could it be?" They start walking again, up the steep incline toward the Junta, a small building next to the Matriz. "Maybe we should talk to the police . . . ?"

Ângela Maria twists her sweater, the way she twists dish towels when nervous. "I don't know if that would do any good. How can we prove anything? They would have to dig Norinha up, and frankly, I don't know they will based on the little bit that we have to say. He hasn't done anything illegal, or even suspect. Growing and using *dedaleira* is not against the law, nor is forgoing mourning."

"I guess you're right, and she could've slipped and hit her head on a rock. We're probably making too much of it. All the same, I think I'll stop by the police station one of these days to ask them if the medical examiner tested her for any poisons." Grace and she go into the church and find seats toward the front.

EASTER

50 DAYS BEFORE PENTACOST SUNDAY

25

IN THE EYE OF A VOLCANO

GRACE

GRACE SITS on the steep slope next to Magnus. The uneven clumps of coarse mown grass are not very comfortable to sit on, and a cold breeze cuts through the sweater Grace wears. If only she'd thought to bring her windbreaker and a blanket to sit on. Aside from physical discomfort, she feels as if she were in a strange dream. There's something surreal about sitting in the eye of a volcano with hundreds of people watching a bullfight, especially this bullfight, which in truth is not a bullfight at all; there is no bull. A not-very-large cow, with horns strapped ridiculously on her head, charges toward the would-be matador, a Spanish dwarf. Several other dwarfs run around the dirt-covered natural arena acting like rodeo clowns, trying to get the angry cow to run at them. Grace can't help but feel—cultural relativism aside—that this display is in extremely poor taste.

Magnus leans over and whispers, "Do you want to leave?"

They paid on the order of twenty dollars apiece to get into this. Such a waste. "What do you want to do?" Grace asks.

"Well, personally, this isn't doing much, and my ass is killing me," Magnus says. "But if you want to stay—for *research* purposes —we can."

Grace, relieved, says, "No, let's get the hell out of here. I'm not really enjoying this too much either." She was eager to see a bull-fight, but an Azorean-style bullfight on the cord, *Tourada à corda*, a bullfighting tradition unique to the Azores. Ângela Maria was right when she said with disdain, *This thing, não presta; it is nothing but a foreign spectacle.*

They climb up to the rim of the *caldeira*. A strong gust of wind almost knocks Grace over. They apparently were somewhat protected where they sat. From the top, they can see Velas below, inviting and warm. They start down the hill.

"Can you believe that cow they're using?" Magnus says. "All skin and bones."

"I know! Poor thing. Such a cruel thing to do . . . Made me worry about my cow, the one for the *jantar*." Grace has been tormented by the idea that she will be responsible for the death of a cow, a poor cow that has done nothing but given to others during her whole life.

"Don't worry, the cow that you bought is nice and fat—a good cow by any standard! I personally have seen to it."

They'd already been through the "it isn't right to kill another animal" conversation, so she would spare him that again. "No, you know what I mean."

Magnus puts his arm around her shoulder. "I *do* know what you mean. Don't worry, these guys are experts at killing—you'll see —it's humane."

Grace shudders. Killing is not *humane*. She supposes she will be there when it happens and will have to witness it herself. Magnus's arm around her shoulder comforts her angst; makes her feel safe.

Since Easter, she and Magnus have been seeing each other at every possible opportunity. Although she fears the pain that loving him might bring, she fears not loving him more. That she has been extremely busy has helped to keep her mind off his departure. In addition to working with Ângela Maria and Zoeta on planning the *jantar*—buying all the ingredients, arranging for tables and chairs and such—she has been invited to observe other people's preparations for coronations.

By day she sits in kitchens gossiping with women and running errands for them, and by night in *impérios*, singing *terços*. She has learned that each brotherhood sings their third, *terço*, of a rosary using proprietary melodies, and she has already managed to record sung *terços* in several different places on the island. Finally, she's doing *real* fieldwork. She has gained a modicum of acceptance among the people. *The magic of a promise*, she thinks.

Still, with each passing day, an inexplicable heaviness descends on Grace. She attributes this feeling to the repetitively unsettling dreams that disturb her sleep nightly. She runs through a complex maze of underground tunnels, chasing a creature that she only ever sees from behind; it has a bushy tail. Once and again, she runs as quickly as she can, but it eludes her. The creature deliberately misleads her, and she always ends up in a dead end.

After giving it much thought, she concludes the dream is about Senhor Estêvão. There's something fox-like about the animal's tail, and it makes sense because of the foxglove connection. The dream, in fact, prompts her to make the trip to the police station, which she has been putting off. Maybe going to the police will bring closure to the issue and bring the dreams to an end.

As Ângela Maria predicted, the police don't take Grace's concerns seriously. The desk officer on duty scoffs, "Of course the medical examiner did a toxin screening!" It is as if he has told her not to worry her little head about it anymore. "We *are* professionals, you know." He and another officer chuckle in a discomforting way, looking at each other in amusement. The desk officer continues, "And your name wouldn't be Jessica Fletcher would it?" Grace laughs with them at this joke to appear to be a good sport. She tells them about the book, the underlined part, that she knows he cultivates *dedaleira*, and also knows how to prepare it. They promise to follow up on her "concerns."

THE WEEK BEFORE THE *JANTAR*, while Grace and Ângela Maria sit at the kitchen table talking, Miguel comes flying through the door.

"Hey! What's the hurry?" Ângela Maria asks. "The island already ends here."

Sweat pours down his face. "I was down at the port, and my brother told me that the police are digging up Senhora Norinha—they think she might have been poisoned." He went to the sink and cupped his hands under the faucet to drink. He must have run the whole way.

Grace and Ângela Maria exchange glances. Grace will let Ângela Maria do the talking for now. Although Miguel seems to have warmed to her a bit, she still doesn't feel entirely comfortable around him. Now, instead of completely ignoring her when he comes into a room, he nods his head and greets her with actual words.

"Really? And where did they get an idea like that?" Ângela Maria catches Grace's eye as she asks.

Miguel sees the look. "I can't believe it," he says as he sits down. "I should have known that you two had something to do with it."

Ângela Maria's face hardens in preparation to defend herself.

"You two are really something," he says, his voice almost warm.

Grace, relieved by his tone, says, "Well, Ângela Maria didn't have anything to do with it. She knew about it, but I am the one who went to the police, and to tell you the truth, I didn't think that they even listened to me."

Miguel studies Grace's face, then Ângela Maria's. "Are you going to tell me what this is all about? Why you think she was murdered?"

After they finish telling Miguel the story of their pre-Easter visit to Senhor Estêvão's, Miguel falls silent for a few moments. He taps his fingers rhythmically on the table as if humming a tune in his mind. "I know you liked that guy, Ângela Maria, but he always gave me the creeps. I think you two might be on to something—so why would he do it? What's the motive?"

"We don't know yet," says Grace. "We think she was holding something over his head. The police must have some reason to dig her up, other than what I told them, don't you think?"

"Yeah, you're probably right." Miguel stands up to go back down to the port to finish working on his boat. As he leaves, he turns and says, "Can you both stay out of trouble, at least until after the *festa*?"

Ângela Maria smiles broadly at him. "We'll try, but you know it won't be easy."

ESTÊVÃO

SENHOR ESTÊVÃO SITS down at his desk in his study to write some letters. The time has come, although much sooner than he anticipated. The visit from the police a week after Easter surprised him. To his horror, they asked him questions concerning his illegitimate son. They also asked about his mother. Who told the police about them? It wasn't Norinha from the grave, and it surely was not Ângela Maria or Grace. Neither of them would know that part of his story. It couldn't have been Padre João either—confession is protected, and Padre João would never bite the hand that feeds him. The police know something, but what?

Before long, his real identity will be known, giving him little choice but to leave this place. Never again will he endure prison, but he is prepared to pay the price. One thing is certain—the American girl possesses more power than he ever imagined: the power to ruin, and the power to save. He places his trust in her. Senhor Estêvão looks out the window, then sets pen to paper.

26

MIRACLE OF TWO RIVERS OF FIRE

MAGNUS

It's April now, and Magnus looks out the window of his house in Topo. Dark, billowy clouds hang overhead. No doubt rain. He hopes the man delivering the cow will arrive soon.

He hasn't spent much time in Topo since returning from Sweden. Being here now only reminds him of the years of work he is throwing away. Is it a mistake to leave? No, it's the right thing to do, his obligation. He needs to be there for his mother in her last years. Sons need their mothers. Mothers need their sons. When his father died, he realized just how little time there is. He wants to be there for her, with her. He resumes packing.

When a horn sounds outside, Magnus steps out and says, "Good afternoon, senhor!" He walks over to have a look at the cow standing in a jerry-rigged trailer. Her coat is a rich rust color. "She looks great!" Magnus reaches through the slats of the trailer and strokes the haunches of the heifer.

"Yeah, she's a good one," the man says.

His brevity reminds Magnus of his own father, who seldom let more than five words pass his lips in any exchange. When Magnus was a young man, it infuriated him that his father was so impossible to talk to. Magnus concluded at one point that he had nothing to say. How wrong he had been.

The man ties a rope around the heifer's neck and carefully backs her down the makeshift ramp. "Well, here you are." He hands the rope to Magnus and goes around to the front of the cow. He puts his mouth next to the cow's ear and says in an audible whisper, "Now remember, no playing with the Holy Spirit!" He pats her on the head. "You are a good one." He turns to Magnus. "You too—*Não se brinca com o Espírito Santo!*" They shake hands, and the man climbs into his truck and heads down the road.

What a beauty, and Grace paid dearly for her, more than she should have. Most people figure she can afford to pay more, being an American and all, and as everyone explained, one pays a premium for the short notice. Magnus enjoyed the task of buying the cow, especially showing off his bovine knowledge. Although an expert at picking out good heifers, he's nothing compared to his father. Buying the cow simultaneously took his mind off his grief and allowed him to grieve fully, for which he is grateful. He leads the cow around to the *quintal*, where he has built a shelter of sorts for her, and ties the rope to a stake amid plenty of juicy grass. He picks up a bucket and goes to fill it in the house.

Grace is on his mind constantly. He knows he's going to miss her. They finally have settled into a comfortable relationship, not complicated by conflicting waves of emotion that were there earlier. They have something real, and their physical desire for each other borders on insane. They have to keep it all in check, though. Grace doesn't have the same freedom to be with him that she'd have in Sweden or the United States. Spending nights with him here would be completely unacceptable from her host family's perspective, so they have had to sneak in their lovemaking under the guise of other activities. Thankfully, over the next week and a half, they will have lots of opportunities to be together as they'll be within walking distance of one another.

Magnus puts the bucket down for the cow. "I think I'll call you Alma," Magnus says as he strokes her one last time before returning to the house to do more packing.

GRACE

Field notes, April 22, Espírito Santo, Topo

"Milagre das duas ribeiras do fogo," as told by Ângela Maria in Zoeta's kitchen, transcribed and translated.

A gente say this is true, and I believe that it is.

There was a man in Urzelina—I'd say about two hundred years ago—it was when the big volcano erupted. Anyway, his wife was pregnant. She was sickly for the whole time, and he had made a promise to the Holy Spirit to keep her and her baby safe. He loved his wife more than anything and could not bear the thought of losing her. He prayed to the Holy Spirit every day.

When the volcano erupted, it threw fiery stones down on the fajãs and villages below. All of the fields were on fire, and most people lost their dwellings, including the man with the pregnant wife. Still, he prayed every day. Some people thought he was a fool. Couldn't he see that they were enduring the wrath of the Holy Spirit? Surely all of the livestock were dead, including the cow planned to sacrifice. Others prayed with him, keeping the faith.

Finally, the day of the feast drew near during Espírito Santo, when the man would repay his promise. The fires subsided. The man went to see if his cow had made it safely through. He had been told that not a single cow in the parish had survived, but he would not believe this until he saw with his own eyes. When he finally got to the field where he had put his cow, he saw her happily grazing on some of the most beautiful green grass he had ever seen. Yet he could not get to her, because the entire field was surrounded by lava that had not yet cooled!

If this is not a miracle enough, listen to what happened next: So the man went back down to Urzelina and told everyone about his cow and asked for ideas about how to get her out of the field. Nobody knew what to do, and the day of sacrifice was near. His faith doubled, and he prayed longer and more vehemently to the Holy Spirit. On the day of the killing, he woke up and found his cow outside the tent where he and his wife were sleeping!

This is what people say.

As Grace piles her duffel bags in a stack for the move up to Zoeta's, she thinks of her Blood and Piegan grandmothers packing their belongings onto wagons to go to the annual Sun Dance encampment. How ironic that she is in another culture sponsoring a religious ceremony when she has never participated in the most sacred ceremonies of her own culture. It's both ironic and a little sad. She has only heard stories about the old Sun Dances from her mother and grandmother.

Her father also speaks of the Sun Dance, but from a white doctor's perspective; he speaks of the self-mutilation, ensuing infections, and resulting deaths. When the Sun Dance was revived, Grace's mother urged Grace to go, but Grace didn't want to. By that time she had lost the idea of herself as anything but white, and besides she thinks of the revival as inauthentic. Still, she imagines that what she's embarking on now is similar to the preparations her grandmothers made for sponsoring a Sun Dance.

She wonders, *Is Tia Carmina right?* Is the Holy Spirit one more name for power lying beyond the grasp of our imagination? The powers that made the universe and continue to shape it? Powers that are simultaneously terrible and kind, like the Sun, like Allah, Jehovah, Zeus, and the countless other named deities crossing space, time, and cultures? Perhaps that was the sort of rhetoric used by the Jesuits to convert so many Blackfeet Indians to Catholicism. Grace's own grandmother, schooled by Jesuits at the boarding school, had little trouble justifying her participation in traditional Blackfeet religion, although she considered herself Catholic.

Until now, Grace hasn't given it much thought. She likes the idea that there is only one God, one Creator. If there is a creator at all, there can only be one, she reasons, and such a god would likely have different aspects called different things in different cultures. Yes, this is something she believes. Where will that get her though? She still doubts that such a creator can be prayed to, talked to, placated, or even bribed.

A COUPLE OF NIGHTS LATER, in Zoeta's living room, which had been turned into a makeshift chapel, voices of Zoeta's neighbors, cousins, and friends sweep Grace away in a monotonous off-key harmony.

> *Lord, show us mercy.*
> *Jesus Christ, show us mercy.*
> *Lord, show us mercy.*
> *Jesus Christ, hear us.*
> *Jesus Christ, attend to us.*
> *God, the Heavenly Father, show us mercy.*
> *God, the Son, Redeemer of the world, show us mercy.*
> *God, the Holy Ghost, show us mercy.*
> *Holy Trinity of God, show us mercy.*

Yes, surely we are to be pitied. Rivulets of sweat run down the sides of her face. Perhaps this is yet another dream.

Zoeta has set up an altar on a small table in front of a window in her sitting room. She has decorated it with handmade white lace, roses, ribbons, and greenery. White candles surround the crown, which sits on a pedestal. A dove graces the point of the crown, and a sword its foot. The women have cleared all furniture from the room and placed two long benches along the walls. In theory it's enough space, but many more people have shown up for Tuesday's *terço* than the previous night's. People stand wall-to-wall, like Portuguese sardines in a tin can. The density creates a powerful and off-kilter sound.

Grace attributes the good attendance at the *terços* to the spectacle of it all; Topenses eager to get a firsthand view of the weird American girl seeking redemption. The details of her promise concerning the boy—including the number of *esmolas*, the number of people invited to the *jantar*, and the name given to the cow by the Swede (assumed to be her fiancé)—are widely known and publicly commended. As people enter, they congratulate her for having the bravery to make such a bold promise. She doesn't feel brave. She feels a bit like a fraud, a fool.

> *Santa Maria, intercede for us.*
> *Holy Virgin of virgins, intercede for us.*
> *Mother of Jesus Christ, intercede for us.*
> *Mother of Divine Grace, intercede for us.*
> *Purest Mother, intercede for us.*

Just as Grace thinks she will faint, a cool breeze wafts into the room. The window remains closed, and yet the breeze comes unmistakably from the direction of the altar. The voices around her drone on, eyes fixed to the front of the room, faces expressionless. Her mouth moves effortlessly with the words, and she suddenly feels lifted and alert. Something white flashes across the window. Perhaps White Owl Woman—*Yes,* she thinks, *surely she knows that I need help.*

> *Holy Ghost. Mercy.*
> *Holy Ghost. Compassion.*
> *Holy Ghost. Grace.*
> *Immaculate Mother of God, Intercede for us.*
> *Immaculate Mother of God, Intercede for us.*

Immaculate Mother of God, Intercede for us.
O Divine Help, stay with us always. So shall it be.

When the *terço* ends, Grace hurries to the kitchen to help with the cookies and drinks for the participants. Magnus leans against the doorjamb in the kitchen. He's already helped himself to a glass of *aguardente*.

"Hey, that's only for people who sang!" Grace says. She pokes Magnus in the ribs.

"Well, believe me, it was work listening!" He smiles. "You know I could hear your singing all the way from my house? That's two kilometers! I bet the Holy Spirit heard you for sure."

"Oh, shut up. You know it isn't wise to joke about Espírito Santo—that's what *the people* say." Grace pretends to sock him in the shoulder, then turns to greet the singers, who start filing into Zoeta's kitchen.

Grace thanks them for their help and invites them back for the next night. Nearly all the singers linger for an hour afterward, drinking and talking. At some point Magnus signals his good-bye to her. She'll see him later tonight, or in the morning. By the time the singers all leave, Grace feels exhausted. Inexplicably, Zoeta and Ângela Maria move energetically between the *sala* and the kitchen as they tidy up. Grace feels like an old woman compared to them. She is stiff and sore from the little bit of work she's done.

"That was incredible!" exclaims Zoeta. She turns on the faucet to fill the sink. "I've never been to a *terço* like that in all my life, and did you see that we were visited? How marvelous!" She turns and looks at Grace with eyes full of excitement.

"Visited?" Grace asks. She was visited, but it didn't occur to her that anyone else saw or felt anything.

Ângela Maria, who's washing the table down, stops. Her eyes fill with tears. "The dove—I felt the wind of its wings—didn't you?" She starts washing the table again. "And look how many people came. A good sign for us Grace, a good sign."

Zoeta drops the little shot glasses and plates into the sink of hot water and begins washing them. "Yes, a good sign for all of us."

"I just hope I survive the week." Grace gets up and grabs a clean dish towel to dry dishes. "I'm already completely drained."

Ângela Maria comes over and rinses her rag off in the hot dishwater. "Ha! This is nothing. After you've made seventy-two loaves of bread, killed a cow, cooked twenty-four batches of sweet rice, made soup, delivered *esmolas*, taken the crown to the church, and fed the children, then you can say you're tired. But remember, you don't have to do it alone. After this is over, you'll sorely miss Senhor Espírito Santo. You'll see."

Right now, all Grace can think about is getting to bed. Tomorrow they will light the wood oven at dawn for the first day of bread baking. They'll make twenty-four loaves of bread for the soup. On Thursday, they'll make twenty-four loaves of bread for the *esmolas*. On Friday, they'll make twelve loaves of table bread to be served at the *jantar*, and twelve loaves of *biscoito* to be served with the sweet rice. More than any other day, Grace dreads Friday, for that's the day the matador will come for Alma.

27

ONE HUNDRED RED ROSES

GRACE

Fieldnotes, April 25, Espírito Santo, Topo

"A história da Rainha Santa Isabel," as told by Ângela Maria with commentary by Zoeta, transcribed and translated.

Zoeta: You know, of course, that the feast of o Divino Espírito Santo began because of a woman, don't you?

Ângela Maria: Listen up and I will tell you the story. It is my turn to tell a story. Zoeta, be quiet. She has the tape machine running—you are wasting her batteries . . . The story begins back during the reign of Dom Dinis—I think this was many centuries ago.

Zoeta: Yes, seven, to be exact.

Ângela Maria: Well, back then there was a lot of poverty in

Portugal, much more than there is today, I think. People were starving to death all over the country, especially the farmers.

Zoeta: And Dinis was the farmer king.

Ângela Maria: The royals, of course, had everything that they needed, and nobility were doing fine too, but in those days, these were only a few people. For the most part, the rich only wanted to take from the poor.

Zoeta: Take and take and take! I, frankly, don't think this has changed.

Ângela Maria: Well, the wife of Dom Dinis, Queen Isabel, felt sorry for the poor and hungry, especially the children, and so she began going out to visit them, bringing with her loaves of bread under her robes.

Zoeta: And she had marvelous robes of velvet and jewels.

Ângela Maria: Yes, and they had lots of room under them. One day, Dom Dinis's servant said to him, "O most venerable and Holy King, your wife is such a generous and kindhearted woman." The king said, "What do you mean by that?" His servant cowered at the sound of the king's voice. "Well, it's just, sir, that she has been feeding the starving children, and the people have grown a little fond of her for it."

Zoeta: Oh, they adored her. When she came out to the villages, the children would climb up on her, and she would tickle and play with them like they were her own!

Ângela Maria: Well, Dom Dinis was not a generous man. In fact, although he was a good, strong king, he was a selfish man. He did not want all of Portugal to love his wife. He instructed her to quit feeding the children at once.

Zoeta: But no, she couldn't do it.

Ângela Maria: Zoeta! This is my story. Well, it wasn't her nature to listen to her husband, so she continued to make her secret trip out into the kingdom. One day, though, she was on her way from one village to the next when she ran into Dom Dinis and his group. Dom Dinis demanded to know what she was doing outside the palace walls.

Zoeta: She was defiant!

Ângela Maria: She stood her ground and said, "I was out

enjoying the king's beautiful countryside!" Dom Dinis looked at her with suspicion. She appeared to have put on some weight, or perhaps she was with child again and had kept it a secret, as she was getting on in years for that sort of thing—if you know what I mean. He said, "Pray thee, wife, that you show me what is under your cloak." Queen Isabel responded, "Oh, husband, you know what is under my cloak—nothing that you haven't had the pleasure of seeing before!" Dom Dinis said, "Humor me, wife—you wouldn't be hiding loaves of bread for the poor, would you?" Isabel feigned an offended look. "Honestly, if I must tell you, I have picked a hundred red roses for your pleasure at the palace, but since you insist on spoiling the surprise, I will show you." Isabel at that moment put her faith in the Holy Spirit and opened her cloak. The one hundred loaves of bread had turned into one hundred of the most beautiful roses the king had ever seen.

Zoeta: I love that story! There are other stories, you know. My favorite is the one about her promise for the life of her son, Afonso.

Ângela Maria: Yes, that is a good one, but it was my turn, and I'm not finished. So, some people say this is why this festival has become so popular in the Azores, because there are so many poor people here. That used to be true, but anymore it isn't. It is getting hard to give alms these days. People get offended. Not like it used to be . . . everything changes.

Alma's eyelid closes and opens over her eye like a camera shutter. Grace wonders what this early-morning world looks like from her point of view. Thick curly black eyelashes frame her beautiful brown eyes. She grazes, completely unaware of her fate. That would be a good way to live—unaware of the future, not caring about the past.

Such a gentle soul. Grace presses her face against the cow's rounded side, breathing in her earthiness. She runs her hand along Alma's back; it feels warm from the sun. Her coat is rougher to the touch than it appears. When Tia Carmina said she would have to make a sacrifice, it didn't occur to her that she would literally make a sacrifice. From her readings on the *festas*, she knows that large quantities of beef are consumed and distributed, but the killing of the cow did not figure as prominently in the literature as one would think, or perhaps it didn't figure prominently in Grace's reading of it.

She supposes that killing one's food is a normal part of life for people here. For the big feasts on Pentecost Sunday and Trinity, as many as five or six cows could be sacrificed at one time. Thankfully, she won't witness something like that. The truth is, she likes meat—meat out of packages; Styrofoam trays with bright-red meat packed under cling wrap. She prefers to think of meat coming from well-lit ice-cold refrigerator cases. The reality of meat is something else. Perhaps she'll give it up.

"Grace." Magnus pulls her away from Alma. "It's time to take her up to Zoeta's."

Grace is suddenly filled with unexpected rage. She pushes Magnus away from her. "What the hell am I doing? This is the most idiotic thing I've ever gotten myself into. And what for?" She begins to cry. "Like killing a fucking cow is going to make a difference to the Almighty Espírito Santo, the Sun, the Creator, or whatever the hell his name is? All of this is really going to save a boy? Why didn't you keep me from doing this? I can't kill Alma. I can't go through with this whole thing." She falls limply to the ground, burying her face in her hands. Magnus sits down next to her, wraps her up in his arms. She keeps crying. He kisses the side of her head and squeezes her tight.

"You know, Grace, sometimes you have to do the right thing," Magnus says quietly as he rocks her back and forth in his arms. "We all have to give up something sometime for the good of others. What I learned from my father's death is that sometimes what we do for the good of others is really for our own good. I know it sounds saccharine, and I'm not that kind of guy. I didn't keep you from doing this, because I think you have to do it, like I have to leave; it's an obligation." Magnus stops rocking her.

As Grace listens to Magnus, her forehead rests on her knees. She studies the earth beneath her. Alma has eaten the grass down to its roots. How has it come about that she owes so much? She could part with the money, and even the research, but being forced to voluntarily kill a living thing . . . this is parting with her*self.* She wasn't forced . . . This is her promise . . . Magnus is right. She owes it to Ângela Maria, Zoeta, Tia Carmina, Elisabete, the people of Topo who have been coming to the *terços* each night. She even owes it in some strange way to Nonna Preta, whose magic has proven futile against other forces at work. She needs to show them she believes in them, that she cares deeply enough about them to give up something meaningful. Perhaps giving up *herself* is enough. She suddenly stands up and takes Alma's lead rope in her hand. "Let's go."

Magnus rises too, dusts off his pants. "That was much quicker than I thought it would be." He looks pleased with himself.

"Well, don't feel too proud of yourself yet. We have a long way to go," Grace says as she pulls Alma to get her moving. She looks over at Magnus and smiles. "Thanks." She gives him a quick little kiss on his cheek.

THE CURRENCY of Grace's trade is gossip—give a little, get a little, sometimes get a lot. On the one hand, as with other precious resources, she has to be careful about spending it wastefully, for the judicious use of gossip can yield critical nuggets of information. Too much gossip, on the other hand, is likely to land her in trouble. Her interest in gossip is not specific, but general. After all, most of the time, she doesn't know the people who are being gossiped about. To her, acts of gossip are simply stories she receives in exchange for the tidbits she offers; they bear the unwritten code of a culture.

Here in Zoeta's kitchen, surrounded by eight loquacious women, Grace finds herself an exceedingly wealthy woman. The kitchen is a constant buzz with stories about—and judgments upon —who married whom, whose husband is cheating, how much this returned Azorean-American emigrant or that one spent on the *gasto* in Ribeira Seca or Norte Pequeno last year, and other such seemingly trivial matters. So many stories are traded simultaneously that Grace manages only to take notes on a few. She feels the moment ripening. She has been dying to find out what people think about Senhor Estêvão, the death of Norinha, and the recent events of her exhumation. Surely, everyone has heard. Surely, they all have an opinion or thought about it. But they have steered so obviously clear of any "dangerous" topics, at least in Grace's presence. Her heart pounds as she thinks about how to drop her tidbit into the ongoing banter, but she can't find a comfortable opening. The conversation is too lighthearted now. She'll wait.

Zoeta has placed the twelfth loaf of *massa sovada* for its second rising on the remaining *roca da velha* leaves. Standing arms akimbo, blue eyes bright and cheerful, she announces, "There! We are making progress. Elisabete—you get to set off the next firecracker when this batch goes into the oven. It is time for us women to eat." She turns to Grace. "You are going to need your strength for the *matança da vaca* this afternoon." She pats Grace on the shoulder and laughs heartily. "I hear you are a bit of a soft one. You know, you don't have to be there, but it might be interesting to you—men's work."

"I have to be there," Grace says firmly. She wants to be there with Magnus, and with Alma.

Ângela Maria and several of the neighbor women are helping scurry around to get lunch set up on the big table in the center of the room. Grace, as usual, feels useless and in the way. Today's lunch consists of bread, cheese, homemade *linguiça*, and *molho do fígado*—all things that Grace likes. Feeling guilty about being the first to sit, Grace says, "Zoeta, you sit down first! You have been working since before dawn without a break."

Ângela Maria brushes past Grace to put glasses on the table.

"Don't worry about her. She's used to hard work—been doing this since she was a girl! How do you think she became a *mestra*?"

"I don't know. How did she?" Grace asks. She has heard the other women referring to Zoeta as *mestra* all week long, but she failed to recognize it as an official status. Grace assumed Zoeta was the boss because this is her kitchen.

Ângela Maria pushes Zoeta toward the table. "Sit down, *mestra*, and tell us your tale." All of the other women quiet down. Everyone sits down and waits for Zoeta to begin talking. Elisabete sits on one side of Grace, and Ângela Maria on the other.

Zoeta sits directly across from them, flanked by her neighbor friends. She busily serves up food as she begins her story. "Well, you all know this story, of course, so I tell it now for the ears of our American friend—so you all won't mind a few embellishments?"

Everyone laughs.

She begins, "My mother and father were extraordinarily poor."

"Yes, yes, very poor," several women agree, as if to convince Grace of the truth.

"We lived in the Portinho, between Calheta proper and Fajã Grande, in a little stone house that isn't there anymore—near the old bakery. My father was a good man and a hard worker. Over the years he worked at gardening for many of the old noble-descended families. You should have seen him in the garden. He could make anything grow. If it weren't for his love of wine, we would have been much better off." Zoeta takes a bite of bread and pauses in her storytelling to swallow it.

"Because we were so poor, I used to go to the bakery at the end of the day. The baker's wife gave me old bread. One day, she asked me if I was interested in learning to make bread. I must have been about seven then. I said yes, and so she instructed me to show up at three in the morning the next day. I knew this wouldn't be a problem. My mother, who was sickly, would be asleep, and my father would be unconscious, so I sneaked over to the bakery every morning and learned to make bread. In exchange for making bread, I received a fresh loaf each day."

"Didn't your parents ever wonder where the bread came from?" Grace asks.

"Oh, my mother was ashamed. She figured I had begged for it, and so she never asked. I never told her, because she would have felt even worse knowing that I had been forced to work so hard at such a young age. She would have blamed herself. My father, well, he never ate that I knew of, and he scarcely knew I existed. When I was nine, my mother died, and I went to live with my godmother's family—the Sousas."

Grace couldn't help herself. She burst with curiosity. "Wasn't that Nor—"

"Yes, the very family. Norinha was a year younger than I. Her parents were wonderful and generous people. They welcomed me into their home, not exactly as their own but still generously enough given that they didn't have to."

Ângela Maria interjects, "Well, as your godmother, she had certain obligations."

"Of course. Anyway, Norinha and I started out being best friends, but her ways were different from mine, and over the years we grew further and further apart. She didn't have the kind spirit that her mother had. She was jealous of the attention her parents paid to me. She constantly tried to get me in trouble, and she worked hard at ruining my reputation through her evil gossiping ways. In the end, she and her parents treated me as little more than a servant. I made the bread for the household each day and did the laundry and cleaned. In exchange, I had a nice room and good food to eat. Other than that, I steered clear of Norinha."

Zoeta takes a sip of wine, leaving a purplish stain on her lips. "When I came of age, Norinha's mother showed me my "freedom" papers. It turns out that my parents were not completely destitute; they had this house up here in Topo, and by law it belonged to me. They moved into the shack in the Portinho because of my mother's health problems. After her death my father lived here. He died when I was twelve, but I didn't know that the house was mine. So the same day Senhora Sousa gave me the papers, I packed up and moved here. I walked almost the whole way, save the last two or three kilometers that I rode on an ox cart. That is when I began my work as a *mestra*. People knew that I was a good person and a good baker, and so I started out helping at the feasts. Pretty soon, people would ask me to come help them. They paid me."

The only sounds to be heard are the clinking of knives and forks on the plates. Finally, one of Zoeta's neighbors, a woman named Ana Maria, breaks the silence. "I've been wanting to tell you how sorry I am about that Norinha . . . God protect her soul." She crosses herself.

Zoeta doesn't seem the least bit upset. "Don't worry about me! I'm not the one they dug up, and there was no love lost between us. Still, I don't suppose she deserved to be murdered, if that is what happened . . . You know, I saw the strangest thing not long ago—been on my mind a lot these past few days. That husband of hers, I saw him here in Topo the week she died. He was talking to Nonna Preta's daughter-in-law—the boy's mother." Zoeta looks over at Grace and Ângela Maria as if maybe they know what it means.

Grace doesn't have a clue. If Senhor Estêvão knew these people, he never gave her a hint of it. Grace looks at Ângela Maria, who has an equally perplexed look on her face.

Zoeta soaks up the liver sauce on her plate with a piece of bread. "Hmm . . . well, there have long been rumors up here in Topo about him . . ."

It's like Zoeta is on some kind of bombing run, waiting to drop her gossip on them like a carefully aimed bomb. Grace can barely stand the anticipation.

"If the rumors that I've heard are true," Zoeta says, "we will all know about it soon enough. São Jorge is not a good place for keeping secrets." She stands up with her plate and looks out the window. "Grace, looks like that matador and his helpers are here, and it's also time for the *massa sovada* to go in the oven. Elisabete, send up a *foguete!*"

Grace looks out the window to see that one of the helpers is Miguel.

28

LEAP OF FAITH

GRACE

THE OLD MAN strokes Alma with one hand and holds the *xopa* with his other. "This is a skinny little runt of a cow, eh?" He smiles raggedly at Grace.

Grace feels embarrassed. Magnus told her just this morning that Alma is a fine-looking cow that anyone would be proud of. "Yeah, I guess so; she's not too big," Grace says, for lack of something else to say. She doesn't know anything about how big they're supposed to be.

One of the other men who came with the matador chimes in, "She looks old!"

Magnus, sounding a little defensive, says, "Hey, she's three!" He laughs.

Miguel says, "Well, you know, maybe Americans eat cows like this." He smiles warmly at Grace for the first time ever.

Bad enough that they are going to kill her, but do they have to insult her too? Magnus moves over by Grace's side. He slides his hand discreetly into hers and squeezes it. He whispers in her ear, "They're pulling your chain."

Alma stands calmly as the matador walks around, feeling up and down her body. More of a mating dance than a prelude to murder. His back facing Grace, the matador appears to embrace her. He steps away from her and she falls silently to the ground with a great thud. The other two men jump back. Grace hears Alma's last breath, as she heard her grandmother's. All is quiet until the matador sends up a shooting firecracker, breaking the deadly silence with a huge crack. To Grace, he says, "That's to let everyone know that we are having a party and that the killing is done." He smiles broadly, eyes bright.

Miguel places his foot on Alma's belly, rhythmically pushing up and down, while the other helper catches blood from a hole in her neck. The matador sharpens knives on a stone. "Most important thing now is to have sharp knives," he says. "You better write this down in your notebook." He nods toward her notebook perched atop a large black rock.

Just as Grace sits down with her notebook, Ana Maria comes over with a big bottle of *angelica* and a shot glass. She offers it to Grace first. "No, no, let these guys drink first—they're doing all the work!" Grace says.

The bottle and the glass pass between the men who encircle the dead cow. Grace takes a few pictures of them. Funny, now that Alma is dead, Grace doesn't feel so bad. The anticipation of her death was so much worse than the reality of it. If only all deaths could be so quick, and so celebrated.

Grace lets her camera dangle as she reaches for the bottle and glass that the matador brings toward her.

"Come, come, you must drink. By tradition we must finish this whole bottle before we're done here." He pours the sweet wine into the cup and places it in her hand.

Magnus, Miguel, and the other helper cheer her on.

The cup is completely covered in bloody fingerprints from the matador's hands. A wave of nausea sweeps over her, but she manages to hold out. Closing her eyes, she swallows the whole glass of *angelica* in one gulp. Good. Its warmth spreads down her throat and across her chest. She forgets about the blood.

The men work quickly, and before long have completely skinned the cow; no longer Alma, but a butchered cow. Each step of the way, the men stop, pass the bottle around, and Grace begins to feel drunk. Perhaps she should stop drinking. In the meantime, Ana Maria runs back and forth between the killing party and the house. With each trip, she takes something from the cow: the feet, the liver, the stomach.

Grace, numb from the alcohol, scarcely notices when they pull the seven-month-old fetus from Alma's belly. She flinches. Magnus runs over to her to see if she is okay. She's fine, ready to pass out, only mildly perturbed at the sight of the tiny, perfect little cow with transparent skin.

The matador jubilantly holds it up. "A sign of good luck!"

Uneasy, Gracy asks, "Will we be eating it?"

"No, but it is good for old people to eat—easy to chew!" he says. Miguel and the other men laugh heartily as if the matador has said something extremely funny. Sometimes Azorean humor goes over her head.

Grace returns to the house before the men have finished the bottle. At the kitchen sink, Ana Maria is doing something with the liver. She has bright-red blood running up her arms to above her elbows. When she sees Grace staring, she holds her arms in front of Grace's face and says, "You know what they say about women here in São Jorge, don't you?" The other women look on in amusement.

"No, I don't know," Grace says. She's tired. Tired of death.

"Women *love* blood." Everyone laughs, except Grace.

MAGNUS

DURING THE SACRIFICE, Magnus watched as Miguel pumped blood from the cow and had little difficulty imagining his brother in that role, or perhaps even himself under different circumstances. He no longer hates cows, but he remains a staunch atheist. The order in the Universe is of man's making through Science. Nothing can change that. Still, he admires Grace for her sincere efforts at understanding the beliefs and religious practices of Azoreans, people with whom she must have nothing, absolutely nothing in common. Magnus understands them better than she ever will, having himself grown up in a dairy land. He grew up Protestant, and that in itself made some difference, but fundamentally, his people and these people are the same—cattle people and fishermen.

As he observed Grace sitting on the large volcanic rock, writing prolifically in her notebook, he felt more attracted to her than ever. A lump formed in his throat. He'll leave in a month, and then what? Will he ever see her again? He asked her if she would consider moving to Sweden. She was noncommittal, saying she would visit for sure, but not until her dissertation is complete . . . He'd expected that answer. *Time will tell,* he thinks.

He feels proud of how she's handled the slaughter of the cow. She showed more fortitude than he expected, given her state prior to bringing Alma to slaughter. She even withstood the teasing of Miguel and the others like a real sport, and at every turn, they tested her ability to tolerate the gore. Although cutting open the stomach was unnecessary, he could see that Grace had a genuine scientific interest in seeing its compacted bright-green contents. She even commented on the strange beauty of it. He most worried about the fetus. That seemed a bit cruel; it even bothered him.

GRACE

ON SATURDAY MORNING, Grace pushes and pulls a large wooden spoon through huge vats of rice pudding cooking over an open fire. Her arms ache, and her sweater, infused with smoke and sweat, reeks.

Zoeta inspects the pots. "Ten more minutes," she says, and hurries down to the *loja*, where Magnus, Miguel, the matador, and his other helper are working at butchering.

Grace doesn't know if she can last ten more minutes. Just then, Ana, Ângela Maria's daughter, comes up, takes the spoon from her. "I can do this. You look like you need a rest."

"Thanks," says Grace. "Ten more minutes." She stands back and watches Ana stir the pot expertly.

"This is usually my job," Ana says. "You know Zoeta does this full-time during Espírito Santo, and sometimes I help her for extra money." Ana switches over to the other pot.

"A lot harder than I thought it would be," Grace says. "I really had no idea what all was involved with one of these things when I volunteered."

"Yes, but when it's over, we will all miss Senhor Espírito Santo, and it will have been worth it, no?" Ana says, smiling big.

Everyone says that, but Grace isn't sure what it means. Has she missed something? Other than an enigmatic flutter at the window during the *terço* on the second night, she hasn't noticed *His* presence. "Here, I can do it again. I want to do it." Grace takes the spoon back.

Ana hovers. "Senhora Graça," she says. "Would it be okay with you if Mário and I distribute the *esmolas*? My dad will drive."

Ana has never called Grace senhora before. Suddenly Grace feels old, like one of the "kitchen ladies." *Respect.* Ana has demonstrated respect for Grace, genuine respect. "Of course! I hope I can go along too!" Grace assumed she would have to do it herself.

Ana bounces up and down with joy. "Of course, senhora! They are your *esmolas*! I'll go tell Mário now."

As Ana runs off, Grace feels happy.

LATER THAT DAY, when the sun begins to descend, its light elongates shadows and intensifies the green of the fields. They wait for the padre to show up to bless the *esmolas*. It's getting late.

Miguel approaches Grace. "He probably doesn't want to bless these, because you aren't Catholic." He sounds a bit sad.

Zoeta overhears and says, "Nonsense. He doesn't like to bless *esmolas* period." She puts her arm around Grace's shoulder. "All that matters is that Espírito Santo is here; we don't need a padre to tell us this is a blessed event." She squeezes before letting go.

A few others chime in with their opinions, and then they collectively decide that the time has come. Best to go before dark. Grace climbs into the cab of the pickup with Miguel and Ângela Maria. The kids pile in behind in the bed, carefully situating themselves among the baskets loaded with twenty-four loaves of bread, forty-eight kilos of meat, and twenty-four liters of wine.

Zoeta has provided them with the list of people who will receive alms—all people in need, including the family of the dying boy. She suggested that Grace remain in the truck as the kids deliver the *esmolas*. *Sometimes* a gente *are embarrassed to see the person who is giving them alms; they appreciate them, but they are ashamed sometimes.* Grace understands. She's seen the same phenomenon on the reservation.

The deliveries go more quickly than Grace expects. Each time they pull up in front of a house, Grace watches as the kids bounce up to the door. The receivers thank the children and disappear into their houses. Not much fanfare. At a couple of houses the people give the children money. The first time this happens, Ângela Maria turns to Grace and says, "You don't think Ana and Mário volunteered for the job out of the pure goodness of their hearts, do you?" She winks.

Nonna Preta's house is last, perhaps by design, perhaps not. By then, the light has grown so dim that the landscape has lost all color. The small house, scarcely more than a shed constructed of loosely piled stones, stands alone in an overgrown fallow field. Grace sees a woman dressed in black sitting on a chair in front. A younger woman hangs clothes on a line, and the girl, whom Grace remembers from the boat, sits on the ground playing with dirt. What a sad scene. She prepared herself for the wicked witch of the east, instead finding an old woman in *luto* struggling to survive. Miguel stops and the kids bound out. The girl and her mother greet them. The old woman remains fixed, staring toward the truck.

Grace feels Nonna Preta's eyes on her but isn't afraid; she feels more pity than fear. She watches as the younger woman takes the meat, bread, and wine. She looks unhappy; she also looks grateful. What choice does she have but to take it? What do they make of this gesture? What do they think of her promise? It has come about for them, and by them. Ana and Mário run back, hop in, and knock on the window to signal their readiness to go home. Grace is ready too.

THE NEXT MORNING, girls in white dresses flit and dance around outside the *sala*, drawn to the presence of the *coroa do Espírito Santo*. Perhaps they hope one day to wear the crown themselves, serving in the capacity of festival queen. Grace closes the curtains to dress. In spite of the cold wind and drizzle, the air burgeons with happy expectation, the expectation of festivities that will last through the afternoon and follow people into the days, weeks, and months to come.

Grace, however, feels an eerie sadness; an inexplicable sense of loss. She slips into the skirt and shirt that Ângela Maria has provided. She runs her hands across the lightweight wool gabardine, smoothing the fitted skirt over her thighs. Not exactly her style, but Ângela Maria insisted on something conservative. It isn't every day that a single American woman, or any woman, for that matter, would have the honor of serving as *mordomo*. Yes, unusual, an event that Zoeta and Ângela Maria say will loom large in the memories of the people of São Jorge.

Grace joins the procession gathering out in front of Zoeta's house. Mário unfurls the large burgundy flag of Espírito Santo, and Grace does the honors of carrying the crown in the procession. The children, taking twelve red rods, one for each apostle, form three squares, one for each aspect of God, and fall into file, beginning their more than two kilometer journey to Nossa Senhora do Rosário where the mass will take place.

As it turns out, Padre João officiates that morning. Although it's nearly impossible, he manages to never once make eye contact with Grace until after the coronation is over, at which point he says to her as she leaves, "I hope you are not making a mockery of us."

To which she replies, "Absolutely not." She wonders, *Is he concerned with anything but appearances?* Obviously not. The covered bald spot, toeing the company line, his worries about what she will ultimately write point to his fears about representation, how she will represent him, represent *his* people. They are *his* people.

She has heard the usual stories about the padre, the age-old stories told by godforsaken parishioners—stories involving young women, young boys, and illegitimate children—but she puts little stock in these. The padre has *something* to hide, but what? Why did he feel compelled to tell her about visiting Nonna Preta's family? There must have been a reason. What did he say about it? He said he didn't know that they had called him there for that reason, because of *olhado*. Suddenly Grace realizes that the priest was not called there at all. He went there of his own accord; he had business with them.

THE DRIZZLE HAS TURNED to rain, hard pelting rain that stings Grace's face. As she heads back to Zoeta's after the procession, she feels disoriented. Everything comes down to this one day. Earlier, when the procession left the house, Grace saw a crowd of onlookers, faces from her saga: Elisabete, Tia Carmina, Magnus, the matador, Zoeta, Ângela Maria, Miguel, Ana, Mário, and others. She finally understands the term *liminal*; she has stepped over a threshold. Her transformation is almost complete.

What, if anything, will Tia Carmina have to say? Has it been enough? Did she do it in faith? Ironic, given her name, that she should spend her life searching for faith. Perhaps if her parents had consulted a proper medicine man on her white name, they would have named her more aptly.

The downpour forces everyone to cram into the house. Hungry, people anxiously await the arrival of food. The *sala*, the kitchen, and the *loja* have all been transformed into dining areas furnished with long banquet tables. The women rush around frantically making last-minute preparations. Dishes and table linens appear on the tables as if from thin air. People crowd into the rooms and find their way to seats.

Grace looks in on the room where the children are being seated. To her surprise, Zulmira helps a young girl to her seat, the girl from the boat, Nonna Preta's granddaughter. Zulmira, as if feeling Grace's eyes upon her, looks up. "This is my goddaughter, Rosa, Rosa Maria," she says, putting her hand on the little girl's head. The girl smiles at Grace with the same sweet smile she had on the cargo boat.

As Grace leaves the room, she muses over her new knowledge: Zulmira is related spiritually to Nonna Preta's family; she was complicit in acquiring her blood out of obligation to the family.

Only the dictates of culture, the unwritten code, are powerful enough to make people act in the ways they do, to feel obligation where none by nature exists.

In the next room, Grace admires plates of bright-yellow rice pudding with their *inhames* leaf patterns sprinkled in cinnamon on top. She goes to retrieve her camera to take a picture of them. Turning into the room where her belongings are stored, she comes face-to-face with Tia Carmina, who sits on the bed as if waiting for her.

"Well, Runs-with-the-Moon, you have done an admirable job with your promise," Tia Carmina says. Of course, she *would* know her Blackfeet name. She should know too that only certain people are allowed to use it. Perhaps she knows that she is one of them.

Grace, embarrassed, says, "I can't take credit for even half of this, even a quarter of it. I feel ashamed of how little I have done." She looks at the floor until Tia Carmina's voice commands her attention.

"Let me ask you this, then: Would Senhor Espírito Santo be here now . . . in this house . . . in this *vila* . . . if it weren't for you?" Tia Carmina rests both of her hands on top of her driftwood cane. Her bushy eyebrows lift up as she asks the question.

Grace takes a deep breath. "I don't know. Is *He* here?" She goes over to her duffel bag and pulls out her camera.

"Have you not felt Him? Have you not felt something? Love? The spirit of giving?" She looks intently at Grace. Standing, she places a gnarled hand on Grace's shoulder. "You didn't bring Him by yourself; it's a collective sort of thing. You gave enough. You *believed* enough. That's *all* there is." She reaches for Grace's hand and squeezes it. "Don't forget to take a picture of the rice pudding; it's perfect." She walks past Grace and out of the room.

Grace feels something, but it doesn't feel complete somehow; she expected more bang for her buck. She thought she would have some sort of ah-ha moment. Has she taken the leap, the feared leap of faith, without even being aware?

After she takes her photos, she joins the main table. She sits at the head. Everyone quiets as Zoeta begins to tell yet another story.

Grace can't bear to listen; she's had enough stories to last a lifetime.

Studying her bowl of Holy Ghost soup, she watches as the dry bread absorbs the broth. *Mushy* best describes the result. She looks toward the end of the table where Magnus sits, apparently having the time of his life. He and Miguel laugh themselves to tears. She sips the broth. Mint. Senhor Estêvão said the *sopas do Espírito Santo* in Topo were the best on the island due to the mint. Mint, he claimed, is good for the digestion and medically proven beneficial. Grace knows that mint is also invasive. Deceptively powerful. She still can feel the place on her shoulder where Tia Carmina squeezed it. For an old woman she has remarkably strong hands. Talons.

ORDINARY TIME

THE REST OF THE TIME

29

FLIES OF SUMMER

On the Monday following the *jantar*, police finally receive the results of forensic testing from the crime lab in Lisbon, the captain and three other officers go swiftly to arrest Senhor Estêvão for the murder of Norinha Maria Sousa, but they are too late—too late by several days. His partially decomposed body dangles stiffly from one of the rafters in his study, in his right hand a crucifix, and in his left a rosary. He had to leave. No amount of prayer could have saved him then or now.

Below him, on a small round table, lie two sealed envelopes: one addressed to a Senhora Lélia Maria Soares Carvalho in Topo and the other to *"O meu filho"* in care of the same woman. The captain carefully opens each of the envelopes and reads aloud to the three other officers.

> *To My Dearest Son:*
>
> *I do not know if you have survived, but if you are reading this, I am in all likelihood dead, and you, in all likelihood, are alive. Good. Stay that way (for your mother's sake). A mother needs her son.*
>
> *You never knew me, which is just as well. I haven't lived a good or honest life. I want you to know I am (I was) not a purely bad or evil man. I am (I was) a man, a man with certain needs, a man who wanted*

too many things, too many things that were not mine to have (including your mother). I hope, my son, that you will be a better man than I ever was. Always remember this: A maldade está nos olhos de cada um. You must guard yourself from the jealous eyes of others, and keep your eyes on your own path always. Do not look at the property of other men, be it money, women, livestock, or children, with eyes of covetousness.

That said, I am writing you this letter now because you should know who you really are—from whom you descend. You should also know that you are the rightful and sole heir of monies and property that I have never been able to claim due to the clandestine life I have chosen to live. I leave the responsibility of the telling of my story, my real story, to my mother, your grandmother, when you are of an appropriate age. Please know that your life has brought me the only pure joy that I have ever known in my adult life.

One more thing, always drink your peppermint tea—it is good for your digestion and will certainly bring you wealth and prosperity; it is tenacious.

Your father in shame,
Afonso Germano Duarte Soares Carvalho

The officers look at each other. "Well, not much need to investigate this one any further," the captain says. He picks up the second letter and reads it aloud.

To My Dearest Mother:

Please forgive me. I know I have been nothing but a disappointment since the day of my imprisonment those many long years ago. I hope you will believe me when I tell you that you have always been my greatest love. I never blamed you and Father for distancing yourselves as you did. As I leave this life, I am only ashamed at how poorly I have provided for you and my son. I did my best, given the circumstances of my unfortunate marriage. When I brought you here to the Azores after Father died, I never imagined how terrible a life it would be for you among these people who were all too willing to believe the gossip about you being a witch. I should have known better than to bring you here. I imagined that having your son near you would be enough to compensate for the isolation. Now I know that I made a mistake. I should have remained lost to you. You were better off with me dead the first time.

I have put all of my papers and accounts in order, as you might expect of an accountant. The documents you need to claim our rightful inheritance can be found in the office at the store in the top drawer of the filing cabinet. I have always thought it a mean turn that Father didn't leave it all in your name, but I suppose in his mind he had a son. Padre João has a key to the store and will assist you. He will not be making his monthly trips to visit you on my behalf now that I am gone.

You are the designated executor of my estate, and I trust that you will take care of yourself, my son, and the others. Under the circumstances, I am uncertain of the disposition of Norinha's significant holdings. She had no heirs besides Estêvão Afonso, but by the time you read this, the world will know my identity and that a man by that name never existed.

Please tell my son the stories of my life, the good stories that you have from memories of me as a young boy and man growing up in Angola. I don't want him to be ashamed of his father. Although I did not marry his mother, he should know that I cared for her as much as I was able to care about any woman.

Finally, I am grateful to you for your assistance in the matter with the American girl. The day she stepped off o barco Espírito Santo, I knew she would bring trouble to this little island, but I never imagined that she would bring so much heartache to me personally. Norinha's penchant for gossip served us both poorly and well; she knew more than I thought she did and was better at spreading the word than I ever imagined. God willing, the white witch's handiwork is as good as the people of São Jorge say.

Your faithful son,
Afonso Germano

Later that day, a crowd gathers outside Sr. Estêvão's house to watch in stone-faced silence as officials remove Senhor Estêvão's body in a plain box, taking it to the unconsecrated part of the cemetery reserved for people who have committed the unpardonable sin of suicide. Within a matter of days, the truth of Senhor

Estêvão's identity and the contents of his suicide notes will become common knowledge, the talk of the island.

ÂNGELA MARIA

A COUPLE of weeks have passed, and already Ângela Maria misses o Espírito Santo. She pushes a needle through the thick waistband of Miguel's pants; he's getting paunchy, and she has to move the button over an inch. She knows for certain that Jaime is at peace in the kingdom of heaven. She's been released from the torture of the guilt she has felt nonstop since his death. Thanks to Zoeta, her sin has finally been forgiven; she is finally able to forgive herself. She misses the Holy Spirit, but she knows she will see Him again in the years to come. Mostly she will miss the intensity of purpose she shared with Zoeta, Grace, Elisabete, and the other women with whom she spent that magical week in Topo.

It's a shame that Grace has to leave early, that her research should end like this, when the festival season only now has begun in earnest. Ângela Maria always looks forward to the arrival of the "flies of summer," the swarms of returned Azorean emigrants from Canada and the United States who arrive in their homeland just when the housefly larvae hatch. Some come to fulfill *out-of-epoch* promises to Espírito Santo, some to Senhor Santo Cristo, others to drink and eat themselves into oblivion at the *churrascarias* and *tascas* at the *festas*.

News of Senhor Estêvão's suicide shocked her, but perhaps not nearly as much as the revelations of Afonso Germano's letters to his son and mother. She marvels that his secrets were so well kept for so long. Like others in Calheta, she prays for his soul, but she suspects it will do little good. No doubt, he will suffer eternally for his covetous and sinful ways.

Ângela Maria holds the pants up to regard her work. There,

that looks good. She lays the pants over the back of the chair and puts her thimble carefully into its special box.

"Miguel, your pants are done!" she calls.

Miguel appears through the door leading from the hallway, wearing his underwear. "Good." He takes the pants from Ângela Maria. "And thanks."

Ângela Maria flushes. "Oh, it's nothing." Until lately, Miguel seldom thanked her for anything, but he has been nicer to her in recent weeks—since the *jantar*. They even made love once, something they haven't done since before Jaime's death. Things *are* different now.

He places his hand on the side of her face and kisses her gently on the forehead. "Just the same, I thank you. Thank you for everything."

Ângela Maria watches him put his pants on. Even Miguel expressed sadness that Grace and Magnus would be leaving soon. Watching Miguel and Magnus become friends has been a pleasure. Friendship doesn't come as readily to men as it does to women. Magnus's and Miguel's awkward conversations amuse her. The two of them spend hours talking about nothing more personal than boats. Miguel plans to buy Magnus's motor boat. He says that it will come in as a handy addition to his fishing boat, but Ângela Maria suspects more sentimental motives.

In the meantime, Magnus and Miguel spend much time in it, fishing and snorkeling. Grace and she went out with them once. Magnus took them on a geophysical tour of São Jorge. Yesterday the two of them brought in a fine haul of baby octopus. Miguel taught Magnus the art of spear fishing.

Miguel tucks his shirt in. "That's much better," he says. "You know, Ângelinha, I've been thinking . . . I know we can't get Magnus to stay, but maybe we can get Grace to. What's one more mouth to feed for four months? And if she were gone, we wouldn't be making any money on the *loja* anyway."

Ângela Maria jumps up and down with joy. "I was hoping you would come to that conclusion! Thank you, Miguel. You are a good man."

MAGNUS

MAGNUS PEEKS through the window of Café da Ilha from outside on the sidewalk before entering. Today is the day he leaves. He spent yesterday in Velas tying up loose ends, and last night at the hostel so he'd be close to the airport for a late-morning flight. He wanted Grace to join him, but she declined. She says she's trying to distance herself from him to preempt a broken heart. She promises she'll meet him in the morning and take him to the airport.

To his relief, Grace is seated at what has become *their* table. Does she feel as much a sense of loss as he does? They haven't talked a lot about his departure, other than those unavoidable times when Miguel and Ângela Maria were making plans for all of them. Then, they glossed over the subject as if it weren't imminent. The month and a half since the *jantar* passed too quickly.

He pushes the door open. Grace looks over at him. *I love her.* As he approaches her for what could be the last time, he knows that she *is* the one. What else could explain the changes that have taken place in him? Suddenly emotional causes take precedence over rational ones. She has changed him.

"Hey!" Grace says cheerfully as she stands up to exchange perfunctory kisses with him.

Magnus holds on to her shoulders a little longer than is customary. "I didn't know whether you would be here." He can't read her face. Probably good; it means she's trying to hide her feelings, which means she *has* feelings. *Does she love me?* He's just doubting himself, making excuses for not doing what he's intending to do.

"I never miss a going away party." She sits back down. "You know how some people hate good-byes? I'm not like that. The way I look at it, if you don't say good-bye, then it is harder to say hello later, and we *will* see each other again. I know we will." She's holding his right hand across the table.

Grace looks at him with soft eyes. He takes a deep breath. "Grace," he says as he reaches out and takes her left hand, "I know this will seem like a rather strange question to ask as I leave, but . . ." His heart pounds. "Will you marry me?"

GRACE

GRACE'S HEART leaps into her throat. "Oh, Magnus, I wasn't expecting this." She stalls, fishing for words. She doesn't want to say no. "I really need to think about it." *Damn it.* Why couldn't she have thought of something better to say? "It's complicated." He blindsided her.

Magnus's face falls. He lets go of her hands. Looking hurt and embarrassed, he says, "Well, I should have known better than to have done that." He forces a smile.

Grace reaches out to him, tries to smooth things over. "Believe me, I want to be with you, and I do love you." She looks at him directly. "I fantasize about spending my life with you every day, but I can't give up everything to follow you to Sweden. That's not the right thing for me now."

Magnus nods. "Well, I had to try. I just don't know how I am going to survive without you."

"You won't be without me! I will visit you, and you will visit me. We can talk every day if you like. There are tons of direct flights between New York and Sweden," Grace says. "Everything will work out the way it is intended—"

"You're probably right. Ironic that I am being so irrational about this," Magnus says.

"Love is not irrational," Grace says. "But, maybe rushing into marriage is."

"On that note," Magnus looks pointedly at his watch, "we had better get going."

Grace helps Magnus collect his belongings, and takes him to the airport. They make light conversation along the way.

At the airport they kiss and hug for a long time. Grace doesn't want him to leave, not because she can't live without him, but rather, because she loves being with him.

Tears run down her face as she watches the SATA flight to Terceira take off. She *does* love him, but having him ask her to marry him is the last thing she expected or wants. *What was he thinking?*

She'll soon be back in New York working on her dissertation for who knows how long. Having a fiancé in Lund does not seem like a recipe for a successful relationship, she knows from experience. She's thought this all through before. No matter how she looks at it, a relationship with Magnus, at least of the sort he proposes, is out of the question for the near future. She hopes that they will stay in touch, even visit each other, and perhaps one day, under the right circumstances, find a life together.

30

OF MOTHERS AND SONS

GRACE

THE SUMMER, half over, passes before Grace's eyes. She looks at her face in the mirror and, for the first time, notices nascent wrinkles; she looks older. Maybe this place does that to people. Her skin is getting darker, and her blond streaks are becoming brighter from the constant sun of summer. Thanks to her ancestry, she doesn't burn. She owes a lot to it, her ancestry, like her high flat cheekbones, and the epicanthic fold that gives her icy-blue eyes an exotic appeal. She blinks. How did she so successfully hide it from herself for so long? Why has her history suddenly emerged on the wings of butterflies here in a foreign land? She washes her face.

A horn honks outside. Grace hurriedly throws her things into her bag and heads out the door. Before rounding the corner of the house, she smells the car's familiar exhaust. The white Opal awaits. Today Zulmira has planned a special outing for her. Since the *jantar*, they have seen each other several times, but they never speak of what happened, about the bogus blood test or about Zulmira's collusion with the police officer (who turned out to be her boyfriend). Grace opens the passenger-side door and slides into the seat.

"Good morning!" Zulmira's smile spreads across her face.

"What are you so happy about?" Grace twists to throw her stuff in the back seat. "And where are you taking me?"

"We're going to visit someone special."

"I was afraid of that." Grace stares out the passenger window so Zulmira won't see her anxiety. She wants to meet Senhora Lélia Maria Soares Carvalho more than anything. She wants to hear her story, to know how she came to be seen as a witch, and to learn more about her son, Afonso Germano. She wants to meet her grandson, the boy for whom Grace sacrificed so little and gained so much. Still, the thought of it fills her with inexplicable fear.

"Don't worry," Zulmira says, as if Grace has spoken her thoughts aloud. "She's a very nice woman. She's an *educated* and *cultured* woman. You'll see." She reaches over and pats Grace's shoulder. "She isn't a witch. She never harbored anything but good wishes for you. She played along with all of this for her son and grandson's sake, nothing more."

The countryside passes silently. They descend into Urzelina, still one of Grace's favorite spots on the island. Zulmira turns down a paved palm-lined lane, passing through heavy iron gates. Beyond the palms, rows and rows of citrus trees—orange, tangerine, lemon, and lime—grow out of rich black soil. The warm air is laden with the scent of blossoms. The sweetness of Azorean summer washes over Grace as they pull into the formal driveway in front of a magnificent house. Finally, she will have her chance to get a glimpse into one of these magnificent monuments. When Ângela Maria had said these homes were *full of woe, unhappiness, death, and even murder,* she was right—at least, this house has such a tale to tell.

Zulmira leads the way through the heavy wooden front door, calling, "Tia! Tia Lélia, we're here!"

From some distant place in the house, a woman's voice responds, "I'll be there in a minute. I'm making some tea for all of us." Children's laughter echoes down the hallway. Grace spies the children peeking out from behind a partially open door.

"Hey, you kids, come out from hiding. Our friend Senhora Grace is here," Zulmira says.

More laughter. Suddenly, they spring into action. They run toward Zulmira, squealing, arms open. Rosa asks, "*Madrinha*, did you bring us any sweets today?"

"No, no. Your mother said no more sweets. Did you say hello to the senhora?"

Rosa turns and says formally, "Bom dia, Senhora Grace."

Grace responds, "And bom dia to you, Rosa. Nice to see you again."

Rosa giggles and turns to cling to Zulmira. The boy, pale and thin, hides shyly behind Zulmira. She lifts him into her arms. "This is Afonsinho." He tucks his face into her neck.

"Nice to meet you, Afonsinho," Grace says.

Zulmira sets him down. "You two run along. We need to talk to your grandmother now." The children turn and run down the hall, passing precariously on either side of their grandmother, who carries a tea tray.

The woman Grace has known as Nonna Preta looks younger than she remembers from the day when they delivered the *esmolas*. Something else strikes Grace: she appears to be of mixed blood— European and African. Like Grace's Indian blood, Lélia's African blood is almost entirely washed out with the paleness of whites. Grace muses, *Maybe skin tones are like spectral light rather than pigments. The more colors that get mixed together, the paler they become.* It explains so much. Racism was at the heart of peoples' willingness to cast this woman as a witch.

"Senhora," Lélia says, "welcome to our home. Come, come, let's sit in here."

"Thank you. Thank you for inviting me." Grace, dumbfounded at the opulence of the house in contrast to where she last saw Lélia, is at a loss for words. She and Zulmira follow Lélia into a large sitting room, furnished with weighty colonial furniture.

Lélia sets the tray down on a table and goes to open the heavy drapes. "This house belonged to my husband—may he rest in peace. I'd never been here until recently. It's been closed up since his death, left to his—our—lost son who you knew as Senhor Estêvão." Light floods into the room. "Well, we have much to talk about, don't we?" She proceeds to pour tea into the cups.

"Yes, there *is* much to talk about," Grace says.

Lélia sits down across from Grace. She reaches an upturned hand out to her. Grace instinctively places her hand in Lélia's. "Grace, I'm sorry for all that you went through. I feel a mixture of shame and triumph for my role in all this."

"Senhora, no need to apologize. I've only gained from my experiences. You are the one who has suffered a loss. For that I am sorry." Grace looks at Lélia, whose eyes have filled with tears.

"Please, let me tell you my side of things." Lélia wipes her eyes before beginning. "When Afonso Germano asked me to play along with being a black witch, I didn't want to. Bad enough that so many people said I was a witch to begin with, but to play the role was another thing. You know, he didn't believe in the evil eye—never had, but when Afonsinho didn't get better, and the doctors gave no definitive answers, he had nothing else to turn to. Rationality failed him. You were the only one who could set things straight in his mind, because you were the thing that had set them awry. He knew that you were on the boat. My son was mentally ill, a fact that eluded me until he murdered Norinha. I *knew* what he had done. I knew that you were falsely under suspicion. Zulmira told me." She gestured toward Zulmira.

"Yes, my boyfriend told me . . . ," Zulmira says.

"I was the one who told the police of my son's and my identity. Afonso Germano thought Norinha had tipped them off in some way before he killed her, but no; it was I. A difficult thing to do, turn your own son in. At first they didn't believe me—the old *mestiça* witch, married into a noble family—likely story." She musters a laugh. "Anyway, you deserve to know the truth. I'm sorry for the deception and deeply grateful to you for what you and your friends did. Not a day goes by that I don't thank God for having brought you here, for having fulfilled your promise."

The blood floods Grace's face. "Well, I'm sure things would

have turned out either way." She isn't *sure*. "And you wouldn't have needed my promise if I hadn't come."

"We will never know, will we?" Lélia asks. "We know the past as it happens, and as we interpret it."

Lélia, Grace, and Zulmira spend several hours talking through the known details of Afonso Germano's life and about Lélia's lost homeland of Angola. At the end of their afternoon together, they agree to meet again. Grace and Zulmira ride back to Calheta in silence.

THAT EVENING, as the sun sets, and the last rays of summer sun vanish from the *loja*, Grace sits down in front of her computer to enter some field notes. Not much in the mood for it, but she's getting behind. Her days have been filled with *festas*, not only in São Jorge, but also in Terceira, Graciosa, Pico, and Faial. With the "flies of summer" came the Cruzeiro das Ilhas, the boat that provides inexpensive transportation between the Central Group islands. Grace has collected more data and taken more photographs than she will ever be able to go through in a lifetime. Thanks to the generosity of Miguel and Ângela Maria, she gets to finish her work.

Her mind buzzes with her conversation earlier in the day with Lélia. So much to absorb. She gazes blankly at the glow of her screen and begins to type hesitantly at first, and then with verve.

> The stories, it turns out, have little to do with me, as Tia Carmina, Magnus, and Ângela Maria have pointed out at various times. They have, however, changed me, the way rites of passage do. Perhaps by stepping onto and then off a cargo boat called the Espírito Santo, I set certain realities into motion, but I was a minor character. The stories of this place are about mothers and sons: the Santa Mãe and Jesus, Ângela Maria and Jaime, Lélia Maria Soares Carvalho and Afonso Germano,

Afonso Germano's mistress and Afonsinho, and yes, even Magnus and his mother. All stories of loss and sadness, stories of women who have carried the burdensome tears of motherhood, tears of stone. The stories of this place are about power, indistinguishably imagined and real.

THE END

ACKNOWLEDGMENTS

Foremost, I would like to thank all of the people of S. Jorge, our "families" and friends, who took ken* and me in and so generously made us a part of their lives. Without their support we would not have survived. I especially would like to thank António, Leonor, Gilda, Sr. Fontes, Arminda, Zulmira, Elisabete, Zé, Pedro, Orlando, Rosa, Magda, Julia, Germano, Paulo, Manuel, Antónia, Vitória, Sr. Jaime, Jorge, Gabriela, Davíd, Maria Eduardo, Maria João, Lúcia, Joe, Nyny, Nelhinha, and Mário Duarte.

Thank you to George Hicks, my friend and advisor, who regretfully died before I wrote this. He was the one who suggested the Azores as a research site for ken and me. George and his wife, Linné, supported ken's and my efforts from the home side entirely —making sure that we had what we needed to get our work done, storing our belongings until our return, depositing checks, lodging us before and after our fieldwork—and gave us endless encouragement in our endeavors.

I owe a debt to Onésimo Almeida, who introduced us to numerous people that were of importance to the success of our work both in the United States and in the Azores. Through him, we met Francisco Sousa, who guided us to the island of S. Jorge and into the open arms of his very large family, who have become our family too.

Through a Haffenreffer Museum collecting grant, facilitated by Shepard Krech III, we were able to travel to six of the other eight islands, attending festivals and interviewing numerous people engaged in the production of textiles. Without this grant we would not have had the opportunity to get a cross-island comparative experience, which was very important to my work on festivals.

Many thanks go to my mother, who has supported me in all my endeavors, not the least of which includes calling me regularly while I was in the field, and who has been the most important role model in my life. She continues to inspire me with the confidence to do the things that I want to do, even when the world seems against me. She is the most courageous and intelligent woman I have ever known.

My children, Zoë and Søren, have helped me finish this work in an indirect way, for having them has taught me much about growth, potential, and the power of perseverance. They sustain me every day, pushing me to achieve as much as they do.

I can't overstate the contributions of my husband, ken anderson. Everything we did in the field was a joint effort: our documentation in the field, our socializing, our misery, our joy, and our sadness. We constantly worked the field from different angles, something neither of us could have done alone. So, although I have written this novel myself, it represents a lot of his sweat equity, both in the field and in earning a living and taking care of our children while I traipsed off in a more leisurely life of working on something I felt passionate about. Thank you, ken, for your immeasurable love and support.

I thank Bill Beeman, who from my beginnings at Brown and as an anthropologist at large, supported me in the breadth of my interests, including theater, music, technology, ritual, religion, and fiction writing. Bill has been my mentor and a living example of how many different people we can be in this one life. Thank you, Bill, for believing in me.

Thank you, Lina Fruzzetti, for having given me valuable feedback on my earliest version. You were right.

Finally, I would like to thank all of my friends and family who read early versions, including my sister, my mother, Judy, Sherry, Marita, Lisa, and more recently, members of my Aristata Press community: Nancy, Ginger, and last but not least, Erin Cusick, my editor.

*ken anderson intentionally spells his name in lowercase

ABOUT THE AUTHOR

Anne Page McClard earned her Ph.D. in Anthropology from Brown University in 2005. Until recently, Anne worked as an applied anthropologist in the technology industry in the field of interaction design. *Butterfly Dreams* is her first novel, the inspiration for which was planted when she did research in the Azores on the annual festival cycle. She currently lives in Portland, Oregon with her ninety-five-year-old mother, husband, daughter, and two dogs.

https://butterflydreams.mcclard.com/
https://anne.mcclard.com/

Interested in booking a bookclub appearance or other event with with the author? Visit https://butterflydreams.mcclard.com/book ing-inquiries/

 instagram.com/amcclard

OTHER ARISTATA PRESS TITLES

LEAVINGS: Memoir of a 1920s Hollywood Love Child, by Megan McClard, 2022

Spanish language edition of: *Tell Mother I'm in Paradise: Memoirs of a Political Prisoner in El Salvador* by Ana Margarita Gasteazoro—*Díganle a mi madre que estoy en el paraíso: Memorias de una prisionera política en El Salvador,* Edited by Judy Blankenship and Andrew Wilson, 2022.

Coming in 2023

This Rough Magic: At Home on the Columbia Slough, by Nancy Henry and Bruce Campbell, illustrated by Amanda Williams, August 2023.

Butterfly Dreams: a Novel, by Anne McClard, September 2023.

Women Caught in the Crossfire: One Woman's Quest for Peace in South Sudan, by Abuk Jervis Makuac and Susan Lynn Clark, October 2023.

Raising Owen: an Extra-ordinary Memoir on Motherhood, by Suzanne Lezotte, October 2023.

Aristata Press is non-profit organization. We depend on charitable contributions and volunteers to keep the lights on. We are a tax exempt–501(c)(3)–organization (EIN 92-0281706), which means that your contributions are tax deductible. Contributions that we receive will go directly to supporting the publications of deserving literary works by authors that for one reason or another would be unlikely to find a home in the for-profit publishing sector.

Please visit us at: https://aristatapress.com

Milton Keynes UK
Ingram Content Group UK Ltd.
UKHW042158181223
434628UK00013B/524/J

9 798987 852453